WOLVES' GAMBIT

P.J. MacLayne

Wolves' Gambit

ISBN-13: 978-0-9985014-8-2

Published in the United States of America.

ACKNOWLEDGMENTS

Cornelia Amiri, for her editorial assistance and friendship

K.M. Guth, for another great cover and other artwork

Amy Atwell at Author E.M.S. for her general support of writers and fine work

WOLVES' GAMBIT

ONE

Behind the bar, Lori Grenville grabbed the ice tongs and slammed them against a metal serving tray. All eyes turned to her. She aimed the tongs at the troublemaker. "Josef! Let go of her. NOW!"

The burly man smirked without letting go of the waitress. "We were just getting to know each other. Right, Princess?" Like many male wolf shifters, Josef's rugged features attracted women, Lori being an exception.

Princess. Stupid name, Lori thought, but it was her job to protect the staff. Yet even on her best day, Lori wouldn't be able to take one slightly drunk male wolf in a physical fight, let alone a bar full of them. Without a weapon, she wouldn't even win in an unfair fight. The situation didn't call for the shotgun stashed under the counter. Not yet, anyway. Her best artillery was her brain, something most of the bar's customers lacked.

With a flick of her wrist, she sent the serving tray hurtling through the air. It flew in a perfect line, narrowly missing another customer and hit Josef's forearm, then clattered to the floor. Instinctively, he let go of Princess to rub the spot.

1

The waitress, a slender redhead, used the momentary distraction to dart out of Josef's reach.

Lori jerked her chin toward the back. "Take a break, Princess."

She waited until the girl made it behind the door marked 'Staff Only' before turning back to Josef. "How many times do I have to tell you, don't manhandle the waitress."

He sneered, and Lori glimpsed his canines, half-extended. "Who the hell do you think you are to ruin my fun, human?"

He meant it as an insult, but it told Lori her disguise held. Between the colored contacts and special soap she used, only a few could detect she was a shifter. She wasn't built like one but those features came naturally. She had human blood in her genes from an uncharted long-ago ancestor, reflected in her blonde hair, a rarity among wolf shifters.

The nearby pitcher of ice water gave her an idea. She clutched it in one hand and stalked to the table where Josef and his friends sat. Tension knotted the muscles in her neck and shoulders as she made her way across the room.

Josef's right cheek twitched. Was he nervous or preparing to shift? Lori couldn't imagine he'd be intimated by her. She'd been described as 'elfin' because she was small even compared to most humans, let alone these wolves. She prided herself on using her size to her advantage.

"You know the rules," she said.

"Rules are for weaklings."

Although her attention focused solely on Josef, Lori sensed bodies around her stiffening in their seats, preparing for action. More trouble or help? She wouldn't find out until she goaded Josef into a fight. One that could see him banned from the bar forever or result in her death. If she didn't stand her ground this and every night, she'd lose her job and fail her mission.

"You're not the alpha. You don't get to make that decision."

"Look at Goldilocks, trying to play tough."

Faster than he could react, she dumped the pitcher of ice water over his head. "You need to cool down. Here, let me help you."

He yelped as the water slid down his back and ice cubes scattered everywhere. At least one fell inside his shirt. A chair screeched as one of his friends pushed away from the table to avoid getting splashed.

"Now go home and don't come back the rest of the week."

A mixture of laughter, growls, and a smattering of applause followed her pronouncement. The laughter encouraged her. She wasn't alone. She planted her hands on her hips. "I don't see you leaving."

To her surprise, he didn't shift. She didn't expect he'd shrink into his seat. A grunt behind her caused her to swivel and identify the source. Behind her stood the biggest man in the pack. No, not the alpha. The alpha's self-image would never allow him to be seen in the rundown bar in the middle of a desolate patch of Wyoming.

But that was all right with Lori. This man was even better for her purposes. No one who valued his or her place in the pack would defy the man who moved to stand beside her—Hyrum, the pack's enforcer.

He put his hand on Josef's shoulder. "Be in my office first thing in the morning," Hyrum said. An unspoken threat echoed in his deep voice, sending a small shiver down Lori's back. Although the gesture appeared friendly, his grip was firm enough to wrinkle Josef's T-shirt. Josef winced, and Hyrum tightened his clasp. "Now go home. I came here to relax and you're ruining the mood."

Josef didn't argue. "This place is lame," he mumbled as he stood. "Who wants to be here, anyway?"

With the problem handled, Lori returned to her spot behind the bar, ignoring the unfriendly finger Josef flipped on his way out the door. By the time Hyrum took a seat, she'd drawn him a beer. She grinned and set it in front of him. "It's on the house."

It was a running joke. The Jaeger Pack owned the forlorn little bar, which closed a year ago when the pack member running it died. Lori had convinced one of the pack's officials to let her re-open and renovate it. Any of the top wolves drank for free if they deigned to enter the establishment. Hyrum was the only one who ever did.

"That was either really brave or stupid." He lifted the chilled mug to his lips and set it back on the bar, half-empty. Lori drew a second one and put it beside the first.

"Or a little of both. What did Princess do now to upset her father?"

Princess and her father—the alpha of the Jaeger pack—rarely saw eye-to-eye anymore. Their disagreement started after her eighteenth birthday when she announced her intention to go to college on the East Coast. Her father had other plans for her. Working in the bar was one of the ways he used to break her spirit.

4

He sniffed and rubbed his nose. "She turned down another suitor—new alpha of a pack in Texas."

Lori snorted. "Isn't he fifty? And bald?"

"Forty-five and his hair is thinning."

"Your great and glorious leader needs to try harder to find a suitable match for her."

"Mouthy little thing, aren't you?"

Lori lowered her voice and leaned across the bar. "At least I can think for myself, unlike most of the women of your pack. But that's the way your alpha likes them, right?"

Hyrum allowed a small snarl to escape between his gritted teeth. "He's the one paying you. If anyone told him what you said... You're pushing your luck, Grenville."

More than Hyrum knew. She'd expected her job to take only a month or so, and she'd been here nearly four. "He may own this joint, but if it weren't for me, it would be boarded up and nothing but a fire hazard. He's paying me, but not near what I'm worth. One of these days, I'll walk away and won't look back." But not before she convinced Princess to go with her.

She snatched up his empty mug and dropped it into the sink filled with soapy water. Then she drew another beer and slammed it on the counter, spilling the foam over the brim of the mug. "Now, if you'll excuse me, I have to go check up on my waitress."

There were times when Lori thought she could get to like Hyrum. He'd backed her up more than once since she'd stepped in to manage the hellhole the pack called a bar. Then he'd go and defend Edgar Jaeger, the pack's alpha, whom she had yet to meet.

It didn't matter. Knowing how Edgar treated the women under his 'care' was all Lori needed to decide he was a waste of oxygen. And so was anyone who stuck up for him.

Sadly, there were other alphas like Jaeger scattered across the country. They kept Lori motivated. She couldn't foresee a time when her talents wouldn't be needed. For now, she'd use them to console a princess.

The harsh noon-day revealed what Lori missed the previous night—a large bruise marring Princess's cheek. It wouldn't do any good to ask about it—Princess would claim she'd run into a door or something—but Lori had no doubt who'd inflicted it. The situation was escalating, and Lori needed to make her move soon.

With the bar closed, the two of them were unloading a delivery. The truck driver was supposed to help them, but he'd taken off on an imaginary errand to the convenience store across the road. Lori didn't mind. It gave her time alone with Princess with no watching eyes.

Outside, no one would hear their conversation. Especially when the typical Wyoming wind blew, masking their voices.

"My father won't even let me keep my tips," Princess complained. "First, he ordered me to work for you for free to show pack spirit, then he said I needed to save my tips to help defray the cost of my wedding. He said he'll save them for me. What if I don't want to get married?"

"Doesn't your father give you everything you need?" Lori passed her a box of new mugs from the back of the truck.

"He only gets me the things *he* wants me to have. I'd like to pick out my own clothes once in a while. Or not have to get my personal supplies from the next-door neighbor, or ask my grandmother." She hesitated. "What I want," she whispered, "is to save enough money to get out of here."

Those were the magic words. "Why don't you?"

"How? I can't just walk away. My father would send every one of his hunters after me to track me and drag me back. I'd never even get across pack boundaries. Then my life would be worse than ever."

"There's a rumor a couple of girls got out recently." More than a rumor. Lori had smuggled them off pack lands and into the hands of friends who could help them create new lives out of Jaeger's reach.

Princess kicked at a tumbleweed skittering across the dirt. "They were low-level pack members. My father claims they weren't worth bringing back because they were ugly and no self-respecting male would ever want to mate with them. He said they were a drain on pack finances. I wasn't allowed to hang out with them, but they seemed like nice girls."

So that was the story he concocted to make the rest of the pack look past his mistakes. Lori's opinion of Jaeger sunk even further, if that was possible. "Where would you go, if you left?"

"I don't know." Princess shrugged. "I've always wanted to see the redwoods."

"From the videos I've seen, they're magnificent." Quite a change from the dusty Wyoming prairie. "Tell you what—any tips you get, give them to me and I'll

7

hold them for you. Will you trust me?" Baby steps. Just enough to give Princess hope.

"My father will notice if I don't bring any money home."

"Then give me half. We'll find a safe place to stash the rest."

"I guess that will work." Princess smiled an uncertain smile. "This is between you and me, right?"

Not that the tips amounted to much. Even combining her tips with half of Princess' netted a measly ten bucks a night. At least she could honestly look Jaeger in the eye and tell him what cheapskates pack members were if he ever asked.

It was a good thing that Princess wouldn't be needing that money to make her escape. No, that would be free.

Princess showing up for work early was the omen Lori needed. "I need a copy of your driver's license," she said, "for insurance paperwork."

Princess shook her head. "I don't have one. My father refused to teach me how to drive. Or let anyone else do it."

"Why not?"

"Because," she raised her hands and drew quotation marks in the air, "When you marry an alpha, he'll drive you everywhere. Or have one of his wolves do it. That's what he told me. He believes that all I'm good for is to be eye candy on some man's arm."

"You're doing a good job here so far."

"Thanks." Princess grinned. "Can you keep a secret? I know how to drive. One of my bodyguards felt sorry for me and taught me."

Bodyguards? Lori's research hadn't found anything about bodyguards. Was someone listening to their conversation? She looked around, but no one was in sight.

"You have bodyguards? I haven't seen them."

"No, he pulled them as part of my punishment. He figures no one will try to attack me as long as I'm on pack land. It's not much of a punishment though, because I like it when they aren't around."

"Why would anyone want to hurt you?" There were dozens of reasons, only a few having anything to do with Princess herself, but she wanted to hear Princess' theory.

"My father is *convinced* if I go anywhere by myself I'll be kidnapped and forced to mate an alpha from a low-level pack. Either that or held hostage and used against him."

Jaeger thought more of himself and his pack than the other packs in the country did. The Jaeger pack ranked near the bottom of the pecking order according to Lori's information. She considered telling Princess that, but it was unlikely a human would be privy to pack politics.

Lori shook her head. "You can never be too careful. Human politics are bad enough, but I really don't understand pack rivalries."

Princess giggled. "We are wolves, after all."

"I'm not so sure. I haven't seen anyone here shift yet. It's like they are trying to pretend I don't know how it works. But I wouldn't have been hired for this job if I was clueless."

"How long have you known about shifters?"

Lori delivered the cover story without a flaw. "I was around ten. There was a pack in the town where I lived, and the kids attended the same school as me. They tried to hide their 'special abilities', but I figured it out."

"How?"

As she picked up the last box of supplies, Lori grinned. "I developed a crush on a boy. He didn't hang around after school, so I never got a chance to talk to him. One day I followed him to see where he went in such a hurry. I stayed far enough back he didn't realize I was tracking him. Anyway, we got to a local park and he headed into a restroom. I hid behind a big old tree and waited. Eventually, a big dog came out." She held up one hand. "No disrespect meant, but when I was ten, I didn't know a dog from a wolf.

"The 'dog' ran away, and I waited until it was time for me to go home. Other boys came and left from the restroom, but he never came out.

"I trailed him a couple more times, and the same thing happened. Then I put two and two together. Of course, he lied when I asked him about it, but his alpha found out and decided I needed to be told the truth."

Lori sighed. "His name was Jimmy. I lost track of him a year later when my family moved."

They entered the bar together, each carrying as much as they could handle. Lori hoped that Princess bought the story. Secrets depended on it.

Two

"Grenville," a voice boomed from behind her. With her earbuds in, and her MP3 player blasting hard rock, Lori hadn't heard the door open. The voice's alpha power compelled her to turn around, lower her eyes and answer.

Her training prevailed, however, and she ignored the voice and continued stocking the shelves behind the bar with cheap liquor. Princess had been sent home to rest before the evening rush, so she and the interloper were alone. The voice sounded female, so not Jaeger. She caught a quick glimpse in the mirror of a gray-haired woman who looked as wrinkled as a used paper towel. The pack's lead female, maybe?

"Grenville," the voice shouted, this time louder. Lori took her time turning around. Not all humans were susceptible to the famed alpha compulsion. This one was weak, anyway, and not a true challenge.

She cocked her head. "Can I help you?"

"Do you not know who I am?"

Lori had to play it cool. Pissing off an alpha, even a female one, was never a good idea. "I'm guessing you aren't here for one of our large collection of fine beers. That makes you the pack leader's mother. Am I right?"

"If you understand that then you should know tradition states you are supposed to present yourself to me."

Lori came out from behind the bar and grabbed a chair from the nearest table. "Have a seat, Honored One. I'd hate to be accused of not showing you the expected courtesy. You want a cup of coffee?"

Sticking to pack protocol, she waited patiently while the old woman lowered herself into the offered chair. "Cream and sugar," the elder stated.

Lori noted the absence of the word 'please.'

It took a minute to fix a fresh pot, and the silence in the bar was overwhelming with only the hiss of the coffeepot providing relief. Lori grabbed her personal creamer from the refrigerator and put it on the table, along with several packets of sugar and the least-stained spoon available.

"I'm sorry for not coming to see you," she said as she poured two cups of coffee. "I guess your son didn't tell you. One condition of my employment is that I stay out of the village."

Only the barest flicker of reaction was evident in the old lady's eyes. Surprise? Anger? Lori couldn't read her facial cues, and found herself admiring the carefully constructed facade.

"I don't think your son wants me corrupting the women of the pack." With a sideways grin, Lori placed one cup down within the reach of the elder. "Me and my crazy human ideas."

"You may call me Madam Rose."

"Thank you, Madame Rose. I didn't want to insult you, but I need this job." Lori allowed a hint of desperation to creep into her voice. It wouldn't hurt to appear weak to the old woman, and less of a threat.

As she took a sip of her coffee, Madame Rose pondered the information. "Yet he trusts you with my granddaughter."

"He's punishing her."

"You treat her badly?"

"Not me. I can't say the same for some of the men who come in here. I try to protect her, but there's only so much I can do."

"The stories have reached me. You do well for not being one of us."

"Thank you."

Lori itched to find out what Madame Rose wanted, but rushing the conversation seemed imprudent. She wanted the female alpha on her side.

"Is she learning anything?"

"She's only been here a few days. She's still getting the hang of the job."

"Would you say she has potential?"

What was Madame Rose hinting about? Did she support the idea of Princess going to college? "She can do better than work in a bar."

"She deserves better than the string of second-rate alphas my son has her parading in front of. Someone like that Fairwood alpha I've heard stories about."

Lori caught her breath. That shot down the college idea. Madame Rose wanted nothing more than to ride on Princess' coattails to a higher standing among packs. "My apologies, Madame, but she deserves to decide for herself what she wants."

"And what would that be?" Madame Rose asked, an edge in her voice.

"Not my place to ask her." Lori shook her head.

"Shouldn't that be your job? Since her mother is dead?"

"Are you telling me what my responsibilities are, human?"

"No. I wouldn't dare."

Lori held her composure as Madame Rose studied her. Her gaze traveled from the top of Lori's head to where her arms rested on the table, then back up again.

Madame Rose sniffed and frowned. "You aren't pure human, are you?"

It wasn't the first time the accusation had been leveled while Lori was in disguise, so she had a canned response. "If there is any shifter blood in my family's history, we haven't been able to trace it. We've checked back as far as we can find records."

Madame Rose harrumphed.

"Sorry to disappoint you."

"Not everyone is as privileged as my family. Our blood line has been traced back to Europe. We are pure shifters."

The old woman spoke as if she was personally responsible for the feat. Lori struggled to come up with a reasonable response. "That's rare, isn't it?"

"Very." Madame Rose slammed her cup on the table and stood. "You will come see me next week. I will tell my son to allow it. This place...." and she sniffed again, "is not suitable."

"I look forward to it." That was the truth. Lori suspected hidden depths and fonts of knowledge all wrapped together in the old lady and wanted to explore them. Madame Rose might be a determining factor in Lori's larger plans.

She made it to the door ahead of the old woman

and held it open for her. Outside, a black limo parked near the entrance to the bar. Lori bit her tongue. She wanted to point out what a waste of money it was, having a limo to go all of a mile.

It was for show, just like the driver running up and extending his arm to help Madame Rose walk the short distance to the open limo door. Who was the old lady trying to impress? Her only audience was Lori and a few pack members at the convenience store across the road.

Madame Rose stopped before getting into the car. She turned and to Lori's disbelief, gave her an exaggerated wink.

Business was picking up and Lori didn't have time to eavesdrop on all the cheerful conversations taking place in every corner of the bar. It had taken a week, but several of the pack females were in the crowd, accompanied by their mates, of course. It didn't take long for Lori to notice that although they might speak to Princess, they kept their eyes turned away from her.

She'd have to solve that puzzle later. She and Princess were too busy keeping the customers happy to do anything more than keep the beer flowing. The tips flowed more freely as well, and Princess' nest egg was growing. Lori needed a new place to hide it. She wasn't comfortable keeping that much cash in the bar.

The upswing in business meant she'd started planning to leave. Soon a pack member would decide they wanted to run the bar and go whining to Jaeger about a human—and a female at that—taking a job away from the pack. A nod from Jaeger and Lori would be out of luck.

Of course, within a few months, the bar would close after the pack member pocketed the profit and didn't put any money back into the business. But she'd be on a new assignment by the time that happened.

She needed to focus on Princess and wrap this one up fast. The ticket had been ordered and the connections were in place. The Free Wolves were waiting to give her a ride in their underground railroad.

A sudden silence caught Lori's attention and she looked up from the sink to see what the problem was. Surely, no one was stupid enough to attempt to rob a bar full of wolf shifters.

The tall man at the doorway didn't look like a robber. Neither did the two men that stood a pace behind him, although they carried rifles slung over their shoulders and pistols tucked into their belts. Lori laid odds there were more weapons hidden.

Several steps behind them, she glimpsed Hyrum. All the pieces fell into place. It was Jaeger, the pack leader, making his appearance. But why?

She expected a rush of alpha power but it didn't come. The men who had claimed the best table in the bar—if there was one—grabbed their beers and abandoned it. They ended up standing against the wall.

Jaeger took his time strolling to the table and sitting. Lori waited until he was settled to walk over and wipe imaginary dirt off the tabletop. Princess seemed frozen in place, as were most of the customers, so it was up to Lori.

"Greetings, Elder Jaeger. Would you care for

something to drink?" she asked politely. No use in antagonizing him. Yet.

One bodyguard leaned over and whispered in the alpha's ear. Jaeger nodded and whispered back.

"Do you have any champagne?" the bodyguard asked.

Champagne? Really? Lori struggled not to laugh. Talk about pretentious. Clearly, they expected her answer to be 'no' but she had an ace up her sleeve. Two of them, actually. She'd found the bottles tucked away in the back of the file cabinet in the office. The previous manager's private stash, was her guess. Likely bought on the pack's dime disguised as something more mundane.

"Will a Pol Roger do?" she asked, her voice saccharin sweet. "It will need time to chill."

Jaeger and the bodyguard conferred again. The bodyguard nodded. "It will be acceptable."

Did Jaeger even know the brand's reputation? Somehow, Lori doubted it. She didn't have a fancy bucket to chill the bottle, but at least she'd found glasses that would do the champagne justice. It seemed silly using the container she used to fill the soda machine's ice dispenser as an ice bucket, but it was the best she could manage.

Mustering faked dignity, she carried the contraption to the front of the bar, placed it on the table, and set a glass alongside it. "Is there something I can get you while it's chilling? A sparkling water perhaps?"

Her voice echoed in the silence that had fallen throughout the bar with Jaeger's arrival. Although the bodyguard leaned over to discuss the offer with Jaeger, Lori noticed their lips didn't move. They were talking mind-to-mind but it was too risky for her to try to listen in.

"He'll wait," the bodyguard announced.

What was she supposed to do in the meantime? Hover around the table waiting for the clock to tick away the seconds? Not her style. Instead, she bestowed a smile on the men. "If there's nothing else, I have a bar to run. I'll return when it's time to pour." She lifted one eyebrow. "Unless you want to do it yourself?"

This time the bodyguard didn't bother checking with Jaeger first. "You can leave," he said, shooing her away with a wave of his hand.

"Arrogant asshole," Lori thought in a tightly controlled tendril of thought that couldn't be overheard. "Just a little impressed with yourself aren't you?" That went for his bodyguard too.

But how did Hyrum fit in? He seemed to be an outlier in the little group. The rest of the bar's customers had recovered from their frozen state, and as Lori filled their orders, she studied Jaeger and his escorts.

All four of them were good-looking in the typical male wolf fashion. Tall and muscular, they each bore just enough stubble to accentuate their chins. They were each outfitted with an expensive white cotton shirt and pleated dress pants, but Jaeger wore a tailored suitcoat over his. Lori had to restrain a giggle as she added up the cost of a replacement wardrobe if any of them shifted without removing his clothes first.

At the fifteen-minute mark, she returned to Jaeger's table, with a clean towel draped over her arm. The two bodyguards had seated themselves, one on either side of their pack leader, while Hyrum remained standing. In a way, she felt bad for him. He was low man on the totem pole. Which struck her as odd, because he looked as if he'd win in a fight with any man in the room. Including Jaeger.

With all the expertise of an experienced sommelier, she removed the bottle from its ice bath and placed it on the table. The foil came off with no problem, and the wire cage followed after a few quick twists of the key. Then came the fine part that would either make or break her reputation in Jaeger's eyes.

After draping the towel over the mouth of the bottle, she gave the bottom a smooth twist. The wine gods smiled on her efforts, and the cork slid into her hand with the merest hiss escaping from the bottle. Effortlessly, she filled the fluted glass just above the halfway point and placed it in front of Jaeger.

He lifted it and held it up to examine its appearance. Lori waited patiently as it was all part of the standard procedure. But when he swirled the liquid in the glass before sniffing it, she swallowed back a groan. He wasn't as sophisticated as he pretended, but she couldn't correct him in front of his pack.

He set it back on the table without taking a sip. He and his number one bodyguard held another silent conversation. "You first," the bodyguard said, glowering at Lori.

She raised both eyebrows. "You want me to pour a second glass or drink from this one?" She had a rule about drinking on the job, but it was time to make an exception.

"This one." The bodyguard pushed it her way.

Whatever. Did Jaeger think she'd found a way to poison a sealed bottle? Was he really that paranoid or was it all part of the show? She wished she knew. It could become an element of her planning. She picked up the glass and took the smallest sip, letting the champagne trickle down her throat. "An excellent vintage," she said, and took a second swallow before swiping the brim clean and setting it in front of him.

There was no standard protocol for the situation, so she had to make it up as she went. She wanted to find that fine line between showing respect and groveling. Jaeger was *a* pack leader after all, but not *her* pack leader.

He could ask for a second glass but how would he know she hadn't poisoned that one? Or he could drink from the first glass and play it safe. Either path could be twisted to show strength or weakness.

Someone in the bar snickered. Or was it a muffled sneeze? It goaded Jaeger into action, and he picked up the glass and drank about half of it. A brief pause, and, still expressionless, he nodded.

She nodded back. Her duties were fulfilled. She'd had the chance to size up Jaeger and he'd failed to impress her. Not once had she felt a trickle of alpha power. Now a roomful of customers needed to be served, and somehow, she needed to convince Princess to find the courage to help her.

THREE

"What can you tell me about Hyrum?" Lori asked Princess as she brought more beer mugs to be washed. Jaeger stayed only long enough to drink a second glass of champagne and when he left, he took the rest of the bottle with him. Even after his departure, the pack members who stayed were subdued and barely touched their drinks so Lori closed the bar early.

"What do you mean?"

Princess still hadn't recovered from the stress of her father's unexpected appearance, and Lori wanted to keep her around as long as possible before sending her home. At least keep her busy until her hands stopped shaking.

"I can't put my finger on it, but he doesn't seem like he belongs."

"You've stumbled on one of our pack secrets. He doesn't."

It was rare, but not unheard of, for an enforcer not to be a pack member. Lori played innocent. "How did that happen?"

Princess scrunched her eyebrows. "I don't know the whole story. Something about an exchange of hostages to prevent a war between our pack and a neighboring pack, the Destins. The Council set it up. You've heard about the Council, right?"

"Bits and pieces from overheard conversations. You wolves are good at keeping secrets." It wouldn't hurt to appeal to Princess' ego.

"Figure the Council is like your Congress. Representatives from the packs get together to hash out differences and settle disagreements. Stops a lot of pack wars and enables us shifters to keep our privacy."

"Makes sense. But hostages?" Lori stacked the clean mugs on the sideboard of the sink.

"Or fosterlings, if you want to be generous. Grandfather and the Destin pack alpha wouldn't follow anything the Council asked. Young men on both sides were getting hurt or killed all the time. So, one night, Council guards raided both camps and snatched a little kid from each. In our case, they grabbed my father's little brother, Randy. Hyrum was snatched from the Destins. They swapped the kids."

It was brilliant and despicable at the same time. "If they kept up the fighting, they'd potentially end up killing a child of their own pack."

"Yep. My uncle is still with the Destins, and Hyrum is here."

"But why make him the enforcer?"

"That's one thing my father did right. He's following the old rule of keeping your friends close and your enemies closer."

"Hyrum stays because the pack war would start all over again if he left."

"Something like that." Princess shrugged. "Plus, he grew up with my father. They aren't as close as brothers, but I don't think he remembers much about his family."

Lori hadn't realized Hyrum was that old. He'd aged well. "Has he picked a mate from your pack?" That would cement the truce. To her surprise, Princess blushed. "You?"

"Nothing serious. We hung out a few times. I suspect Hyrum felt sorry for me because my father restricted who I could be friends with. When my father found out, he threatened to marry me off right away if we didn't break it up. So, we did. It hurt, but I got over it."

"Is that why he shows up here so often?"

"He keeps an eye on me, but haven't you noticed the way he looks at you?"

Lori dropped the mug she was washing and water splashed onto her shirt. She ignored the wet spots soaking through to her skin. "Me? You're imagining things. Besides, I've never seen a successful shifter-human relationship." Getting involved with any male in the pack was a bad idea.

"My father wouldn't approve it, anyway."

"Who's your boyfriend now?"

"You're funny. No male wants to get involved with me because of my father. Most of them buy into his rules without a question. They don't want anything to do with strong-willed females. The old ways are better as far as they are concerned."

"You don't agree."

Princess lowered her voice. "Times are changing. Rumors suggest even women are taking positions in pack leadership. My father would have a heart attack if I suggested such a thing."

Lori didn't have time to respond because Princess'

escort home strode in the door. That was okay. Baby steps. The wheels turned in Lori's head. She needed to firm up her plans.

Lori put down the pen on top of the stack of orders on her desk, pushed her chair back, and yawned. The last two weeks she'd been working non-stop and she needed a day off. Several days would be better. Although she closed the bar every Tuesday to visit Madame Rose, it wasn't enough. Even with Princess helping her, most duties still fell on Lori's shoulders. But it was Princess' first job so Lori tried to be patient with her.

At least Princess was starting to make friends among the few steady female customers. The men treated her better as well. How much of that was due to Madame Rose's influence Lori wasn't sure, but it didn't matter. Princess was breaking out of the shell her father had encased her in, and Lori counted that as a win.

Did he know how much this job was doing for her? It was no longer a punishment. Lori hoped he wouldn't find out and force her to quit. Lori enjoyed having Princess around.

Still, she needed to get out of Jaeger pack territory. She didn't dare shift where she might be spotted, and her wolf was protesting its forced hibernation. Besides, she wanted to check in with friends and couldn't do that where she might be overheard. She lost herself in memories of acres of wooded lands with a sparkling stream meandering through it, a perfect place to let her wolf run free.

The squeal of the back door opening jerked her back to the present. "We're closed," she called.

"Sorry." A young man stuck his head in the office doorway. A quick sniff told Lori he was a wolf shifter, so that meant he was a Jaeger. "Are you hiring?"

She took her time studying him. Average height, brown hair and a slender build meant he wasn't part of the upper echelon of the pack. A smattering of pimples on his face revealed a human ancestor and his youth. Despite Madame Rose's pride in her lineage, the entire pack didn't claim to be pure bloods. "Why do you want to work here?"

His face reddened, and Lori thought he was cute in a human sort of way. "The pack leaders haven't found a position for me, and I don't have the funds to leave. Since you aren't part of the pack, I thought you might hire me. I can't promise you how long I'll stick around, but I'll work hard while I'm here."

Lori tented her fingertips and considered his statement. She'd heard of the tactic before and felt sorry for him. Not giving jobs to the weakest members of the pack ensured the strongest would have less competition for mates. She could find something for him to do. "What do you want to do when you leave the pack?"

His one-sided grin made him look even younger. "I'm a geek," he said. "I want to do something technology related. Programming maybe, or networking. I don't know which I'd be better at."

The pack was light-years behind in technology. The bar still had an old-fashioned cash register, and she'd had to spend her own money to get a computer for the office and her internet access crawled. No wonder the young man wanted to get out. She was just the person to help him.

"What's your name?"

"Ralph. But my friends call me Steve."

"Steve?"

"As in Steve Jobs." His face turned a deeper shade of red.

"Two more questions, Steve. First, does your alpha need to approve this?" She wondered if Jaeger was even aware of Steve's existence.

"I don't think so, but I can ask my parents."

Lori decided she'd ask her contact with the pack as well, to be on the safe side. "Okay, second, do you have any issues taking orders from a woman?"

He hesitated. "I've never had to. I think I'd be okay taking orders from you."

"How about from Princess?"

Steve arched an eyebrow. "Really?"

"Really. She has seniority."

He scrunched his face. "I guess so."

"Come back tomorrow and I'll have paperwork for you to fill out."

"Does that mean I have a shot at a job? With pack approval, of course."

Lori smiled. "That means you're hired."

He waited until he was back outside to let out a triumphant holler. Lori smiled and returned to her paperwork. She'd made someone's day.

The little town of Charity didn't offer much more than a small grocery store, post office, and a diner, but it was the closest piece of civilization to pack territory. Inhabited by retired ranchers and Californian expatriots, its citizens knew not to question the occasional appearance of pack members. Most looked away as Lori, Princess and her bodyguard stocked up on a few supplies.

As she opened the trunk of her car after exiting the grocery store, she admired the motorcycle parked next to her. It looked like it had just come off a showroom floor, with only a few specks of road dirt marring its shiny paint job. Her car, on the other hand, had seen better days and looked as if the deep coating of dust held the body together. It was on loan from the pack.

"Nice bike," she said to the motorcycle's rider.

"Thanks." The man removed his helmet and ran one hand through his short hair.

He looked as if he belonged on the same showroom floor as a model, Lori decided after a quick appraisal. Tall and elegant, the scruff on his chin added to his appeal. His motorcycle leathers clung to his frame and accentuated the muscles underneath. His dark eyes swirled with yellow streaks. He was all wolf, although not an alpha.

He placed the helmet on the seat of his bike and grabbed a case of soda from the bottom of Lori's cart. "You look like you could use a hand."

Lori glanced around to see if any pack members were within sight. Princess and her escort should be back at any time. Although she welcomed the chance to talk to someone outside of the pack, the interaction would be frowned upon. "Sure."

He had to lean over to place the soda in the trunk. Before straightening, he slipped a piece of paper out of his jacket's pocket and slipped it under the cardboard case. Their eyes met, and he nodded. "Not much of a grocery store," he said.

"It's the only one in town." She knew Dmitri Gromav of the Fairwood pack from the short time she'd spent with them. Gavin Fairwood, CEO of Fairwood Enterprises and alpha of the Fairwood pack, didn't get involved in low-level efforts. His time was normally spent trying to influence the Council to modernize.

Their arms bumped as they reached for the same bag. He grinned and picked up another one. That brief moment was all it took for a connection to be made. They'd be able to 'talk' without being overheard.

"You couldn't go to Fairwood so he sent me. Are you doing okay?" he sent.

"It's been too easy. I'm worried."

"Say the word and I'll contact Wind to pull you out of here."

"Not a chance. I've got two potentials. One is the alpha's daughter."

Lori shut down contact when a member of the pack exited the store. She hoped the young woman wouldn't report the incident. Any interaction with a shifter outside of the pack could be interpreted as a threat. "Thanks for your help," she said.

"No problem. Are there any good restaurants in town?"

"You might try Joy's. It's not fancy, but everything is homemade." She pointed down the street. "Two blocks east. You can't miss it."

He nodded. "I'll check it out. Thanks." He turned and went into the small store.

Rearranging her bags to throw off anyone keeping an eye on her, she retrieved the slip of paper and stuck it in her bra. She'd wait until she was alone to read it. Her hand struck something small but hard where it didn't belong. She couldn't restrain her curiosity and shoved aside a bag to uncover a metal case.

Lori hid a smile as she slammed shut the trunk, the object in her hand. A burner phone. How had he managed to drop it without her catching him in the act? She was supposed to be the master undercover artist. He was just the muscle. Too bad he was taken. She shoved the thought into a back corner of her mind. He was more useful as an ally than a lover.

When she saw Princess and her bodyguard leaving the drugstore across the street, she stuffed the phone into her purse. She'd find a good place to hide it later.

FOUR

The office was cramped to begin with, but add one large and angry enforcer and there wasn't enough air to fill Lori's lungs. Hyrum had pulled her away from the bar leaving Princess and Steve to cover.

"Who was he?" Hyrum demanded. Someone had informed him of her encounter in Charity.

"I didn't ask. He wasn't a pack member, so it was none of my business."

"What did you talk about?"

"The grocery store. Joy's Diner." Hyrum stood too close for Lori's comfort. She put her hands on his chest and pushed. She wasn't strong enough to make him budge but she was trying to convey an unspoken message. His superior strength didn't intimidate her—much.

Hyrum didn't back off. "He was kin."

"You mean shifter? Yeah. My guess is wolf. But as big as he was, he could be bear."

"What do you know about bear shifters?" A small snarl escaped his throat.

So, the Jaeger pack held on to the old prejudices against any shifter group besides wolves. They fell another couple of points in Lori's book. "I've met two or three. Never had the opportunity to sit down and chat with one."

"Did you tell him about us?"

Lori crossed her arms. "Why would I do that?"

His lip curled. "Profit. The Jaegers have many enemies who would pay for inside information."

With one finger, she jabbed him in the ribs. "Look. I have no desire to get involved in a pack feud. I'd be the first one to end up dead. I'm smart enough to not risk my life for any amount of money." Although she risked it every day for the cause. "Money doesn't mean a whole lot out here anyway."

Hyrum studied her, his probing gaze another intimidation tactic. "I can't read you and I don't like it. I don't trust you."

"You mean that whole 'thinking at each other' thing you guys do? You're not the only one who can't tell what's on my mind. I can't explain why. Maybe it's because I'm human and my brain works differently than yours does." Or the months of training that taught her how to close her mind to all but the most powerful alphas.

"You make me nervous. I'm not good to be around when I'm nervous."

"You make it sound like I'm some kind of threat. Little ol' me? That's almost funny."

His growl reverberated in the office. "I take my job seriously."

Not the most opportune time, but Lori grabbed the opening. "Why?"

He blinked several times at the unexpected change of direction. "Why what?"

"Why are you so committed to the Jaegers? I've

watched how they treat you. They don't abuse you as far as can see, but they don't respect you either. Why do you stay here? Haven't you ever considered returning to your pack?"

He reacted as if she'd slapped him, taking a step backward. "Who said I'm not respected?"

"No one has to say anything. Jaeger is using you. It's clear by the way he treats you. You're disposable."

"This pack raised me. I owe them."

"This pack ripped you from your family. You are an adult now. You're free to make decisions for yourself. If you want to leave, you can."

Lori didn't expect to see a shadow of sadness cross his face. "There's no place for me to go. My pack of birth doesn't want me. They believe I'll be a spy for the Jaeger's."

"I'm sorry, Hyrum." She meant it sincerely. "Have you ever considered going packless?"

"And go where? I don't have the skills to hold a human job. How would I live?"

"You must be good at something."

"I'm an enforcer. That's who I am and I'm proud of it."

She didn't want to make him angrier. "You're right. I'm sorry. I overstepped. I've never heard anyone say you weren't good at your job."

"As long as you understand that and don't get in my way, Grenville. I still think you're hiding something. If you remember anything else about the stranger, you'll tell me, right?"

"Absolutely." Not. "Can I get back to work now?"

He jerked his head towards the door. "Go."

As she squeezed past him, he grabbed her arm. "One more thing. I may only be the pack's enforcer, but you're nothing but a bartender. Understand?"

She pulled away, ignoring the pain. She'd have a bruise in the morning. "I may be a bartender, but at least I respect myself. Do you?"

"Are you sure that was a good idea?" Princess asked as Lori drew several beers. The bar's patrons eyed her as if expecting Hyrum to return and continue the show.

Lori frowned. "How much did you hear?"

"Little bits and pieces. Enough to know you made him angry."

"What was your first clue? The way he stomped through here on his way out? I've been known to rub people the wrong way."

"Be careful. Rumor is the last couple of people who got on his bad side disappeared. No one knows what happened to them."

"I'll be fine, Princess, but thanks for worrying about me. At least he won't show up here and ruin the mood anymore."

"No. Now we get to worry about him not being here when Floyd gets drunk and causes problems. That puts us on the losing side of the argument." She grabbed the tray, sloshing the beer, and clomped off.

Lori sighed. Now Princess was mad at her too. Not her best night.

"*New stop*," the note read. "D*evil's Tower. Ranger Abraham.*"

That was all well and fine but didn't do Lori a whole lot of good because it was hours away from Jaeger pack territory. It certainly wasn't worth Fairwood taking the risk of making contact. There had to be more.

She held the paper up to the light over her kitchen table. Squinting her eyes just right revealed faint marks that could be writing, but she needed a brighter source of light. And more privacy. Anyone could be peeking through the crack of the curtains that covered the small window over the sink.

The bare bulb in the windowless bathroom would do the trick. If, as she suspected, there was a second message written in lemon juice, the heat from the bulb would reveal it. Sometimes the simplest methods of hiding communication were the best.

"*Randy Jaeger dead. Possible murder.*"

Who was Randy Jaeger? She didn't remember any of her customers being named Randy. Who killed him? And what did that have to do with her?

With the note held over the sink and the fan turned on, she lit a match and set fire to one corner. She held it as long as possible and dropped the tiny scrap remaining at the last moment. The full force of the opened faucet washed the ashes down the drain.

As she got ready for bed, she finally remembered. Randy Jaeger, the alpha's younger brother and the other side of the Destin-Jaeger hostage swap. No wonder Fairwood had wanted to warn her.

Hyrum needed to be told. How to get word to him?

Fireworks? Lori rolled over to check her alarm clock. Who in hell was setting off fireworks at four in the morning?

She fluffed her meager pillow and pulled the blanket around her shoulders. There was still plenty of time for her to get back to sleep. She needed it because she hadn't been resting well. Hyrum hadn't shown up at the bar since their argument, and she had no way to reach out to him. Her weekly visit with Madame Rose got canceled at the last minute, so even that hoped-for opportunity vanished.

As she drifted back to sleep, another burst of explosions and light brought her to an upright position. She reached over and raised the blinds so that she could peer out the window. The red-orange glow that colored the night sky had nothing to do with a celebration or the rising of the morning sun. The months she served overseas rushed back to her.

It took every ounce of Lori's self-control to fight back the instinct to shift and join the battle. Fully awake now, she realized the long truce between the Jaegers and the Destins had ended. Whose side was she on?

Neither was her immediate answer. But she'd still offer her skills in first aid. The pack didn't have a clinic or doctor, and she'd trained as a medic in the Army.

She pulled on the jeans and shirt she'd left on the floor before crawling into bed. With the small first aid kit from her bathroom tucked under her arm, she dashed down the stairs to her car. It contained next to nothing but was better than going in empty-handed. Otherwise, she'd need to make do with whatever she could scrounge up from the village.

Mid-morning, Lori rotated her shoulders as she washed her hands for the umpteenth time. It was a good thing shifters healed quickly. No one died in the raid which ended at sunrise, but many earned their first battle scars. The Jaeger's younger generation had come of age, and the older ones had added to their collection of war stories.

The pack's abandoned schoolhouse was transformed into a triage unit. The desks had been shoved against the walls to make room for the injured to sit or lay on the floor. The mix of blood and dust bunnies created a hazard but she deemed it better than treating the wounded outside in the cold air.

As she and other women stitched up each shifter, the wounded returned to their homes to rest and heal. The Destins had proven their point—only one small outbuilding had been destroyed, but they were capable of inflicting heavier damage. The advantage was theirs.

Only a few more patients remained, and they were being taken care of, for the most part. A young man Lori didn't recognize slumped in the corner, staring at the floor. Underweight and clothed only in shorts, his face, arms, and legs were bloodied, but no one hovered near him. Her heart cried for him. Clearly an Omega.

The situation screamed trouble, but Lori was too tired to pay attention. She filled her bucket with fresh water and snagged a clean washcloth. The last bottle of rubbing alcohol lay open and emptied on the floor.

"Hey there." She knelt in front of him. He raised his weary eyes and blinked. "Let's get you cleaned up so I can see what the damage is."

"Don't touch him," Madame Rose snapped as she entered the room. Hyrum trailed behind her. She hadn't participated in the battle but had been one of the first to work with Lori to treat the pack's wounds. Hyrum had a few scratches but escaped major injuries.

Lori ignored her and dipped the cloth into the water. She cupped the young man's chin in one hand and wiped the blood from his face.

"Why not?" she asked, her back to the old lady, a huge breach of protocol.

"He's a Destin."

That explained everything. "He's also hurt."

Madame Rose cackled. "He'll be hurting a lot more before my son is done with him."

With only a few minor cuts on the Destin's face, Lori started to clean his arm. He warily watched her every move.

"I thought that was against the rules of combat."

"Who's going to stop us?"

Lori stood, the bloodied cloth clenched in her hand. Not giving herself time to change her mind, she turned to face Madame Rose. "I am. I claim sanctuary for him."

FIVE

"You're a fool," Hyrum repeated.

He was right, but when Lori made a commitment, she stuck by it. Only the three of them remained in the schoolhouse although guards patrolled outside to make sure the prisoner didn't escape. Lori didn't think he'd be able to because she'd discovered an injury needing stitches on one leg needing stitches.

"Don't you have any sympathy for him?" Lori asked. "Chances are the two of you are related." The captive still hadn't spoken.

"No, no sympathy. He chose his path."

"And I've chosen mine. At least I have honor. It's pretty sad when a human follows pack rules better than a pack does."

Hyrum growled. "You don't get to define what we call honor."

"Okay, tell me how you define it." Lori had no doubt Hyrum would parrot the textbook answer word for word.

"Pack first," he said. "Pack above self. Pack above all."

"Have the Jaegers formally accepted you into the

pack, Hyrum? Which pack should you be putting above all?"

"I support those who support me. The Jaegers."

If that's how he felt, nothing Lori said would change his mind.

"But why are you doing this? He's not your pack."

"I've always been a sucker for the underdog," she said.

"But to risk your life for someone you don't even know?" Hyrum cocked his head.

The concept of sanctuary was just that. Lori pledged her own life for the safety of the Destin. No further harm would come to him as long as he remained in Jaeger territory, but if he left, her life would be forfeit. At least he'd be safe until his pack arranged for ransom.

"It was the right thing to do." She turned back to the young man. "I'm out of supplies and that wound on your leg needs stitches. It's deep enough that even your healing powers won't fix it. I'll take you back to my place to work on it. No one here will give me what I need."

"You can't leave," Hyrum crossed his arms.

Lori was too tired to care about his intimidation tactic. "The pack owns the bar and my apartment, so I won't be leaving. I'll just be changing locations. That still meets the standards for sanctuary."

She turned back to the prisoner. "What's your name?"

He licked his lips. She wished for cold water to give him, but there were no glasses available and no clean containers for him to drink from. "Eugene," he forced out between parched lips.

"Eugene, can you make it to my car?"

"If it's not too far."

"You can lean on me."

He managed a small grin. "You don't look strong enough to be much help."

"If you hop on one foot, we'll make it. First, let's get you up."

She was surprised when Hyrum pushed past her. "I've got you," he said, leaning over and effortlessly picking up the prisoner.

Hyrum carried Eugene up the wooden stairs to Lori's apartment and stuck around while she stitched up the gash with regular sewing thread. By then it was midday and time to open the bar. She wondered if anyone would even show up.

Eugene had fallen asleep on her bed. She yawned as she peered in on him. "I think I'll keep the bar closed today," she whispered to Hyrum, who had taken up a guard position by her apartment's front door.

He nodded. "I don't think you'll have any customers today, anyway."

Probably not. "How can I get word to Princess and Steve?"

"I'll handle it. You get some rest."

There wasn't any place for her to lie down beside the small couch and she wasn't sure she'd get any sleep with Hyrum hovering nearby. "I should stay awake to make sure Eugene is okay."

"If he has a problem, I'll wake you."

She needed to wash off the blood, grime and sweat,

and use the special soap that hid her scent. If Hyrum caught a whiff of her *other* self, there'd be hell to pay. "I'm going to take a shower first. Do you want to wait outside?"

"I'll wait here where I can keep an eye on the prisoner. I won't peek if that's got you worried."

It hadn't even crossed her mind. Now that he'd mentioned it, she'd have to lock the bathroom door. If it had a lock. She'd never checked.

"There's water in the fridge and a coffeepot on the counter. Help yourself." She covered her mouth as she yawned again. "I won't be long."

When she came out, he was on the phone. The couch looked more comfortable than usual, and she curled up on it, bending her legs so she'd fit. She yawned again and didn't hide it. She really should check on Eugene. In a minute.

"It's about time you woke up," Madame Rose said.

Lori squeezed her eyes shut. She wasn't up to dealing with her.

"Don't pretend you're still sleeping."

"I'd like to be. I had a rough night."

"We all did. But we need to talk."

Lori shifted to a sitting position and stretched. "I need to check on my guest first."

"I already did. He's doing fine."

This wasn't going the way Lori wanted. "Would you like something to drink?"

"Hyrum made me tea before I sent him downstairs."

All the social niceties taken care of, Lori couldn't

think of any other ways to delay the upcoming conversation. "Why are you here, Madame Rose?"

Madame Rose leaned forward. Someone, probably Hyrum, had brought a chair upstairs from the bar for her. "I am here to warn you."

"How many enemies did I make today?"

"It is not how many, it is whom."

"Your son being on the top of the list, I suppose." A chill ran down Lori's spine.

Madame Rose's lips narrowed to a slit. "Yes."

"And you're a close second."

"I changed my mind. When I considered what you did for the pack, I found myself liking you. You could have hidden here and not gotten involved."

"I don't work that way."

Madame Rose nodded. "You would be an asset to the pack. But your actions regarding the Destin pup have made that impossible unless you take back your claim."

"I won't do that."

"Your refusal may cost you your job."

Or her life. Either would make Lori's mission impossible to finish. "I'm aware of that, but I won't change my mind. What is it about the Destin that makes him such a prize?"

"You really don't know?" Madame Rose sat back. "If our information is correct, he is Elex, son of Sereh, daughter of the Destin alpha. And the son of Randy Jaeger. My grandson. And rightful alpha of this pack."

It was too much for Lori's tired brain. "Wait a minute. I thought Elder Jaeger was the oldest of your sons."

"He is. But my mate designated our second son, Randy, as his heir."

Lori had heard of that happening before, but it was rare. "But Randy never claimed the position even as an adult."

"No. He chose to stay with the Destins and Sereh, his mate. He was officially accepted into the Destin pack on the same day as their marriage."

"Wouldn't that have ended his claim to the alpha position here?"

"Not if we joined the two packs. I have always hoped Hyrum would find a mate here."

"You?" Lori sputtered. "You suggested the swap to the Council?"

"I did. But it didn't quite go the way I expected."

The wheels churned slowly in Lori's head. "You wanted Elder Edgar to go to the Destins."

"It seemed like an obvious solution. He was not happy about his brother being named alpha-heir and did everything possible to make his brother's life miserable. Even hurting him in unfair fights. Separating them seemed to be the only choice."

"What happened?"

Madame Rose sighed. "I don't know. The Council representatives showed up a day early and I was gone when they arrived. My mate may have changed his mind about sending Edgar at the last minute. He would never discuss it with me. He was against the arrangement from the beginning."

There was more to the story. "Or?" she prompted.

"Or Edgar figured out what was going on and somehow convinced Randy to switch places with him. Randy adored his big brother, so it is possible."

"Or Elder Jaeger lied to his brother about what was going on."

"Yes." Madame Rose inclined her head. "The thought crossed my mind many times."

"Why didn't you do something about it?"

"By the time I got back it was too late. I'd gone into Casper to buy Edgar new clothes and toys to take with him. I wanted him to have things to remember me by."

"You never got to say goodbye to Randy."

"No. I told myself that it was all right, that we would reconnect when he grew up but now the chance has been taken from me." Moisture formed in Madame Rose's eyes and she hastily blinked it away. "Why am I telling you this? I have never mentioned it to anyone, not even my closest friends."

"Because seeing the captive woke up old memories and telling me is safe. It's in my best interests to keep your secret and it won't make you look weak to the pack. There's only one problem."

"What's that?"

"The young man told me his name is Eugene, not Elex. You've got the wrong Destin."

They'd argued for a few minutes about moving Eugene to Madame Rose's house. Madame Rose pointed out he'd be in a more comfortable bed and cleaner surroundings. Lori pointed out that it would place him closer to pack members who wanted to hurt him. She finally convinced the old lady, based on her somewhat exaggerated medical background, the move would be detrimental to his recovery. They did reach a compromise—Madame Rose promised to send over a new bed, one Eugene could stretch out on, and Lori would allow her to provide trusted pack members to guard the apartment.

With the guards came a bonus—food. Pre-cooked meals to warm up in the small microwave Lori moved from the bar to her apartment when she'd bought a bigger one for the business. She didn't think Eugene would appreciate her usual diet of salads and fruit.

After Madame Rose left, Lori went downstairs to get more ice to use on Eugene's injuries. To her surprise, Hyrum wasn't hanging around. He'd hinted about wanting to question Eugene. Which was impossible while Eugene slept.

And that worried Lori. Had she missed an injury when she examined Eugene? She'd been so focused on cleaning all the cuts and gashes, she hadn't checked for the signs of a concussion. After returning to the apartment and putting the ice in her freezer, she decided to check on him. The bedroom was dark now that night had fallen, and although she'd left the door open a crack, she couldn't see inside very well.

She intended to be silent but the door hinges squeaked as she opened it a bit wider. The light trickling in from the front room barely cast a glow on the bed. It was enough, however, to reveal that Eugene wasn't in it.

His hands shot towards her throat. Her inhuman speed and his injuries allowed her to avoid the explosive onslaught. Her upper canines dropped instinctively. The missed attack caused him to stumble. Unable to balance himself, he slammed into the wall.

She sprang to his side and caught him before he slid to the floor. "Hold onto me," she ordered. "I'm here to help you."

The gold streaks in his eye spun wildly. "Who *are* you?" he hissed.

Alpha power radiated from him, demanding an answer. Lori fought the dual need to both obey and ignore it. She was more concerned with the underlying pain that reached through her mental shields. How had she missed that he was alpha—and a strong one—when she treated his injuries?

"Why don't you sit down before you collapse?" she suggested, sending him a mental nudge to cooperate. She kept it almost non-existent so no one outside the room would pick up on it.

Leaning his full weight against her, he shuffled back to the bed and sat. "Who *are* you?" he asked again, this time more with curiosity than anger.

She flipped the light switch and held up one finger. "Follow it with your eyes," she said. "Don't move your head."

"I'm not drunk," he protested, but obeyed her instructions.

Next, she ran a hand over his face. "Those cuts are mostly healed, and there's no sign of infection. Hold out your arms so I can check them. Do you have a headache?"

"Not anymore."

A quick once-over assured her that even the deepest wounds were healing quickly and he showed no signs of a concussion. "Now your leg." She dropped to her knees.

The sharp intake of breath at her slight touch to lift the dressing was all she needed to know. "I did the best I could with it," she said, "but I'd be happier if a doctor took a look at it."

"No doctors," he said between gritted teeth.

"The pack doesn't have one anyway, and the retired nurse in Charity refuses to treat shifters so you're stuck with me." She got to her feet. "It's not infected but will take a while to heal."

"I'm not going anywhere, am I?"

Lori let out a deep breath. "Neither of us are."

"I'm not sure whether to thank you or curse you."

"Better dead than a prisoner?" she asked quietly.

"Something like that. But you still haven't told me who you are. I want to know who I'm hating." A slight smile on his face made a lie of his words.

"Lori Grenville. I run the bar for the Jaeger pack." She stuck her hand out. "And you are? Not Eugene, I suspect."

"We'll leave it as Eugene for now." The smile left his face and he ignored her outstretched hand.

Lori pulled it back. The refusal stung, but she understood why he didn't trust her. "Whatever you say. I'll help you get to the bathroom and then see what I can put together for supper. You need to keep your strength up."

"A raw steak sounds good."

Yeah, he was all wolf, she thought, helping him to his feet.

SIX

A week crawled by without another raid by the Destins. They had also not responded to Jaeger's demand for a large ransom for Eugene. Lori had become accustomed to having the young man around as he made himself useful, helping her with cleaning in the mornings. With Princess now banned from the premises, she needed his help.

During business hours, he remained confined to her apartment with guards stationed at the bottom of the outside stairwell. The few members of the pack who ventured to the bar seemed more curious than hostile. Business had dropped drastically. Lori wasn't sure if it was because her former customers feared being seen with her or if they were preparing for another raid. Or a retaliatory one.

Even Madame Rose avoided her. Lori had assumed she'd be visiting Eugene on a regular basis, trying to get to know him better. Her absence worried Lori.

She wondered if anyone had alerted the Council to the situation. If a Council representative took custody of Eugene, she'd be off the hook. But she'd been unable to use the burner phone to call any of her contacts to inform them of what was going on. All the extra people hanging around meant she never had a moment of privacy.

"Break time," she announced. She and Eugene were outside, refinishing the bar tables, cleaning off years of accumulated grime and sanding off surface damage before applying new varnish. Although almost healed, he still tired easily.

He straightened and stretched. "It's looking better."

"I'll claim this one is antiqued," she said. "Those burn marks are too deep to get rid of."

"It's old enough to be an antique. At least it's older than me."

She handed him a glass of water and poured one for herself. He refused to drink alcohol, even in the beginning when she'd offered it to him to ease the pain. "That's not saying much. I'm ancient compared to you."

Joking around eased the tension. They were keeping secrets from each other, but it was more uncomfortable when they didn't talk at all.

"That's right, you were around when they built the pyramids." Eugene tipped his head back and poured half of the ice water over his face.

Lori grinned. "And I came to America on the Mayflower." Tradition claimed some of the original settlers were wolf shifters.

"Elder Destin says one of his ancestors was with the first settlers in Virginia."

"Elder Destin? Your grandfather?" she asked in an undertone. The guards were inside, out of the heat and sun, keeping an eye on them through the windows.

"Who told you that?" He gripped the glass so

tightly Lori feared it would shatter. Eugene had no control of his emotions.

"Back off, Eugene. I'm your friend." Lori fought back her own anger at his emotional display. No pack should neglect such basic training for its young.

His eyes widened at her resistance. "I don't know that."

"You're right. You don't know that and you don't know me." Lori opened her hands and held them at waist level. It was a symbol of submission used in public places around non-shifters. "But you're an alpha. Even if you don't trust me, trust your *other*. What does your wolf suggest?"

His eyes widened further in recognition of her action and her plea. "I'm not an alpha."

"Whoever told you that lied. You may not be trained, but there is no doubt you are alpha. Why didn't the pack tell you?"

"I'm not pure Destin and my family history is unwritten. I'm only an Omega. How could I lead the pack?"

His birth was unrecorded? Lori wondered if he realized what he had revealed. She tucked the information away in a corner of her brain for safekeeping. "Didn't they give you battle training?"

"Not since my first shift. They said I was too undisciplined and weak for warrior status." The hurt that had caused showed in the strain of his neck muscles and leaked out in the tightness of his voice.

Lori shook her head. "An untrained alpha is far more dangerous than one who knows what he is capable of and how to control it."

"So says the human. And I'm not alpha."

"So says the battlefield tactician. You'd be

surprised at how much human military strategy applies to wolves. Doesn't the Destin pack encourage its young men to join the service?"

"Most of us go to work in the oil fields as soon as we are old enough. We bring money back to the pack to support our parents and grandparents. There isn't much else we can do. The silver mine that used to support the pack played out years ago, and it's not like we can take up ranching. Have you ever seen how cattle react to our presence?"

"They're a bit on the skittish side, I bet." Lori grinned.

Eugene released a slow breath. "That's an understatement."

Worried the guards would get suspicious of the lull in work, Lori tackled the chore of sanding the tabletop again. Eugene finished off his water and then joined her. "I can help you better if you tell me the truth," she said.

"Help me how?" He glanced towards the bar. The guards had come outside for a smoke break. "It seems as if we are both prisoners here."

"They serve two purposes. They are making sure we don't leave but they're also here so no one tries to hurt you." Or worse.

"Why would anyone want to protect us?"

"You, mostly. I'm expendable. But if you are Madame Rose's grandson, she's got a huge stake in keeping you alive. Those guards," she jerked her chin towards them, "are supplied by her."

"I'm not who she thinks I am."

Lori twitched as she resisted another surge of raw alpha power. He needed to learn control, and she couldn't help him while staying undercover. "That's between you and her. My opinion doesn't count. Since the Destin pack hasn't offered ransom for you yet, at least not that we've heard about, it makes me wonder. Why don't they value you, Eugene?"

She had no power to make him respond, but she knew a trick or two. She stared at him. It would make him uncomfortable to be challenged.

"I told you, I'm not pure Destin," he snapped.

"The strongest alphas I've ever run into were the result of alliances between two packs. In fact, bringing in new bloodlines makes a pack more resilient."

"Name one."

"The Fairwood pack back East. The alpha's mother was from a pack in New England somewhere." Gavin Fairwood never spoke of his mother, and she'd never heard the whole story. "In fact, he's mated to a woman with no pack affiliation. One of his seconds is from still another pack, and the other trained with a pack from Maine. Now they're one of the most powerful packs in the area."

"An East Coast alpha wouldn't survive the challenges that we deal with here on a daily basis. They're too civilized."

"That's another lie someone fed you. I've seen Elder Fairwood tear apart an enemy that threatened his mate."

Eugene smirked. "Words don't count."

"In wolf form, Eugene. Combat wolf to wolf by the old rules. Death to the loser. Elder Fairwood is still alive, so that tells you how the fight ended."

"They allowed you, a human, to watch the fight? You're lying." His eyes narrowed.

Lori's mouth twitched. "They didn't exactly allow me. Let's just say I was with a friend that night, and we just happened to end up in the right place at the right time."

"Like you happened to be in the right place to claim sanctuary and spare my life."

"That was no coincidence at all. I'm familiar with the sounds of battle, and I'm no coward. I could have stayed here in my apartment and not gotten involved but it goes against my ethics. The coincidence was you. How were you captured anyway?"

Eugene tipped the heavy table over, scattering tools everywhere. Lori stumbled backward, barely escaping getting hit by a hammer. A silent growl reverberated in her skull, followed instantly by a pounding headache. His fangs descended and hair sprouted from his hands, clenched in tight fists.

At breakneck speeds, the three guards came running, one shifting on the way. "Control your guest," the first one demanded as he helped Lori to her feet.

"Eugene, take a deep breath. Do it, Eugene."

The yellow streaks in his eyes spiraled wildly.

"Eugene," she shouted, "Deep breaths, now!" She wondered if she dared to touch him. Would it break through the trance he was in?

A wolf prowled just outside her range of vision. If he was good, he could kill Eugene in the vulnerable moment when shifting. But would the guard react swiftly enough to save her life if Eugene attacked?

She took the chance. "Eugene," she said, softening her voice, "look at me." The speed at which the streaks in his eyes whirled slowed and she took a step closer. "Focus on me, Eugene. I'm safe, right? I couldn't hurt you if I wanted to." She'd heard stories of shifters getting stuck mid-shift, and the results weren't pretty.

His eyes started to focus and his breathing slowed. "I'm going to touch you now, Eugene. You'll feel me stroking your hand."

A shudder ran through his body. She reached out and laid her cool hand on his burning hot one. Slowly, she ran her fingers across his hands and along his wrist, then moved them up to his arm. When his breathing was normal again, she rested her hand on his shoulder.

He blinked several times and focused his eyes on her face. His canines retracted and his pupils dilated. He licked his lips. "I'm sorry." The anguish in his voice tore through her.

She resisted the urge to throw her arms around him. "We've got to work on your control, but first you need to go for a run and work off some of that energy." She turned to the guards. "I'm not equipped to handle that. Can you guys help out?"

They held a silent conference, the one in wolf's form prowled in a tight circle around the little group. "We're not authorized to allow it," the head guard said.

"Well then, use your mind-talking magic and contact Madame Rose. See if she'll okay it."

The guard's face got the standard blank stare that told Lori he'd made contact. She waited impatiently, leaving her hand on Eugene's shoulder so she could track his physical state.

"How will you guarantee his good behavior? He's proven that he is unstable."

It was a valid concern. Would Eugene go rogue in her absence?

The answer was simple. Silver. Silver would inhibit Eugene enough to make him less dangerous, without stripping him of all his abilities. It was a bad solution, but the only one she had.

She held up the thin silver necklace a friend gave her years ago. The silver content was low and she was able to wear it for short amounts of time, creating a convincing display of her humanness. "Once you've shifted, I'll wrap this around your leg. I'm told it feels like a mosquito bite, irritating, but not painful unless you scratch it. Here, touch it."

Eugene poked it then jerked his hand away. "More like a horde of no-see-ums."

"You want to test it?" Lori asked the guards. Having four large men crowded into her apartment reminded her how small it was.

The head guard grinned and grabbed the necklace with one hand. He quickly tossed it back to Lori. "I'm not going to be the one to put it on him," he said, jerking his head towards Eugene.

The other guards held up their hands in a 'not me' gesture.

"I'll do it then," Lori said. Cowards. Leave it to the human.

The plan was for two of the guards to shift with Eugene. The third, who was staying in human form, was equipped with a handgun loaded with silver bullets. A fourth pack member was on his way to stay with Lori. If anything went wrong, it would be his duty to kill her. It seemed excessive, but if it would help Eugene control his wolf, it was all good.

The head guard's face went blank for a moment, but that was replaced by a look of surprise. "I didn't expect *him*," he muttered at the sound of footsteps on the stairs. He walked over, unlocked and opened the door.

Lori caught her breath when she saw who stood there. Hyrum.

"I'm against this." His glare stabbed each person in turn. "I don't like it at all."

"I'm sure you don't but Madame Rose approved it. She sent you, right?" Lori asked.

"Against my wishes."

"Look at the bright side." Lori put her hands on her hips. "If Eugene tries to escape, you get to kill me. Doesn't that make you feel better?"

"The only thing that would make me feel better is to cancel this ridiculousness." Hyrum crossed his arms.

"If you want to change your mind, I'll understand," Eugene told Lori.

"Nope. We made a deal. If you can put up with the silver I can put up with him." She pointed at Hyrum. "So, let's get this show on the road."

There wasn't enough room for all three men to shift at the same time. They'd do it one at a time, with Eugene going last. The guards pulled off their clothes and tossed them on the couch, but Eugene hesitated.

"I've seen you naked before if that's what's bothering you," Lori pointed out.

"It's not that. It's the idea of shifting in front of a human. That's taboo."

"I've seen if before, but if it makes you more comfortable, I'll turn around and promise not to peek." She matched her actions to her words and grinned when another set of clothing joined the others.

She'd wanted to watch him shift. It was a way she could judge how much training he'd received and how much work he needed. Hopefully, there would be more opportunities.

SEVEN

The unmistakable crunch of bones cracking and reforming as bodies changed shape filled Lori's ears. It sounded worse than it was, at least in her experience. But she'd trained with one of the best.

At least the noise helped her track the transitions. Two close together, then a short delay before the third. Eugene's shift seemed faster than the first two, or was that wishful thinking?

"You can turn around now," Hyrum said.

She didn't need help identifying which wolf was Eugene. He was larger than the others. His eyes shone more gold than the others and power emanated from his even stare. But she had to pretend. She had a secret to protect.

"Okay, who's the lucky wolf who gets to wear this thing?" she asked, dangling the necklace from her fingertips.

The two wolves who weren't Eugene curled their lips in a wolfish approximation of a grin. Eugene looked mournful as he shuffled forward on large paws. Lori knelt before him on two knees, well aware of the symbolism. An offer to serve him, although only temporarily, not a lifetime commitment. He didn't react to the gesture but Lori didn't regret making it.

It took only a moment to secure the necklace around his front leg. It dangled loosely, but his leg was too big for her to wrap it around it twice. As large as his paws were, there was no danger the slim silver strand would fall off.

"Does anyone want to check my work?" Lori stood and made a point of stretching. Hyrum pushed by her and nudged the necklace with his foot. He grunted his approval.

"All right then, you boys run along. See you in an hour or two. Play nice!" Lori waved her hands, shooing them towards the door. "You're getting hair everywhere and I just cleaned."

Behind her, Hyrum stifled a chuckle. She whirled to face him. "Don't laugh or I'll put you to work. You can start by sweeping while I dust."

One guard raised his muzzle and howled then bolted down the stairs. Eugene echoed the howl and followed him. Soon the room was empty, except for her and Hyrum. She took a deep breath. She'd be alone for the first time in over a week if she got rid of him.

"I'm serious," she said. "You stay, you clean. Or go sit at the bottom of the stairs and contemplate your belly button."

He shocked her by grabbing the broom from the rack behind the door. "You dust, I'll sweep," he said, "and we'll get this done in no time."

He was true to his word. Between the two of them, they knocked out all the chores that Lori had been putting off while she was acting as nurse to Eugene.

She even had time for a hot shower before the group was due to return.

Hyrum had gone downstairs to watch TV in the bar, giving her a few moments of privacy. As she pulled fresh clothes out her footlocker, her hand encountered the burner phone and she hesitated. Did she have time to make a call?

Voices from the bar below filtered up through the floor and she put the phone back in its hiding place, secure between the layers of a folded-up sweatshirt. It was a good thing she did because when she came out of the bedroom, pulling on a clean t-shirt, Hyrum was in the kitchen.

"You were low on soda so I brought some up for you," he said, closing the refrigerator door.

"Thanks." This new side of Hyrum made her nervous. What was his motivation?

"Why do you do that?" he asked suddenly.

"Do what?"

He sniffed and frowned. "Use a soap that washes away your natural odor. Don't human males appreciate the female's scent?"

"Not really. Most women wear perfume. I used to, but it bothers shifters, so I stopped."

"I don't understand it." He shook his head. "How do they identify their mate if they can't smell her?"

"Maybe that's why there are so many divorces."

"Not every wolf pairing succeeds."

"True. But how many of those are arranged and not true matings?"

"Sometimes the need of the pack outweighs the need of the individual."

"I don't believe that. Isn't it the pack's duty to help each member be happy?"

He frowned. "The alpha needs to weigh the two sides and determine the balance."

"There are lots of shifters that don't accept that. Too many alphas that put their own needs above that of the pack or its members."

"Being alpha doesn't make them perfect."

She'd heard the same old excuses too many times in too many places. "Don't you think pack members should have a choice? Whether to be in a pack or not?"

"We can't survive outside the pack."

"You're wrong. Times are changing. There have always been shifters who have left a pack or been thrown out and now they're banding together. Working together like a pack does, but no one gives them orders."

"Misfits, rebels, and malcontents."

Lori gave up. She wasn't going to change Hyrum's mind.

Rain pounded against the windows. Wyoming wasn't supposed to be this wet. Hyrum paced from the front of the bar to the back, pausing to stare outside at each end. Lori's calm demeanor as she meticulously examined each beer mug for cracks and chips was a sham. Everything had gone so well the first three days. What had changed besides the weather?

"They were supposed to be back forty-five minutes ago," Hyrum said, breaking his pacing long enough to glare at the clock on the wall.

Her stomach churned as she held up another mug to the light. Watching the second-hand tick away the passing time wouldn't make it go any faster. The slightest wrong move might set Hyrum off. Even in her *other* form, she didn't stand a chance if he attacked.

"Can't you hear them? With your mind-talking trick?" She didn't dare reach out herself. Hyrum might be able to overhear anything she *sent*.

He pounded his hand against the wall so hard that the nearby window rattled. Or was that due to the clap of thunder that reverberated at the same moment? "If they've crossed out of pack territory, I can't reach them," he said.

Eugene wouldn't break their agreement, would he? Lori didn't think so. Besides, his guards were there to act as guides as well. It was their duty to keep him on trails within the set boundaries. But in this storm, familiar landmarks might be difficult to locate. Had they accidentally strayed onto forbidden ground?

She considered offering Hyrum one more beer to calm him down, but he'd already had three. Shifters had a higher tolerance for alcohol than humans but she wasn't willing to take the risk that Hyrum might be a mean drunk.

"I'm going to make a fresh pot of coffee. You want a cup?" Lori asked. She took his answering grunt as a 'yes' and added another scoop of coffee grounds to the filter. Although she didn't see him as a cream and sugar kind of guy, she dug both of them out of the cabinet and put them on the counter alongside two cups.

"They've probably holed up somewhere waiting for the storm to pass," she suggested. She hoped.

Hyrum sat on a stool across the bar from her. It groaned underneath his bulk. "I don't want to kill you, you know," he said gloomily.

"Well, I should hope not!" Her tone was light, but her heart sank. When she claimed sanctuary for Eugene, she never expected that her life would be endangered. But that was the price to pay if Eugene didn't return.

"I will do it if necessary."

Her hand trembled as she filled his cup with the freshly brewed coffee and wondered if it would be the last time she savored the aroma. He placed his hands on hers and steadied it. Her skin tingled and she almost jerked away.

"It isn't my choice."

"There's always a choice," Lori said. "At least that's what a wise woman once told me. I made my choice when I demanded sanctuary for Eugene, and I don't regret it. Will you regret yours?"

"I don't get a choice. My orders came directly from Elder Jaeger."

You choose to follow him, she thought. "Not every order that an alpha gives is good."

"Sometimes they are necessary for the pack to prosper. The alpha must make unpopular decisions." He let go of her hand to pick up his cup.

As suspected, he drank his coffee black. She filed that bit of information away for future reference, but would she ever have a chance to use it? After pouring her own cup, she set the carafe back on the warmer.

How could he be so casual about the prospect of killing her? Didn't he have any empathy? She blinked back the rush of unwelcome tears and busied herself with arranging the same glasses she'd looked at a few minutes earlier. The legs of his stool screeched against the floor and footsteps heading away told her he'd returned to his pacing.

She tracked the sound to the front where they paused as he stared out the window. She didn't know how much longer she could stand the building tension. Surely, they'd hear from the guards soon. How long would Hyrum wait before claiming sanctuary was broken? Or would Elder Jaeger be the one to make the decision?

The footsteps returned to their measured cadence. This time, they stopped before they reached the back. She turned to see Hyrum standing inches away. "What?" she snapped.

He put a finger under her chin and lifted it so she was looking at him. "I promise I'll make it painless. That's the best I can do. Believe it or not, I admire you. You've shown much bravery and I'll miss you, human."

The words held little comfort. Dead was still dead.

He ran a finger down her cheek and leaned forward. "You've been crying."

"Allergies."

"Don't lie."

"So, I'm not ready to die. Big deal."

"Neither am I. That's my problem. If the Destin escapes and I don't kill you, Elder Jaeger will have me killed along with you. He won't be as merciful as I will be."

"He told you that?"

Hyrum nodded.

"I'm sorry. I didn't want anyone else involved. If there was a way to fix this, I would." Short of killing Jaeger, she couldn't see a way out. She patted his shoulder. "It'll be all right. Eugene will make it back. We're jumping at shadows. This storm has us freaked out, that's all."

He snorted. "This storm is nothing. You may trust Eugene, but I don't."

"I know. So, I'll do the trusting for both of us."

He ran a gentle finger across her lips. "From your mouth to the ears of whatever gods might be listening."

For a fleeting moment, Lori thought he might try to kiss her. Instead, he stiffened and his face went blank. She hoped for good news.

He exhaled loudly, blinked, and a smile creased his face. "They were hunting. Took down two antelopes. The village will feast tonight."

Her knees wobbled and Lori clutched the counter to support herself. She bent her head to hide a second wave of tears—these ones of relief.

"Will Eugene be invited?" She knew she wouldn't be on the guest list. Humans never were. She'd gotten use to the snub long ago.

"He made one of the kills so tradition demands his presence. I don't know how we can guarantee his safety. It would be better if he didn't go."

"Who would try to hurt him?"

"You want a list? Only about half the pack."

"The Jaegers hate him because he's a Destin, the Destins don't want him back—how can I help him?"

"You've mentioned wolves going rogue and leaving their pack. How much do you know about that?

More than she'd tell him—or anyone. "I have a friend I could ask. But I can't do it from here, and I can't go into town because Eugene can't go. Besides, you and I would have to leave too. It wouldn't be a problem for me but you're a different story. If Jaeger knew you took part in our disappearance and wanted to be vindictive, he'd send his men after you. Or hire someone else to track you down and kill you." Another reason the Free Wolves maintained their network of hiding places.

"What other choice is there?"

She reached for the thread of an idea and lost it. It tickled in the back of her head and she coaxed it to the front. There was another way, Lori realized. One that would relieve both her and Hyrum from any responsibility for Eugene. It went against much of what she stood for, but would make it impossible for Jaeger to object. "The Council," she said, "we request the Council take charge of Eugene. In fact, we ask that they send a representative to come and get him."

Since Eugene couldn't go to the village for the celebration, a few members of the pack brought the celebration to him. They finagled an entire leg away from one of the carcasses and brought it to the bar. Not *into* the bar, but to the empty field behind the building.

In misery, Lori watched from her apartment. She'd joined them for a few minutes, but it was too much for her *other* to bear. Between the sight and smell of the raw meat and the playful yelping and howling of the wolves, she almost lost control and shifted. It had been too long.

But Eugene seemed to be enjoying himself. He was the largest of the wolves there, bigger than even Hyrum, but his antics were those of a pup. At least someone was having fun, she thought, turning away from the window.

She considered locking the door and shifting for a minute or two. No one could get in and she wouldn't be able to get out in wolf form. But the urge to howl with the others would be too great, and she wasn't sure she'd be able to pass up the temptation.

Instead, she downed a double shot of rum to ease the pain and fell into her own bed. Eugene wouldn't need it tonight. He'd sleep with the others, as a wolf, under the stars. At least he'd have one night of happiness.

EIGHT

Lori grabbed the dashboard to steady herself as the truck hit another pothole. Two days after the storm, and the road was still nothing but washouts and potholes. She was convinced Rory was hitting them on purpose.

He didn't like her. She didn't remember ever seeing him in the bar, and a frown marred his face ever since they'd met an hour ago. His presence was Madame Rose's doing, but his loyalty lie with Elder Jaeger.

Lori had gone to Madame Rose, pleading her need to make a trip into town for personal items not stocked in the pack's warehouse. Madame Rose listened and worked out her little scheme.

Under the watchful eye of Hyrum, Eugene was spending the day at Madame Rose's house. That gave the elderly lady most of the day to manipulate Eugene into revealing the true information about his identity. Meanwhile, Lori got to go to Charity, even if it meant enduring the company of Rory.

Who hadn't even spoken to her yet. When they were introduced, he'd looked her up and down, refused to shake her hand, and grunted. She'd stopped trying to make conversation with him ten miles back. It was not going to be a fun day.

As they bumped along the road, she worked on a plan to ditch him as quickly as possible. The burner phone hid in her purse, buried beneath the carefully planted clutter of lipsticks, assorted old receipts, and tissues.

He didn't look the type to take kindly to being asked to wait in the truck while she ran her errands. Charity didn't offer enough activities to allow her to lose him in a crowd, one of her specialties. It didn't have a shoe store where she could bore him into leaving after watching her try on shoe after shoe after shoe. But another kind of purchase practically guaranteed he'd go running back to the safety of the truck.

Her shopping began in the grocery store. She needed napkins and paper towels for the bar and that aisle was a convincing place to start. Then she moved on to the snacks. Although she always kept the bar stocked with chips and pretzels, today she'd treat herself to personal favorites. At least that's what she wanted Rory to believe.

After pretending to study a display of dusty Christmas decorations, she moved on to her real target. Feminine products. As she'd hoped, Rory paused as she entered the aisle. "This will take a few minutes," she said, "if you want to wait for outside, I'll understand. I promise I'll be good."

He hesitated for a moment before turning around and disappearing out the front door. Lori grinned. It had been too easy. If she wanted to leave, she could walk out the back door and vanish. She'd done it before. Not this time.

After taking her time to select one of the small choices of offerings, she dug the burner phone out of her purse and steered her cart towards the back. Although the bathroom didn't offer total privacy, it was better than making the call in the middle of the store. Luckily, there was no line of customers waiting to use the facilities. She entered, making sure she locked the door behind her.

The number was engraved on her brain. Her heart pounded as she dialed and waited for an answer.

"Wind here," said the woman's voice.

"Shadow here," Lori responded. Her primary connection to the Free Wolves was a woman she'd never met. She'd only talked to 'Wind' on the phone. But their connection grew stronger each time they talked.

"How many passengers?"

"No passengers."

"Extraction?"

"No. Just listen, because you won't believe what you're about to hear."

Lori explained the situation in as few words as possible. Her time was limited, she didn't know how long she had before Rory came looking for her. When she finished, she waited for Wind's response.

She didn't expect a giggle. Then a snort. Then a full-out belly laugh. "You had me going there for a minute. What do you really want, Shadow?"

"I'm serious. The Council needs to step in. I've got two potential passengers, and I can't get them a ticket while I'm tied to sanctuary."

"Okay, we'll take it from here. We have friends who have friends. Do you need a callback to confirm?"

"No. I'm following strict deniability protocol on this

one." That meant as soon as the call was over, the phone would be destroyed.

"Roger that. Good luck, Shadow."

With nothing but dead air in her ear, Lori went to work. She took the back of the phone and removed the battery and the SIM card. The SIM was dropped into the toilet and flushed away. She shoved the battery into her pocket. There were other uses for it. She removed the lid from the toilet tank and dropped the phone inside, making sure it didn't lodge against any moving parts. The job done, she replaced the lid.

She took a minute to wash her hands. The bathroom was less than spotless and she didn't want to carry any germs back. When she spotted Rory in the hallway as she exited, she didn't have to invent an excuse for her disappearance.

"Get tired of waiting for me?" she asked with a bright smile.

Rory grunted, uncrossed his arms and jerked his head towards the front of the store. Lori took the hint. She retrieved her cart and resumed her shopping.

As far as she was concerned, there was no need to hurry back to pack territory. She'd been stuck there since Eugene's arrival and even a trip to Charity seemed like a mini-vacation.

After piling her purchases into the back of the truck, she turned to Rory with a smile. "How about some pie and ice cream at Joy's? My treat."

To her surprise, he nodded. "Okay," he said. Baby steps. She still had a chance to turn him into an ally.

Willpower. That's all it took, Lori reminded herself. Don't keep looking at the road, No one is coming.

It had been her mantra for the past week. At first, she had daydreams of Counselor Carlson, the head of the Wolves' Council, arriving in a shiny white limo to snatch Eugene away. At this point, she'd be satisfied with the lowest level representative sending a message asking to begin negotiations.

Which, in actuality, could have happened already. Chances of her hearing about it were slim. Top level pack politics were a closely kept secret. Since Hyrum had been avoiding her, little gossip reached her.

At least Steve hadn't abandoned her. With Princess no longer helping out, he'd become her second-in-command. Unfortunately, his low pack status meant he wasn't hearing any rumors either.

Eugene was out somewhere with his guards, hunting again. They'd been tasked with bringing in fresh game for Elder Jaeger's birthday. Jaeger had requested venison even if it was out of season. If Lori's wish came true, he'd have to settle for old rabbit.

The sound of a vehicle pulling into the parking lot broke her willpower and she craned her neck to see who it was. Her hopes were crushed when she recognized Rory's truck.

Her efforts to make him an ally resulted in an unintended side effect. He had a crush on her. She recognized the signs although he hadn't said anything about it. He'd started coming to the bar, sitting at the counter, ordering a beer, and watching her while he drank it. At least he didn't get in her way although she'd caught him glaring at other men who paid her too much attention. Or the wrong kind of attention.

"He's back," Steve said as he brought a tray of dirty mugs to the sink.

"I noticed."

"You want that I should get rid of him?"

A sweet offer, but in a physical confrontation Steve would be no match for Rory. "Thanks, but if he gets to be a problem, I'll handle it."

Steve shrugged. "Your call. But I've got your back, Boss."

Lori had a beer waiting for him by the time Rory took his normal seat. "What's up?" she asked, expecting his normal grunt in return.

Instead, he leaned forward and said quietly, "There's a rumor going around they're going to make a play for your friend Eugene. Maybe tonight."

She made a show of wiping up a non-existent spill. "Who?"

He lifted the mug to his lips. "I don't know. Nobody's talking."

That meant they ranked high in the pack structure. They might be working directly for Jaeger.

"What am I going to do?"

"Your best bet is to run."

She couldn't do that without abandoning Eugene. "No."

"Figured as much. Don't say I didn't warn you." He swiveled so he faced the room instead of her.

At Steve's next trip to the bar, she grabbed him by the sleeve. "I need to talk to you. In the office."

His eyes widened. "Did I do something wrong?"

"No. It'll only take a minute."

She handed him an empty box from behind the bar to cloak the reason for their disappearance. Once in the office, she closed the door behind them. "I need your help."

"Okay?"

"How good are your telepathic abilities?"

"I can reach farther than any of my friends," he said.

"I want you to contact Eugene. Tell him not to come back tonight. Come up with an excuse so his guards stay with him. Maybe he can fake an injury."

"You want to tell me why?"

"Why do you think? Not everyone honors sanctuary."

Steve's face paled. Lori hadn't wanted to place this responsibility on him, but didn't know what else to do. "I'll handle it," he said as he straightened his usual slumping posture.

"Thanks. Good luck." She hoped the plan would work. If Eugene and his guards spent the night in wolf form, they'd be fine. Although the nights were getting chillier, they were still manageable for a furry creature.

Rory's empty mug and four one dollar bills were all that was left to show he'd been there. Lori noted a few other customers also left in that short amount of time. Of those who stayed, she counted how many would fight for her and how many were neutral. The totals didn't look good. She hoped Eugene got the message and went along with the plan. It was the only way she had to protect him.

She had the bar locked up for the night when she detected voices outside. She'd even sent Steve home, although he'd offered to stay. A foolish move on her part, but she didn't want to turn the attack into a civil war within the pack. Besides, it was only speculation that the attack would be that night. The voices could easily be some kids out for a midnight stroll.

Still, she dropped to the floor and crawled over to the light switches. With the room darkened, she gained an advantage. She could use her *other's* heightened sense of sight without actually shifting.

Unfortunately, that meant anyone keeping an eye on the bar knew her location. Not for long. Bending low, she scurried over to the window and peeked outside.

The lights in the parking lot revealed the shapes of six men. Two or three of them she recognized. They'd been the worst troublemakers in the bar when she first took it over. They'd stopped showing up after Hyrum objected to their bullying tactics.

"Come out, come out, wherever you are," one taunted.

"Hand over the Destin and we won't hurt you," another called, slurring his words.

"Much!" yelled a third. He was met with scattered laughter from the rest of the group. Lori didn't find him funny. If they were drunk, their behavior would be more unpredictable. Bad for her.

She wondered if they knew about the gun behind the bar, her ace-in-the-hole. She'd never resorted to using the short-stock sawed-off double shotgun before, but there was a first for everything.

The real benefit of the weapon came in the special ammo she'd bought. To the casual observer, it appeared to be regular birdshot, but each bead contained pure silver. Not enough to kill a shifter, but a well-placed shot could put one down until each pellet was removed.

She double-checked the lock on the front door and wrestled the nearest table in front of it. Its legs screeched against the floor, protesting. There wasn't much she could do about the back door other than lock it. On her way to the back, she made a detour to grab the gun. As she turned the lock, the front door rattled.

"Let us in, little human, or we'll huff and we'll puff and we'll blow your house down." A roar of laughter followed.

Hilarious. Lori wondered how drunk the men were. But she had others to worry about.

Steve hadn't been sure he'd reached Eugene. He hadn't received an acknowledgment. She wasn't sure if that was good or bad. If Eugene and his guards showed up, they'd help even the odds. If they chose to fight at all. On the other hand, she didn't want Eugene injured or killed in a battle not of his making. Did she dare to drop her cover and try to reach him?

One other person might be willing to help. Hyrum was closer; but riskier. She had no way to disguise her mind-voice, but would he identify it as hers?

She didn't even consciously make the decision before she opened her mind. A torrent of voices overwhelmed her. She'd expected the pack members to be asleep, but instead everyone seemed to be shouting at the top of their 'voices.' Lori caught excitement and fear and puzzlement and rage in the brief moment before she quieted the hubbub. What was going on?

Telepathy worked so much better if the initial connection was established face to face, but Lori didn't have that luxury. She opened her mind again, filtering out the voices of women and children. Still, how would she find Hyrum among all the men? Did she dare send out a blanket call for help? And would it even be heard among the confusion?

Pounding on the back door broke her trance. "Lori! Let me in!"

Instinct dictated her response. "Get out of here, Eugene, before they hear you."

"Open the door, Grenville." A surge of power swept over her. She reached for the lock to follow its orders. At the last second, she shook herself free from the compulsion. "I'll deal with this. Go away, Eugene."

He threw himself against the door. It creaked and the window shook but held. "Let me in!" he demanded.

A second blow might tear the door apart, leaving her more vulnerable. She unlocked and opened it. Eugene rushed in, knocking her down in the process. He slammed the door shut and locked it before helping her to her feet.

"Where are your guards?" she asked.

"Trying to find help."

"What's going on in the village?"

"No idea. We've got bigger problems here."

A rock crashed through the front window. The shattered glass tinkled as it hit the floor. "This is your last chance, human," called one of the men.

"We can't wait for help," she said to Eugene. "You need to fight as your wolf. Slip outside and circle around so you can attack them from their rear. I'll hold them off in here." She lifted the gun in a salute. "First blood wins."

A slow grin spread across his face. "I like this version of you." His bones popped and crackled, the air shimmered and he was *other*. She opened the door for him and he slipped into the night. "Good hunting," she whispered and she turned the lock.

"*Good hunting,*" echoed back to her. She'd forgotten to close her mind to mental speech. Had Eugene known or was his response a force of habit? She closed the connection as a wolf crashed through the broken window.

With a smooth motion, she swung the shotgun to her shoulder. Without taking time to aim, she squeezed the trigger. The recoil pushed her against the wall, which held her up. The wolf, still advancing, snarled and tightened the muscles in his hindquarters. Lori didn't have time to figure out his plan of attack. She fired the second barrel. He dropped to the floor, whined, and crawled under a table.

She retrieved two more shells from her pocket and reloaded. Outside, a lone wolf howled. It echoed in the night but received no answer. Surely Eugene hadn't taken down an enemy already? Or had he abandoned her?

With her back against the wall, she took a deep breath and braced herself for another attack. An oppressive silence, broken only by her breathing and the soft whimpering of the wolf she'd shot, blanketed the bar. Lori jerked her head, trying to shake a few stray hairs away from her eyes. She didn't dare loosen her grip on the gun.

Then two wolves, side by side, emerged from the darkness outside and hurtled through the window frame. A third followed. The first two paced towards her shoulder to shoulder. When she pulled the trigger, the scatter of one shot hit both of them. One stumbled for a fraction of a second, but didn't stop. In two steps, they'd be on her.

She fired again, the recoil pushing her hard against the wall. The double damage at close range forced them back. One limped to the window and crawled out. The other sought refuge behind the bar.

She still had the third wolf to deal with and empty chambers. She broke open the gun and dumped the spent casings. They clattered to the floor, rolling towards the center of the room. The last wolf gathered himself for his onrush. Her hands shaking, Lori pulled more ammo from her pocket. One slipped from her fingers and rattled to the floor. There was no time to get another. She dropped the lone round in the chamber. A surge of power hit them, demanding compliance. To what? It staggered her and the wolf paused and shook his head, swatting his ear like he'd been bitten by a horsefly. She regained her balance first. The power didn't feel like Eugene's, but the distraction gave her the time needed to finish loading. She'd figure out who released it later.

The wolf shuddered, snarled, and backed up a few steps. Lori slid the bolt closed and raised the shotgun to her shoulder. What was he waiting for?

A chorus of howls shattered the silence. They sang of safety and peace. The last wolf dropped to the floor, rolled over and exposed his belly. Lori fought the urge to lower the gun but lost.

NINE

Lori had seen Counselor Carlson once before, back when Gavin Fairwood rescued his mate from the rivals who planned to take over her company. But when Carlson strode through the door of her ruined bar, followed by his contingent of bodyguards, she realized how much power he controlled. She fought the urge to shift and crawl on her belly to lick his feet.

"Lights, please," he said, and the spell broke. One bodyguard ran his hand across the wall until he located the switch. Lori blinked at the sudden brightness. Carlson glanced around, examining the situation.

Lori had stayed hidden in the darkness during their previous encounter. As he assessed his surrounding, she studied him. He hadn't changed. A large muscular man, he kept his graying hair short and neatly trimmed. His eyes landed in her.

"It would make me feel better if you'd drop the gun," he said with a smile. "If you don't mind."

One of his guards stepped forward and held out his hand, but Lori found her courage again.

"I'd kinda like to hold onto it," she said, "at least until I know what your intentions are."

He laughed. "I'm sorry, I should introduce myself. I forget that not all humans know who I am. Obviously, you're familiar with shifters, so maybe you've heard of me. I'm Counselor Adam Carlson, head of the Wolves' Council. By the way, what have you got loaded in that gun?"

"I'm familiar with who you are and your reputation. That's why I want to hang onto this." She raised the gun. "It's loaded with silver buckshot."

His guards tensed. One growled. "Aha," Carlson said. "That explains a lot. How can I make you comfortable enough to hand it over?"

"Tell me what you're doing here." She knew the answer but needed to protect her cover story.

He smiled. "I got a message from the wind that there was a young man here I needed to meet. So here I am."

"Thank you for your kind offer, but I wouldn't dream of asking Miss Grenville to move out of her accommodations," Counselor Carlson told Jaeger. Jaeger's offer to allow Carlson's group to stay in the village had been turned down on the grounds of maintaining neutrality in the upcoming discussions. Lori was angry that Jaeger then suggested Carlson make use of her apartment without talking to her first but she kept her mouth shut as she refilled the Counselor's water glass. "Besides, we have made arrangements for quarters."

She wondered where. Charity hosted only one old, ratty motel and she couldn't imagine the counselor and his entourage staying there.

Jaeger shot her a dirty look which she ignored. He wasn't top dog anymore.

"You aren't staying with the Destins, are you?" Jaeger asked, sounding like a spoiled little boy that someone refused to give candy to.

"You insult my integrity." Although his voice was emotionless, Lori caught the tightening of the tendons in Carlson's throat. "No, my staff is bringing in motor homes. We'll park here. I'm sure Miss Grenville won't mind if we hook up to the bar's electricity. Correct, Miss Grenville?"

Was he trying to upset Jaeger by deferring to her? It was the pack's bar, she was only running it. "Of course not," she answered. The truth was, the continued presence of Carlson and his guards made her nervous. To have them outside day and night for an unknown period made her queasy.

One of Carlson's staff leaned over and whispered in his ear. His face brightened, "I've just been informed the RVs will be here shortly." He stood and held out his hand. "It's been a pleasure, Elder Jaeger. We will contact you when were are ready to begin discussions."

It was as clear of a dismissal as Lori had ever seen and although Jaeger didn't argue, he took a moment to accept Carlson's hand. "The Destin will be coming with me." Eugene sat between two of Carlson's men on the far side of the bar. They'd patched up the various scratches and scrapes he received in the fight.

"Absolutely not. He is my guest, and I am taking over the responsibility of sanctuary while we investigate the problem. Miss Grenville is released of all obligation in the matter."

Lori silently cheered. That meant she could return

to her original mission. Or leave, if events demanded it.

"Of course, I anticipate depending on her for her advice as she has worked closely with him the last few weeks and may have insight in this matter."

So she wasn't off the hook entirely. Rats.

"She's not one of us," Jaeger objected.

"I'm aware of that." Carlson shot a glance her way and she caught her breath. Had he figured out her secret? "And that makes this situation all the more interesting. Good night, Elder Jaeger."

It was a direct order, and Lori caught the minuscule amount of power that Carlson put behind the words. Jaeger, shoulders hunched, all but bowed before leaving, followed by the few pack members who'd accompanied him.

A hint of dawn colored the sky through the empty window frame and Lori covered a yawn. She needed to get upstairs and to her own bed without seeming rude. She looked forward to being alone again.

"Miss Grenville," Carlson said, "If you don't mind, I'd like to ask you a few questions."

She did mind. As exhausted as she was, it would be too easy to slip and reveal more than she wanted to. "I'm sorry," she said. "Can't it wait until morning? At least, much later in the morning?"

He grinned and sent a soothing nudge of power her way. "I'll let you sleep soon, I promise."

She didn't want to play his game. "Look. Both you and I realize you could compel me to answer your questions if you wanted to. But you and I also know it's against the ethical code you promised to adhere to when you took your oath of office. Am I right? So let's call it a night. I'll be in a much better mood later on."

"You know more than you're telling."

He wanted to keep her talking. She recognized the technique. "Good night, Counselor. Please feel free to make use of the bar until your RVs arrive. Make sure to lock up when you're done."

One of his guards covered his mouth and coughed. Or was that a chuckle?

"If you want anything to drink besides water, just keep track of it. I'll run a tab for you," Lori said. "Good night."

As she headed up the stairs to her apartment, Lori was certain it *was* laughter she heard.

Lori hadn't expected Carlson's staff to cook breakfast for her when she emerged from her apartment, well-rested and freshly showered. She'd lathered extra well, hoping to preserve her image as human. She doubted it would work.

He was off in meetings, so her questioning was delayed. She'd been awakened by a stream of motor coaches somewhere around sunrise. She'd seen TV shows about million-dollar RVs, but to have eight of them in a line outside her door stretched the limits of her belief.

Rested and fed, she got ready to head to the bar and figure out how to repair the damage. It would take several pieces of plywood to cover the broken window until she could round up enough cash to replace the glass. She'd decided to not try to pry the silver pellets out of the walls. They'd add a distinctive touch to the decor, a unique reminder of the night's event.

As she stepped out of the kitchen RV, she was greeted by the buzz of an electric saw coming from the bar. Two delivery trucks parked outside the front door as well as a pickup from a local carpentry shop. The front window was already boarded up.

Inside, the sight of stacks of wood and several men measuring the walls greeted her. Another man was cutting boards. "What's going on here?" she asked, yelling to be heard over the noise of the saw.

"You must be Miss Grenville." The man using the saw turned off the blade. "I'm Xavier. Counselor Carson wants to use your facility for the upcoming talks so we're doing minor repair work."

Lori looked him over. All wolf. Even though he'd put down the board he was working on, his massive shoulders stretched the sleeves of his T-shirt. "I don't remember anyone asking for permission."

He grinned sheepishly. "Sorry. We thought you'd appreciate the help. Someone did a lot of damage here."

"That would be me," she snapped. The bar had become a bit of a sanctuary for Lori, and all the 'invaders' had destroyed her peace of mind.

"Nice!"

She hadn't anticipated his approval. But then, some male wolves took pride in their mates being able to fight on their own. She'd been hanging around the Jaegers for too long.

"So you took out half a dozen wolves?" asked one of the other men.

"Only three," she admitted.

"What did you use?"

"Shotgun. Sawed off, double-barreled."

"Silver birdshot too," Xavier held up one of the pellets. "They're all over the place. Great combination for self-defense."

Lori was impressed that they didn't question her ability to use the gun. Most people looked at her size and assumed she was harmless. She felt a bit more charitable towards them. Maybe they could collaborate. It was on Counselor's Carlson's dime, after all. "I'd like to see what you have planned. There's a few changes I've wanted to make since I got here."

With the bar closed for normal business, Lori needed something to do. Now that the repair work was being tackled in earnest, she was in the way. She tried to catch up on some reading, but the noise from downstairs distracted her every few pages.

Mid-afternoon, she drowsed off into a light sleep. The banging of hammers and nails kept her from drifting into a deep slumber. In her fitful dreams, the banging downstairs morphed into a wolf hurling itself against her door, and, half-awake, she reached for the shotgun.

And finally woke up enough to realize someone was knocking on her door. "Miss Grenville, are you there?"

It appeared her meeting with Counselor Carlson was about to happen. She was out of time and excuses. As she stumbled towards the door, she wished she had time to take another shower and renew the protective soap. "Coming."

She expected him to be accompanied by his ever-present bodyguards, so she was shocked when she opened the door. He stood there alone, in a pair of tightly fitting jeans and crisp cotton shirt instead of his suit. In one hand was a bottle of wine, in the other a large picnic basket. "They told me you missed lunch," Carlson said. His eyes sparkled. "So I brought you supper. If I'm going to grill you, you need to keep your energy up."

"Is this a trick?" She put her hands on her hips and cocked her head to study him. "The outfit doesn't match your reputation."

"I was trying to fit in with the locals."

"You look like New York City's interpretation of a cowboy, minus the hat and boots." For some reason, he was wearing his dress shoes. "But if what you have in that picnic basket tastes as good as it smells, I'll forgive you. Come on in."

There was only one chair for her kitchen table, so they sat on the couch and spread the food he'd brought on the rickety coffee table. Lori's mouth salivated at the sight of the steaks still dripping red juices. Thankfully, he'd brought wine glasses with him because she didn't own any. She didn't even have to supply plates and silverware because they'd been tucked into the basket.

"Your staff thinks of everything," she said.

"They take good care of me, but not enough came on this trip to cover the serving duties during the conference. Can you make any suggestions? I'll pay them, of course."

She gave him points for a smooth transition between handling the obligatory niceties and getting down to business. "I assume you'll want representatives from both packs. There are a couple of people I can suggest from the Jaegers, but I haven't met any of the Destins. Eugene might be able to help you."

Carlson nodded. "I'll ask him."

"From the Jaegers, you'll want to ask for a kid who goes by Steve although his name is Ralph. He'll be happy doing pretty much whatever he's asked to do, as long as he gets paid. He's saving his money to get out of here."

Carlson's lips twitched. "Anyone else?"

"Princess."

His eyebrows arched. "Elder Jaeger's daughter?"

"The one and only. She's fed up with being the sacrificial lamb offered to help expand her father's influence and wants to expand her horizons. But you'll want to make sure you're never alone with her. Her father will try to manipulate the occasion to make you choose her as a mate."

"You don't have a very good opinion of him."

"I only met him once before last night. My opinion of him is based on hearsay." And her personal suspicion that he was either the weakest alpha she'd ever dealt with or a beta masquerading as an alpha.

"And your disdain of the pack system."

"I didn't say that," she said, quickly on alert.

"You didn't have to. I've worked with the Free Wolves enough to understand the prevailing philosophy. You are a Free Wolf, aren't you, Miss Grenville?"

"What makes you say that?" She fought the rising panic. The risk of death grew with every person who discovered her secret.

"Why else would someone with your talents take a position in the middle of Nowhere, Wyoming? I must say, you're one of the best-trained operatives I've had the pleasure of meeting. I assume you're wearing contacts but I can't imagine how you hide your scent as well as you do."

It made sense as the alpha's alpha he'd see through her disguise.

Carlson continued without waiting for an answer. "If I have to guess, I'd say you're hoping to get Steve and Princess away from the pack. And since one method is as good as another, you're hoping that I'll hire them permanently."

Things were moving too fast for Lori's comfort. "This is between us, right? You're not wired, and no one is listening in?"

"I give you my word." He held his arms wide open. "You can frisk me."

Lori decided she didn't need to. Sometimes honesty was a good policy. "Steve, no. He'll never be as strong as your bodyguards, and his interest is computers. He's the perfect fit for Miss Lapahie's school." Dot Lapahie, another of the Free Wolves, ran a training facility for computer-related fields.

"I'll let you handle his escape then. And Princess?"

"She's been raised to be eye-candy and nothing more than a fancy breeder. She doesn't know what she wants and hasn't been given the chance to explore anything beyond the narrow choices her father has given her. I'm afraid she'll be overwhelmed by the freedom that the Free Wolves offer."

"An interesting observation. I'll think it over and then we can collaborate on a solution. What about her mother?"

Lori shrugged. "No one talks about her. I suspect she either left the pack or is dead. Madame Rose is too busy being the alpha female of the pack to give Princess much support."

He nodded thoughtfully and cut into his steak. Lori followed suit. The juices dripped onto her plate and her wolf wanted to lick them up. It had been too long. But her reverie broke when Carlson spoke again.

"What about Eugene?"

TEN

Lori took her time answering Carlson's question. "What has Eugene told you?"

"Next to nothing. I don't have the time to spend with him, and he doesn't trust me." Carlson seemed unperturbed by the confession.

Smart call on Eugene's part. "So why aren't you having supper with him tonight?"

"Timing and appearances. It's all politics. I need to make it seem as if my visit is more about arbitrating old differences between the packs than focused on Eugene."

"How I do I fit into your scheme?"

"I need to decide. My intel didn't tell me about you. Hence, supper." He waved his hand over the bounty.

"It'll take a lot more than one supper to buy my loyalty."

"I suspect there isn't enough money in the world to buy your loyalty, Miss Grenville, but I hope we can be allies in this endeavor."

"When it suits my purposes. I don't know your end-game yet."

"Meaning?"

"You've got two alphas at war. It's easy enough to say you're here to negotiate a truce. Now throw in a young alpha without training that may or may not be heir to both packs although no one will acknowledge him."

She tore off a piece of her roll and smeared it with butter. It wouldn't hurt to throw him off-balance. "Don't forget to factor in that this whole mess was caused by the Council the last time they tried to resolve the pack rivalry. You've got your hands full, Counselor. Forgive me if I don't want to align myself with any one side."

Carlson nodded, unperturbed. "I understand. But that leads us back to Eugene. Are you sure that his training has been neglected?"

"Non-existent might be a better description. He uses his power without even knowing he's doing it. I'm surprised he didn't kill anyone last night."

"He's untrained and you encouraged him to fight?"

Lori grunted. "Encouraged him? No. I couldn't talk him out of it. Besides, before he showed up, it was me against six men. What other option did I have?"

Carlson got the familiar blank look on his face. It lasted for only a moment. "His training needs are noted. It isn't the first time we've come across an untrained alpha, although usually, we place them with a nearby pack. We'll have to look further away this time."

"Gavin Fairwood." Her favorite alpha.

"I'm aware of the unique skills Elder Fairwood has, but he might not be the best mentor for Eugene. Besides, he has his hands full planning a wedding."

Lori dropped her fork. "He's getting married? I thought he was happy being mated to Dot."

"The two of them are very happy. They decided that

they wanted to make it legal in the human community, not just on pack terms."

"Well, I'll be darned. What's the date?" She'd been out of the loop for too long.

"It's still in negotiations." Carlson buried his face in his hands and groaned. "Pack wars I can handle, but being asked to come up with a date that doesn't conflict with Council activities is impossible. They asked me to officiate."

Underneath his hands, Lori detected a smile. She giggled.

"At least they agreed to hold the wedding in Atlanta so it will be neutral territory, and both pack members and Free Wolves can attend. But somehow I got suckered into helping them find a location for the ceremony and reception." He shook his head and blew out a loud breath.

Lori chuckled.

"Even that wouldn't be bad but then I got on a conference call to hammer out the details and they started talking about dress designers and shoes and makeup. It was terrible!"

Lori laughed. "You poor thing! It's not like you have a staff who does that sort of thing all the time. You know, the folks who conjure up RVs in the middle of the night and pack amazing picnics on the fly. You should trust them to pull together the wedding of the century, right?"

"That's what I keep telling myself." Carlson sighed dramatically. "It gives me the chills just thinking about it. Can we get back to business?"

"What else do we need to talk about?"

"How much to pay you, for one."

She stiffened. "You aren't buying me."

"I phrased that badly, I'm sorry. To help maintain your cover, I'll request Elder Jaeger temporarily assigns you to work for me. He'll try to pump you for info, but I trust you won't reveal anything of any importance. I hope that you'll coordinate the locals we hire as serving staff, so that will allow you to keep an eye on your friends. And I will pay you to make it appear official."

"I can't be on the books."

"Why not?"

"It's simple. I don't exist. No birth certificate, no social security number, no driver's license. There's no official documentation that a Lori Grenville has ever walked the earth, and I don't plan to change that now. Not for you or anyone else. I'll take cash, or you can make a donation to the Lapahie school."

He nodded. "Cash it is. If you ever want to change your undocumented status, I have the connections."

So did the Free Wolves, but it was a kind offer. Besides, her other identity had all the needed paperwork. "Thanks. I'll keep it in mind."

"Also, after tonight, I'll need to limit direct contact with you. I'll assign one of my staff to relay messages back and forth. I can't be seen as treating you any differently than anyone else from either pack."

If she needed to talk to him, she'd find a way. She didn't go by the moniker 'Shadow' for no reason.

"Is there anything else you can think of that we should discuss?"

A tendril of concern chewed at her. "Hyrum."

Carlson's eyebrow raised. "The Jaeger's enforcer? Another alpha?"

"Yep. Him. He's not an alpha, but he's not a Jaeger either."

"Many packs choose their enforcer from outside pack ranks."

"Yeah, but he's a Destin. In fact, he's the other side of the hostage swap."

"Go on. Is he a Free Wolves candidate?"

Lori shook her head. "No. He claims he's happy with being part of the Jaeger pack. But he's not. Part of the pack, that is. They never formally accepted him. And I'm not so sure about the happy part either."

"What do you want me to do?"

"I wonder if he's being compelled or blackmailed somehow. I've got no proof, it's purely a reaction at an instinctive level. He's loyal to Jaeger and I don't understand it. Talk to him and see what you think."

"That can be arranged. But you can do me a favor in return."

Lori was used to trading favors for favors, but she was wary about swapping favors with someone in his position. "What?"

"I need to go for a run tonight. My wolf wants to stretch his legs. Will you come along? Several of my bodyguards will accompany us, so you'll be chaperoned. And the combination of our scents will cover yours, so no one will be able to detect your *other*."

It was an offer Lori didn't want to refuse, but one she wouldn't accept either. "As much as I'd like to, no. The more people that know my secret, the less of a secret it is. And that's a risk I can't take."

Behind the bar, Lori grabbed the ice tongs and dropped two small ice cubes and only two cubes into a crystal whiskey glass. After two days of negotiations, she knew exactly how Counselor Carlson liked his drink. Bartending for him wasn't much different than serving anywhere else except the drinks were of better quality and so were the customers. Most of them anyway. She still hadn't made up her mind about Elder Destin, and Jaeger had done nothing to improve her opinion of him.

The two of them wouldn't even sit at the same table. Destin claimed a table on one side of the bar for him and his staff, and Jaeger and his advisers sat as far across the room as possible at another. Carlson and his people formed a barrier in the middle.

The negotiations on seating arrangements had made Lori's head spin, so she didn't expect much from the discussions on the actual issues. Neither Jaeger nor Destin seemed to want a solution. They'd be happier continuing to hate each other.

Lori gave Carlson a lot of credit, however. He'd found a beginning point they agreed on, and kept hammering away at other issues that, if settled, would benefit both packs. Like supporting the small businesses of Charity instead of ordering supplies on-line. Or helping to establish a medical clinic there, so the basic needs of pack members could be treated closer to home.

But no matter how many hours were spent debating, Carlson didn't seem to be making any progress on the question or the raids or the status of Eugene. Lori didn't even know where Eugene was. She hadn't seen him since the night of Carlson's arrival.

Drink in hand, she made her way to Carlson's seat. Only she was allowed to make his drinks and serve him. Although he played it off as an idiosyncrasy, he had a right to be wary. His position as the most powerful wolf shifter in North America brought an inherent set of risks, and assassination attempts were one of them. Lori hadn't been screened in the normal fashion because she didn't exist in those databases, but Carlson vouched for her, to his bodyguards' dismay.

She winked at the nearest guard. He glared at her and crossed his arms. She didn't expect they'd ever be friends and she didn't have the time to change his mind. Being down one server meant she had to work extra hard and extra hours. She covered her mouth to hide her yawn. It didn't look as if she'd get to bed early. At least the bar closed after the days discussions were over, and became off-limits for everyone but Carlson's people.

Her wait staff was down to three, the two Destins and Princess. Steve had been whisked away the first day to 'help' with laying computer wiring. That was the story, anyway. Lori heard he'd packed up his clothes after the second day and moved into the RV that housed the technology staff. One less passenger for her to stress about.

Back at her station, she watched as one of the Destins waiters, Rupert, flawlessly refilled the water glass of his pack leader. Lori needed to make time to chat with him away from the bar. He'd complained once that he wanted to study literature and become a writer and Elder Destin wouldn't allow it. If he was thinking about leaving the pack, Lori could help.

On the other side of the bar, Princess hesitated as she neared her father's table. The water in her pitcher sloshed and almost spilled over the top. Josef, seated beside Elder Jaeger, sneered.

"You can't do anything right, can you?" he said. "Not even pour water without spilling it. Some waitress. Here, let me show you how to do it." He shoved his chair back and stood.

Lori couldn't get to Princess fast enough to stop whatever Josef had planned. The last time he 'helped' her, he dumped an almost-empty pitcher on Princess' feet. He'd been finding ways to embarrass her all week long and there wasn't anything she could do to put end to it.

One of Carlson's guards got to Princess first. He stepped between her and Josef and took the pitcher from her shaking hands. He turned, and without a word, filled Josef's water glass to the brim. His glare dared Josef to complain.

Lori held her breath. She wouldn't put it past Josef to attempt to interrupt the proceedings. Both sides had been trying to all week. Carlson shut down each attempt, but she wondered when he'd reach his breaking point.

She'd reached hers. No matter what happened, Princess wouldn't be serving the Jaeger delegation anymore. Lori would either keep her behind the counter making drinks or have her serve the Destins. She'd have to clear that move with Carlson.

At least Josef seemed to get the hint—this time. Frowning, he took his seat and carefully picked up the glass and took a sip. Lori got satisfaction out of seeing that he spilled a few drops in the process.

Conversation in the room resumed and the guard, after giving the pitcher back to Princess, retook his position. She gulped, but filled the rest of the water glasses before scuttling back to the bar.

As normal, Lori was the last person in the bar at the end of the day, except for the guard who stayed all night long to ensure nothing was touched. She brewed one last pot of coffee and left in on the warmer for him. Although he never acknowledged the action, the pot was always emptied and cleaned in the morning. "Good night," she said as she pulled off her apron and tucked it under the counter before heading out the back door.

The crisp night air wrapped itself around her as she stepped outside. Stars glittered in the sky, slightly faded out by the lights from the RVs. The Milky Way swept from one side of the horizon to the other and Lori paused to enjoy the show.

But something was off. The wind carried a scent that didn't belong. It mingled with smells of sage and dirt and diesel and she couldn't isolate it. She considered returning to the bar and asking the guard to walk her upstairs.

It would have been a good choice. But in that moment of hesitation, a large form, as black as the night itself, emerged from the darkness and sprang.

She didn't have time to shift. Instead, Lori threw herself to the ground and rolled. The wolf missed, but swiveled on its back paws, bunched its muscles, and prepared for a second attack. Without a weapon, she could only hold it off for a few seconds.

So she did what any human would do. She screamed. Only she dropped the pretense and screamed with her mental voice. The sound of a rabbit's dying scream. The shrill, high-pitched cry for help didn't need to be aimed at only one person. It would wake everyone within range. There'd be a lot of headaches in a very short time.

The wolf stopped in its tracks and shook its head. That was all the time Lori needed. A metal snow shovel had been left leaning against the building after the last snow months ago, and she grabbed it. She gripped it in both hands and swung.

Her aim was true. The shovel thudded against the side of the wolf's head and it staggered. But Lori knew of a more vulnerable spot. She adjusted the direction of the next swing. The awkward angle resulted in a less forceful blow, but still, she hit the tender nose.

The wolf snarled, its teeth glistening, and leaped.

She whirled out the way and swung the shovel at the same time. The blade met the wolf's front haunches. A cracking sound sent a chill down Lori's spine. The wooden handle was breaking. She'd only get one more hit. It had to be a good one.

The wolf heard it too. Out of reach of her makeshift weapon, it paced, tongue hanging from its mouth. Left to right, right to left. Only Lori's eyes followed it. She watched for the telltale signs. The tightening of muscles, the focusing of the eyes, a lowering of the head. The wolf was toying with her. Her heartbeat kept pace with the wolf's steps. Too fast.

But where was the guard? He'd had time to come to her rescue. Was this one of Carlson's men? She'd been a fool to trust him. He was just another pack leader. Take advantage of those less powerful and discard them when they are no longer useful.

She wondered how sharp the edge of the blade was.

Sharp enough to rip through flesh? There was no time to check. She needed to stay alert for every twitch.

The charge happened in the blink of an eye. One second he was on the ground, the next flying towards her. She didn't wait. With a loud cry, she held the shovel straight in front of her like a lance and ran to meet the attack.

The shaft of the shovel splintered as it met the wolf's forehead. She dropped to the ground, still holding the broken end. The wolf landed on top of her. A claw pressed into her thigh. She gathered her strength and thrust upward. Wood penetrated fur and she pushed harder. Flesh tore and she kept pushing until wood found bone.

A howl ripped through the night as a heavy weight settled on top of Lori. Her face was buried in fur and she couldn't breathe. Instinctively, she opened her mouth to draw in air and tasted blood. Shifting was impossible under his dead weight. She struggled to push the heavy bulk off her chest, but her arms failed her. How ironic, she thought, to be smothered to death by an opponent she'd defeated.

ELEVEN

"Breathe, dammit, breathe!"

Hands pounded on her chest. A spasm ran through her body and she gasped. Air rushed to her aching lungs. She struggled to breathe but her throat was blocked. She couldn't stop coughing and bile rose. It settled at the back of her mouth. The acid mingled with the sweet flavor of blood and her stomach churned. She retched and a seizure wracked her body.

She was rolled on one side, too weak to protest. Her hair was gently brushed away from her face. She took a shuddering breath and spit, trying to get the bitter tang out of her mouth.

"I've got you," a low voice said.

She *heard* the words both with her ears and her mind. She slammed the blocks into place. It was too risky to reveal herself when she had no defense against an attack.

A trickle of water slipped across her lips and her tongue darted out to capture it. "More," she pleaded, and then coughed again.

"I'm going to sit you up so you can have a proper sip. Don't worry, I have you, little human."

Strong arms wrapped around her and brought her to a sitting position. The screaming pain in her leg settled into a dull ache. A warm body behind her gave her something to lean against. A cool object was pressed to her lips and she tilted her head back as water slipped into her mouth.

"Spit it out," ordered a new voice.

Reluctantly, she did so. It seemed a shame to waste perfectly fine water.

"This time, swish it around and rinse out your mouth." It seemed like a good idea. She didn't want the bitterness of blood to ruin the water's freshness. She spat out the third sip as well, and the coughing started again.

"It'll get better. You can swallow this time."

She lapped greedily as the water bottle touched her lips, demanding more. It was pulled away far too soon. She whined in disappointment.

"A little at a time."

The swallow was bigger this time. She tried to open her eyes but they were glued shut. Like a tired child, she raised her fists to rub them. Someone grabbed her arms to stop her and she groaned.

"Let me wash your face first. We need to see what the damage is and don't want to injure your eyes." Another new voice. How many people were there?

While wet fabric stroked her face, she listened. She counted the breathing of four people close to her, but quiet murmurs told her there were many more nearby. A soft buzz in her head was either the beginning of a massive headache or a sign of many unheard conversations going on.

"Try to open your eyes now."

She blinked and forced her eyes open, but a light

shining directly into them forced her to shut them again. "Too bright," she croaked after licking her dry lips to wet them.

She caught the distinctive click.

"It's off now. Try again."

Lori blinked to adjust her vision to the semi-darkness and looked around. So many people. Most of them she recognized as Carlson's staff. Carlson himself was nowhere to be seen. Who held her?

If he talked more, maybe it would jog her memory. What could she ask that would force him to respond?

"Ready for another drink of water?"

Hyrum?

Lori tried to twist in his arms but he held her tightly. "They want to take a look at your leg. Hold still."

"We're going to have to cut your jeans. Sorry about that," said the third man.

Lori wanted to argue it was only a scratch and not worth bothering with, but he'd started cutting along the outside seam. Besides, now that she paid attention to it, her left leg hurt like hell. She wondered what it looked like, and what she would recommend as treatment.

As the jeans fabric broke free from the wound, she gritted her teeth. Crying wasn't an option. Not in front of all of these men.

"She's going to need stitches," the man announced. "But I only have medical supplies to treat shifters." He looked Lori in the eyes. "If you were a shifter I wouldn't be so worried, but humans don't heal as fast as we do. I'd like to get you in more light so I can get a better look."

"Lead the way," Hyrum said. Lori found herself scooped up and in the air, cradled in his arms.

Lori had only been in one of the RV's, the one designated at the kitchen. While nice, its setup was fairly basic. When Hyrum carried her in to this RV, the chandelier hanging from the ceiling caught her eye. Then the maple cupboards. She worried about getting dirt and blood on everything she touched.

With great care, Hyrum laid her on a leather couch. "What can I do to help?" he asked.

"We'll take it from here," said one of the men.

"I'm not leaving her."

"Hyrum, I'll be fine." If he left, she could share her secret with Carlson's men. They'd never tell.

"No. Until we know why Lori was attacked, I'm not going anywhere."

Lori wanted to know the answer as well. At the moment, she had other things to worry about. The two men—she assumed they were Carlson's medical staff—prodding at her leg.

"We're going to have to undress her. Do you mind waiting outside?"

From the look on his face, Hyrum did mind. Lori was used to naked men getting ready to shift, but shyness went with in her human role. "I'll be fine, Hyrum. It won't take long."

When he was gone, the tension in the room lifted slightly. "He's scary, isn't he? I'm Billy, by the way, and this is Gordon. Let's get you out of that shirt so I can make sure you don't have any scratches we've missed. Counselor Carlson wouldn't take kindly to us being anything but thorough."

The shirt had been provided by Carlson to the serving staff, but hers wouldn't be good for anything anymore, not even rags. The bloodstains would never come out. She didn't protest as they cut it away from her body.

"The Counselor will be here in a minute," Billy said. "Anything you want to tell us first?" He rubbed her back with a wet washcloth, removing the dried blood that clung to her skin. The warmth of the cloth eased the ache of her strained muscles.

"Nothing that he doesn't already know." Lori winced as Gordon wiped her leg with an antiseptic. It burned almost as bad as her wounds. "He's aware of my nature."

"Wolf."

"Yes. Free Wolf by affiliation."

"It's a dangerous game you're playing. Who else knows? The big guy outside? Is he your boyfriend?"

"No one else knows. Especially not him. And no, he's not my boyfriend. He's the enforcer for the Jaeger pack. I have no idea what he's doing here." To keep the bar as neutral territory, no one from either pack was allowed on site once the daily meeting had ended, except for those hired as support staff.

Billy and Gordon exchanged glances. "We'll let the Counselor sort it out," Billy said. "As far as your leg goes, I'd like to put in a couple of stitches to aid in the recovery and help maintain your cover story. I don't have any topical anesthesia, so it's going to hurt. Probably worse than it did when the claws penetrated. Are you okay with that?"

"If that's what it takes. Do I get a bullet or a wooden stick to bite on?"

Gordon chuckled. "Why don't we start without anything and see how it goes?"

"Or I could use my power—with your permission, of course—to make it so you don't feel anything," Counselor Carlson suggested from behind Billy's shoulder.

Lori hadn't even heard him come in. She rolled over and sat up halfway, supporting herself on her elbows. "You can do that?" she asked in surprise.

"I can't stop the pain totally but I can inhibit it. You'll have to let me into your mind, of course."

Of course. It was an easy decision and she dropped the block. He had the ability to force his way past it anyway. "Go for it."

"Gentleman, let me know when you're ready," Carlson said.

Gordon and Billy hustled around the RV, gathering needed supplies. "We're ready, Counselor."

Carlson nodded and put his hand on top of Lori's head. She felt a surge of power followed by a lighter-than-air sensation. She was dimly aware of Gordon threading a needle and handing it to Billy. There was pressure on her leg, and a pinch. Several pinches, but nothing more than the gentle play-bite of a cub.

When Carlson removed his hand, she was exhausted. He looked tired as well. "You didn't mention how it would wear you out," she whispered.

He quirked his mouth. "That's why I don't do it except in extreme emergencies. Go to sleep now, Miss Grenville. Let your natural healing begin. I'll make time to talk to you tomorrow."

"Who will serve you?" she worried.

He chuckled. "Don't worry. We'll handle it."

By the fourth day, Lori had enough of sitting around and doing nothing. As luxurious as the RV was, it was still a prison. She wasn't allowed to leave, both for medical reasons and because no one was sure she wasn't still in danger. Her attacker hadn't regained consciousness so, they hadn't been able to question him. The amount of blood he'd lost was the issue, and since he was still in wolf form they couldn't take him to a hospital and give him transfusions. But Billy and Gordon assured her he would eventually recover.

To keep her cover, she couldn't go back to work although all that was left of her injury was an ugly bruise. So, she and the two medical techs concocted a daring plan. They retrieved her special soap from her apartment and got her a wheelchair. Once they wheeled her into the building, she could sit behind the bar and make herself useful mixing drinks.

Only Counselor Carlson was in on the plan. Lori had wanted to surprise him too, but Gordon and Billy talked her out of it. Claimed it would be disrespectful. They knew him better than she did, so she took their advice. He took it a step farther. It would be the perfect opportunity to find out if the wolf that attacked her had any co-conspirators. As long as she showed up when he wasn't distracted, he'd be able to sense people's reactions to her appearance. If the plan worked, he'd be able to identify the guilty parties.

Billy was the first one out of the RV. If she slipped on her way down the stairs, he'd be there to catch her. Gordon was to follow in case she fell backward. The wheelchair was strategically placed at the bottom of the stairs.

Lori knew Hyrum wasn't going to like it.

He was convinced the attack was his fault. There had been mumblings that no human should be present at an official gathering of the Council. What was Counselor Carlson thinking, and how was Lori controlling him. Hyrum was sure it was all talk and meant nothing. But the attacker hadn't been a Jaeger pack member.

Hyrum had been the one to find her. He'd been patrolling the perimeter of the temporary neutral zone to make sure no one snuck onto pack lands, and heard the call. Like so many others, he'd thought it was a child screaming. While the search effort was being organized, he'd stumbled across the wolf and seen Lori's feet sticking out from under it. When he'd rolled the wolf off her, she wasn't breathing.

Rumors said the bodyguard ignored her scream, deciding his duty to keep an eye on the meeting room and keep it secure was more important than investigating the sounds of the fight. Either that, or he didn't hear anything over the rock music streaming from his MP3 player. Rumors also said he no longer had the honor of serving Counselor Carlson.

Hyrum wasn't around twenty-four hours a day, but he seemed to be there every time she looked around. Enough that it made her and the medical techs uncomfortable. She shouldn't have been surprised that he was sitting on the bottom step of the RV when they open the door.

"Out for some fresh air?" he asked.

"Nope. Going to work. I'm already late." Lori replied as Billy helped her get settled in the nearby wheelchair.

"You can't even walk!"

"Don't need to. I can make drinks just as well sitting down as I can standing up."

"You're letting her do this?" Hyrum asked Gordon.

"As approved by Counselor Carlson." Gordon grinned. "He mentioned that only she seems to know how he likes his drinks."

"In that case, I'm coming along."

"You can't. Against the rules of the negotiations. You're not a delegate or official security," Billy pointed out.

The muscles in Hyrum's neck tightened and he clenched his fists. "They didn't do their job before, did they? Why do you trust them now?"

A small part of Lori agreed. How had an unknown wolf gotten that close to the bar? And to Counselor Carlson? It should have been stopped before it ever stepped foot into the neutral zone.

"I'll be fine," she assured him. Another part of her worried that Hyrum was involved. Over the years, he'd run patrol over each rise and gully. Had he used a hidden path to sneak in undetected, bringing along her attacker?

Billy tucked the blanket he was carrying around her legs. The chill in the air was enough to justify it, but it served a dual purpose. Billy had slipped a revolver into her lap. One loaded with silver bullets. It had been Gordon's suggestion, and Carlson himself had provided the weapon.

Leaving Hyrum to trail behind, Billy and Gordon rolled her over the gravel parking lot to the front door because the back door wouldn't accommodate the width of the wheelchair. All eyes swung her direction as the door creaked open and Lori wished she were somewhere else. As Billy pushed her behind the bar, she put on a fake smile, refusing to allow anyone to see her discomfort.

It started with one of the Destin servers. It spread to Carlson's staff, then to the Jaeger pack delegates. Even the Destin officials joined in. A slow clap that turned into a standing ovation.

Lori had heard of such accolades before, when a wolf claimed victory over a more experienced opponent. She'd never seen one and hadn't realized the story of her fight had spread. She'd only told Carlson and his lead bodyguard. Oh, and Billy and Gordon. As she blushed and smiled broadly, she pretended not to notice the one unhappy person in the room. He'd been the last one to clap, the last one to stand. Jaeger.

TWELVE

Lori rejoiced at being back in her own apartment even though it featured a guard at the bottom the stairs. Someone upgraded the place while Lori stayed in the RV healing, and it now contained a full set of chairs for the table and curtains for all the windows. Oh, and a security camera aimed at her door.

After a week and a half, her attacker died without ever regaining consciousness. The precautions were in place although there'd been no further attacks or threats against her. That was the good news. The bad news was that she'd earned a new nickname. Buffy. As in 'The Vampire Slayer.' Because who else would use a wooden stake to kill a wolf?

She sighed as she kicked off her shoes. Her heel, bruised by the pebble she'd placed in the insert, throbbed. Walking on it made her limp as if her injury hadn't healed yet. A good soaking would help relieve the ache, at least for an hour or two.

A strong drink might be what she needed to cure the ache in her head because nothing else worked. She never drank on the job, but spending two weeks listening to the so-far-fruitless negotiations drove her to consider it. How did Carlson maintain his calm demeanor day after day?

In her heart, Lori didn't believe Jaeger and Destin wanted to settle their differences. She suspected they preferred an all-out pack war, fighting until one pack was so weak that it would disband, its men would scatter, leaving the women and children as easy pickings for the conquerors. Such was the way of history. She learned long ago she couldn't rescue all of them, especially those who didn't want to be rescued.

Why did she stick around? Perhaps it was a misplaced loyalty to Carlson, payment for his services and kindness. Steve had traveled in style to the Lapahie school instead of having to run from safe house to safe house, courtesy of the Counselor. Princess, on the other hand, seemed to enjoy the interest she was receiving now that Jaeger's men no longer hassled her on a daily basis. More than once, Lori caught her flirting with Carlson's security guards. It might be a different story once Carlson and his staff were gone, but at the moment, there wasn't any way to convince her to leave.

She'd seen Eugene around the RVs twice. Both times he was accompanied by a member of Carlson's staff, making it impossible to talk to him privately.

It happened that way once in a while. Months of setup to have a mission fail in the end. A first for Lori but she didn't foresee the outcome changing. Time to plan her exit.

It would be tough with all the added security, but she'd earned the right to be called Shadow. As she relaxed, sipping on a beer and soaking in the hot water, she plotted her escape.

She'd need to slip through two layers of security— Carlson's and the Jaegers. She didn't think she could arrange a trip to Charity without having company, and she doubted Rory would be assigned to her this time. On one occasion, she'd faked an illness requiring hospitalization, but since Carlson was in on her secret of being a shifter, that wouldn't work either. It looked as if she'd have to resort to the most direct approach—leave everything behind except for one change of clothes and a few items stuffed in a small pack and sneak out in wolf form.

Timing was everything. The full moon graced the sky two days ago, so she needed to wait at least a week. A rainy night made tracking harder, but she wouldn't be able to wait for one of those. Not in the desert of Wyoming.

Maybe she'd make the run to Devil's Tower, hole up with the ranger, take a break, and enjoy the scenery. She'd take time to recoup and heal her wounded pride before taking on another mission.

With luck, her next job would take her somewhere with trees. She missed the hardwood forests and running in wolf form along leaf-covered age-old trails and through gurgling steams.

She woke with a start at the sound of footsteps on her stairs. It must be Billy. He always stopped in after she got off work to check her leg and make sure she hadn't put too much strain on it. He was totally devoted to Counselor Carlson, so she didn't think she could leverage their friendship to make her escape.

The gauntlet had been thrown and the challenge accepted. Exactly what the doctor ordered. The thrill of the chase and the capture of the target. Lori counted cadence with the guard's steps as he circled the RV.

When Billy conveyed Carlson's request to see her it came off as a demand. Perhaps Carlson was tired and didn't use the right words, but it was time to remind him she was a Free Wolf. He had no right to order her to do anything. She'd go to see him, but on her own terms.

She hadn't spent her time in the medical RV without learning a few things about her surroundings. The arrangement of the rooms. The location of the electrical connections and the storage areas. The loose panel under the bed in the master bedroom. From the outside, all the RVs appeared to have the same basic floor plan.

The mottled-gray catsuit clung to her like a second skin as she worked her way around the parking lot. She'd retrieved it from its hiding place in the crawl space above her apartment. It was her only possession she had an attachment to. One of the original Free Wolves made it specifically for her.

She belly-crawled closer to Carlson's RV. His guards were the best she'd ever seen, but she was better. They should have him rotate RVs instead of staying in the same one. They should guard every RV instead of only his. That would make it harder to determine which one he was in. If she came away happy from the meeting, she might share her intel with him. If he pissed her off, she'd keep to herself.

Too many lights lit the target RV and the shadows of people moving around inside darkened the curtains. Didn't Carlson ever sleep? As long as the lights in the bedroom stayed dark, she was good. She shifted into a crouching position and prepared to make her move.

The guard stopped and sniffed. She hit the ground and held her breath. Had he scented her? He sniffed again and sneezed. Three times. The dry Wyoming air did that to people until they adjusted to it.

Damn. She'd lost track of her count and needed to start over. As long as Carlson stayed in the main living area of the RV, she was good. She could wait.

It took a few minutes for the man to get back in sync with the guard on the other side. When it happened, she sprang like a jumping jack out of the box and rolled under the RV just as the guard turned. Phase One complete.

Phase Two was trickier and dependent upon the luggage area under the RV being unlocked. In Lori's observations, they were left closed but not secured to make it easier to get things in and out. Because they were rentals, there wasn't much stored in them. At least not in the one assigned to Carlson.

The pick-locks sewn into the seam of her outfit would work on almost anything and the locks on the outside storage doors would be easy to pick, if she had the time. Which she didn't. Getting into the storage area unseen would use every available second.

The moment the guard turned his back, she popped out from under the RV. She tugged at the storage door. It didn't budge. Crap. She pulled again and felt the slightest give. The latches on either side were horizontal, and she flipped one of them to a vertical position before ducking back under the RV.

She watched the guard's shoes as they stopped at the end of the RV. A smile came to her face as she considered reaching out and untying them, then tying them together. His reaction would be hilarious.

Focus. She needed to stay focused. As he turned

and marched away, she darted out. She flipped the other latch and jerked the door open. Her size worked to her advantage. She slipped inside the storage area, swiveled, and yanked the door closed. From there she couldn't do anything about the latches, she could only hope that no one would notice the difference.

Footsteps overhead signaled a new problem. Of all the rotten luck. If Carlson went to bed now, her work would be for nothing. If she hopped out from under his bed, his initial reaction would be to strike first and ask questions later. *If* she survived the attack.

A drawer open and closed and paper rustled. Maybe he wasn't going to bed after all. The footsteps trailed out of the room and she let out a silent sigh of relief. She reached up and pushed. Right where she belonged. The access hatch under the bed.

The last part of the journey was the most hazardous. She prayed the room was empty and the door closed. If luggage or anything else was piled on the bed, her plan would be spoiled by the sound of it falling on the floor. It was a chance she had to take.

With her shoulder, she pushed up on the plywood. And held her breath as she peeked through the resulting crack.

At least he'd left the light on. So instead of waiting in the dark, Lori leaned against the backboard with a book from the nightstand. Three pages in, she yawned, regretting her decision and wondering if there was something else to do.

"What are you doing in my bed, Miss Grenville?"

She tossed the book at him and Carlson caught it one-handed. "I can't believe you're actually reading that. Or do you use it to get to sleep at night?" She yawned again. "Because if you hadn't shown up, I'd be asleep in a few minutes."

He sat on the bottom of the bed. "I find the international political climate before World War One fascinating. I can apply many of the lessons learned to the current political squabbles among the packs."

"That's why you've been reading it for a year and a half." She'd found a dated note written in the margins. "I hear you wanted to see me. In fact, the message I got said I *had* to come see you."

"And here you are."

"Yep."

"How did you get in? Obviously not by the standard method," he said, checking out her outfit.

She shrugged. "I have my ways. I could share them, depending upon how this meeting goes."

"I could make you tell me."

"I'm sure you could. But you won't. It goes against your ethics."

"You think you have me figured out." His fangs descended partway.

"Nope. I understand your public face, but I don't know anything about your private one. And you shouldn't tell me either. I might use it against you."

"I'm beginning to understand that. You're not as innocent as you appear, Miss Grenville. Although if anyone else showed up in my bed in *that* outfit this late at night, I'd think they were trying to seduce me."

"No offense but you're not my type. But I am giving you a gift."

"What would that be?"

"Plausible deniability, Counselor. When I disappear, there's no proof I was ever here. You won't be the last one to see me, so you can't be accused of harming me."

His left eyebrow arched. "You're leaving?"

"Making plans. There's no reason for me to stay."

"If I order you to?"

"You forget. You may be paying my salary, but my loyalty can't be bought. I'm a Free Wolf and I answer only to myself."

"Sometimes I forget you're a wolf at all, you hide it so well."

"If that's a compliment, I'll take it. However, it won't change my mind. Tell me why I'm here." She swung her legs over the edge of the bed.

"I have a problem and I hoped you would help me."

"From what I can see, you have a lot of problems with the current negotiations and they're all above my pay grade. What do you want from me?"

Carlson grimaced. "To my great consternation, I'm getting nowhere with the packs. But that's not why I wanted to talk to you."

Lori was in no mood to play games. "You can get to the point anytime."

"Eugene. I need help with Eugene."

THIRTEEN

"I'm surprised Eugene's still here. Can't you find a pack leader to mentor him?" Lori asked. Hadn't that been the plan?

Counselor Carlson let out a loud breath. "Call it hubris. When I saw his immense potential, I decided to mentor him myself. It hasn't worked out so well. I don't have enough time to give him and he doesn't trust me."

"Imagine that."

"I can't even get him to admit he's Randy Jaeger's son."

"There's a story behind that and he won't share it. I had him this close..." Lori held her thumb and forefinger only a hair-width apart, "one day when we were interrupted. I'm not sure if he's Elex or not."

"Does he trust you?"

"I don't think so."

"So where does that leave us?"

"You. Where does that leave you? I've got no stake in this game. Not anymore."

Carlson's mouth twitched. "Sure you do. When you claimed sanctuary, you created a bond between the two of you. Even though I took over sanctuary officially, the bond still exists. You might deny it, but ask your *other*."

Lori didn't need to ask. That explained why she hadn't left yet. "I'll concede the point. So where does that leave us?"

"The same place we were five minutes ago. Nowhere."

They sat in silence for a minute. "Here's a crazy thought," Lori said. "What if he isn't Elex? All we've got to go on is rumors and guesses. If he is Elex, why wasn't he trained? Surely his father would make sure his first-born son was acknowledged and trained."

"It would be a severe breach of pack protocol," Carlson agreed. "So if he isn't Elex, who is he?"

"Can you use your authority to demand the Destins produce Elex? Bring him to a meeting or something?"

He shook his head.

"I could sneak into the Destin village and try to locate their records."

"While I don't doubt that you could do it given the proper time to prepare, we don't have the time."

"So, what's your plan?"

"I'm cutting your hours. We claim work has been too hard on you and you want to build your strength up gradually. The extra time you spend with Eugene. Everyone will be busy in the meeting and won't know."

"You want me to reveal my *other*? No. I need to maintain my cover."

"That's fine. Maybe you can go on walks together with him acting as your guard."

"It feels dirty manipulating him."

"I suspect you aren't above manipulating people and situations when you're pulling a 'rescue.' That is the correct word, isn't it?"

Close enough. "And now you're trying to manipulate me."

"It comes with the job, Miss Grenville. Consider Eugene as one of your rescues. What would you do to help him?"

Everything possible. "All right, I'm in. But I'll do it my way."

"I don't know any more than I did when I started," Lori told Carlson. She'd come in through the front door, supposedly to deliver some paperwork. "I'm not so sure he doesn't want to tell me as much as he doesn't remember and won't admit it."

"Amnesia?"

"Yeah, but wouldn't our healing powers fix that too?"

"I've never heard of a shifter having amnesia."

"It sounds like a bad plot device in an old movie."

"Or like some veterans with PTSD and missing chunks of memory." He poured himself another cup of coffee. Lori figured he was planning on a long night and needed the caffeine. She was ready for bed as soon as she could get back to her apartment. Between spending half the day bartending and the other half babysitting Eugene, she was exhausted.

"He's never mentioned serving in the military. He's not old enough."

"I've got contacts in DC who can verify that, but you can acquire a form of PTSD from other things. Like childhood abuse or a life-threatening event. I knew a man who was in a car accident and wasn't found for two days who was diagnosed with it."

In most packs, children were regarded as sacred. Lori discarded the notion that Eugene had been abused. "I'll see if I can get him to remember being in an accident. Would Billy and Gordon be able to diagnose him?"

"Their medical training isn't that in-depth. They're more like EMTs. We need a psychiatrist's opinion."

"Of course, you know someone."

"I'll get in touch with him tomorrow."

Lori stood, ready to head back to her apartment. "That still doesn't explain why the Destins didn't want to acknowledge him or ransom him."

"Unless they see it as an easy way to cull a weak member from the pack."

"Weak is not the word I'd use to describe Eugene." Under the care of Carlson's staff, he was getting stronger every day.

"Agreed. But if we can't solve the riddle behind Eugene, he'll become a liability."

Lori stiffened. "What makes you say that?"

"We're running out of time, Miss Grenville."

"I didn't know I had a deadline."

"I phrased that poorly. *I'm* running out of time. There are rumors both Elder Jaeger and Elder Destin are using these negotiations to cover their true intentions."

It didn't take a genius to figure out the implication. "War," Lori said.

Carlson nodded. "With an added twist. They are both convinced they can take me down and send the entire country into chaos. Just like the 'good' old days."

"Can that happen?"

The transformation happened in a flash. Carlson no longer looked like a mild politician. Even without a full shift, all the strongest features of his wolf came out. His fangs descended, his eyes darkened, his cheeks sank in, his hair got longer and he seemed to increase in bulk. When he snarled, Lori instinctively took a step away.

"I'm not just a pretty face," he growled, "and I didn't get this position in a popularity contest. I'm more than capable of defending myself. Shit, I don't even need to shift to take down Jaeger. He's the weakest alpha I've ever met."

She held up her hands. "Okay. I got it. You can put that face away now." He'd confirmed what she suspected all along—that Jaeger held on to his position through methods other than the traditional alpha powers.

His features softened until he looked 'normal' again. "Only a few of my staff are aware of the threat. I'd appreciate it if you would keep it to yourself until we see how this plays out."

"Why tell me?"

"So you can prepare to leave. I won't involve you in a pack war."

"One of the reasons the Free Wolves exist in the first place."

He nodded.

"This may sound strange but take it for what it's worth," Lori said. "I'll help. Surveillance, undercover work, minor disturbances for distraction—they're all up my alley. I've got too many friends in too many packs to allow the progress that's been made in the past few years to go to hell."

"I'll regret saying this, but no thanks. I can't let you risk your life for something that isn't your cause."

"But it is. In the past few years, the Free Wolves

have been able to come out from the shadows. Not all the way, but most of us don't look over our shoulders every minute of every day anymore, worrying that someone from our packs will drag us back. You've made it possible, and I'm not about to let a Neanderthal like Jaeger ruin it." She talked faster and faster and at the end, she stopped to catch her breath.

"That was quite a speech, Miss Grenville. You've convinced me. If it gets to that point, and I hope it won't, you're in."

Learning the schedule of the target was key. If Lori waited until Carlson asked for her help to do her research, it would be too late. Since the Destin village was a good distance away, she needed to be wolf.

Although the Jaeger pack had added extra sentries and switched up their schedules after the Destin raid, Lori had plenty of information about the layout of the village, like where the food and weapons were stored. She'd made practice runs on both for the fun of it when she started working for the pack. The Destins, however, were unknown.

She'd tried to pump the two Destins servers for information and got nowhere. The one Destin she'd made inroads with early during the negotiation was no longer there. In fact, she found herself training new members of the pack for server duties every few days. In light of Carlson's revelations, that wasn't a good sign.

Jaeger and Destin lands didn't share any common boundaries, so she had to slip by sentries of both to observe the village. She'd memorized a map provided by Carlson before setting off at midnight. This first run was a test, planned when Hyrum wasn't on duty and a less knowledgeable pack member was.

In her night camouflage suit, she wormed her way down a gully. She'd observed the sentries bypass it on their rounds on a regular basis. The barbed wire fence that marked the boundary didn't follow the dip, so there was plenty of room to slip under the wire.

Once out of sight of the guard, she stripped off her clothes and stuffed them into a small backpack. She reached for that glorious sense of other and felt her body change. Wolf now, she began the long trot across the desert, carrying the backpack in her mouth.

There were unforeseen obstacles and she noted their locations for future reference. A ranch house with dogs that barked as her scent reached them. A four-lane highway carrying more traffic than she'd anticipated. The creek bed that was marked as dry on the map but wasn't. At least it had been narrow enough that she was able to leap across it.

By the time she got to Destin territory, it was too late—or too early in the morning—to slip inside. The color of the sky was changing from the dark of night to the pale gray of a cloudy morning. She found a spot on the top of a rise that allowed her to track the sentries as they made their rounds along that section.

It didn't take her long to spot the pattern of movement. When she was ready, she'd be able to sneak across the border. The next trip, she'd allow herself enough time to actually get inside.

The first time Lori ran this trail it wasn't much more than a rabbit trail. She and Eugene had run it enough that it now looked more like a deer trail. She padded along it now with Eugene, in wolf form, at her heels.

The run was much more than exercise. It was a statement that she still had a claim in Eugene's sanctuary and messing with him meant dealing with her. Lori wasn't above taking advantage of the fact that her kill had gained her a small group of loyal fans.

Eugene believed he was guarding her, and he was, in a fashion. If a wild animal attacked her, he'd chase it away. It wasn't likely to happen, but she hoped it would give Eugene a touch of self-confidence.

Besides, there was a rumor that Jaeger wanted to get rid of her. Her source had been one of the Destin servers, so she didn't give it too much credence but it didn't hurt to take precautions anyway. She hadn't told Carlson because she didn't want him to worry. She'd take care of herself.

She worked on gaining Eugene's trust, telling stories about her childhood and hoping he'd reciprocate. When he returned to human form, of course, but so far it hadn't happened. But every now and then, she caught echoes of his thoughts, so she still had hope.

They went a little further than normal, and Lori was out of breath when they reached the top of a hill. She knelt and rested her hands on her knees while she recovered. Behind her, she heard Eugene shifting back to human form.

"You okay?"

"I'm out of shape. I should be able to get up this hill without a problem."

He sat beside her, his breathing perfectly even. "I've never felt this good."

"Didn't you go running on your pack lands? Patrolling or even for fun?"

"They said it would kill me."

"Bad heart? You're doing fine now. But maybe we should have Billy check it out."

"He has and found nothing wrong."

"They lied to you?"

"It appears that way."

"Who lied to you, Eugene?"

"My foster mother. She was very protective of me."

Or over-protective, Lori thought. Fostering was a rare occurrence. Even when a cub's mother died, there were always family members willing to take the cub and raise it as their own.

"Is she the one who wouldn't allow you to be battle trained?"

"Or let me leave pack territory to find a job. I lied to you. I've never worked in the oil fields."

"Was the raid your first experience away from your village?"

"I got to go on school trips once in a while. Of course, my foster mother, Felina, came along as a chaperone."

"So, you were an easy target. That's why you got captured."

"No. I was betrayed."

The anguish in his voice tore at Lori's heart. She had no doubt he was telling the truth, no matter how far-fetched it sounded. "What happened?"

He stared at the ground. "I was permitted to come along as a sort of water boy. My job was to carry ammunition where it was needed. I wasn't supposed to fight. It didn't make me happy, but I figured it was a first step in gaining the pack's trust, so I did it.

"During the raid, I took ammo to Ivan, one of the pack's strongest men, and one of my biggest bullies. Even as I brought him what he needed, he taunted me and called me a weakling. When I turned to go back to the staging area, he hit me from behind and shoved me. I fell into a hole and I guess I lost consciousness."

They sat in silence for a long time. Lori hid her tears because she could see Eugene was fighting back his. His pack deliberately turned their backs on him. There was no comfort she could offer him that would make a difference.

He cleared his throat, "When I came to, the battle line had moved and the Jaegers were all around me. Although I shifted, I couldn't fight five of them at once. I didn't even know how to fight one of them. They should have killed me that night and then none of this would be happening. I'm dead anyway. A lone wolf has no chance of surviving. I don't know why you and the Counselor waste your time on me."

Lori hated to push when Eugene seemed so vulnerable, but it might be the only chance to get the answer she needed. "Why does the alpha female think you are Elex?"

"How am I supposed to know? She's nuts. Elex is in New York. He was sent to a pack there to learn how to manage money and make us rich. He's supposed to be a bigshot stock broker on Wall Street. If he's doing so well, why do our men have to give the pack their paychecks? Why doesn't the pack have money to fix up the school and hire a teacher? We had a real teacher when I was young, but she left after a few years and now one of the elders teaches when he can be bothered."

"Why didn't you tell us before?"

Eugene took a deep breath. "If Madame Rose thinks I'm Elex, I get to stay alive. All my life I've been teased about being Elex's weak and ugly clone. They even dress me up and make me pretend I'm him when we get visitors from other packs. I wave from a distance and then I'm hurried out of the way. There's always an excuse why Elex can't sit at meals with guests. So, this time I'm using it to my advantage. Maybe that's wrong, but why should I care? The pack doesn't care about me."

"You didn't have any friends?"

"Oh sure, we Omegas stuck together. Unless there was a chance to get in good with one of the betas. Then it was everyone for themselves."

In what crazy world was Eugene considered an omega? There was so much she needed to discuss with Carlson.

"You know, you aren't weak and you aren't ugly," she said. "I don't know if you've looked in a mirror lately, but with all the running you've been doing, you've put on a lot of muscle. You've packed on a few pounds too, and it's going to all the right places. Does Carlson's staff have you lifting weights when I'm not around?"

His eyes darkened. "Now you are teasing me. I thought you were my friend."

"I am your friend." Lori grabbed his arm and squeezed. "That doesn't feel like a weakling's arm."

"Everyone is strong compared to you."

Lori chuckled. "True. But that doesn't make me an omega, does it?"

"I don't know what you are. But I've never spent much time with humans, so I don't understand how you work."

"Fair enough." She needed to try a new tactic to get through to him. This one wasn't working. "What does your wolf tell you?"

"How are you going to talk to my wolf?"

"Not me. You. Don't you know how to talk to your *other* without shifting? I'm no expert, but from what I've been told, it's like meditation. Shut out all the outside distractions and listen for your inner voice."

Eugene frowned and closed his eyes. "Are you sure about this?"

Fourteen

"That's what my friends told me. Obviously, I've never tried it." Lori hated herself for the lie, but too much was riding on her to blow her cover.

With his eyes squeezed shut, Eugene took a deep breath and exhaled. Fingers crossed, Lori waited. His face lengthened and long whiskers sprouted from his cheeks. The shift had begun. It wasn't what she hoped for.

She waited until the shift was complete to speak. "I guess my information was wrong. Sorry."

He shifted back to man form. "It would be nice to talk to my wolf."

"Is there anyone else you can ask for help?"

"No."

The answer was short and sharp, and Lori read the hidden pain. She had several suggestions, but didn't think he'd like any of them, so she kept her mouth shut. None of them involved the man currently creeping up the side of the hill.

How long had Hyrum been spying on them? She tapped Eugene on the shoulder and raised a finger to her lips. He looked puzzled but nodded. In a loud voice, she called. "How's it going, Hyrum?"

"Can't you two find a better place to admire the scenery?" he grumbled when he reached the top. "No one knew where you were and Elder Jaeger is screaming about you having left pack lands and breaking the rules of sanctuary."

"I'll take the blame. I pushed myself too far today and needed to rest, but as you can see, we are still within the set boundaries." She pointed to the barbed-wire fence across a small gully, barely within sight.

Hyrum nodded and got the familiar blank look on his face. Lori wondered if he was communicating with Jaeger or with one of his betas. She was struck with a sudden flash off inspiration.

"Can you do me a favor, Hyrum?" she asked sweetly.

"What?"

"Teach Eugene how to talk to his wolf without shifting. You can do that, right?"

"Every cub knows how," Hyrum scoffed. "It is one of the beginning lessons when they reach the age of first shift."

Lori put a hand on Eugene's shoulder to keep him calm. "Not every cub gets that lesson."

"I'm an enforcer, not a teacher. Ask someone else to do it."

"Do you see anyone else to ask?" Lori indicated the wide-open spaces with a sweep of her other hand.

"He won't help," Eugene said in resignation. "I'm not worth his time."

"Or maybe he's afraid to try," Lori said. Oldest taunt in the books, but would Hyrum fall for it?

"I'll do it," Hyrum mumbled after a long moment.

"Not because I like him, but because it's not fair to his wolf."

Lori didn't care what his excuse was. If Hyrum could help Eugene, her battle to convince Eugene that he was worthwhile would be easier. Baby steps.

"I thought I was crazy for hearing voices in my head." Eugene, in man form, wearing the clothes she'd carried for him, trotted alongside Lori on the way back to the neutral zone. "It was my wolf, the whole time!"

"I'm glad you got that straightened out, I suggest you find somewhere quiet when we get back where you can sit and have a long conversation with your wolf. See what he has to tell you."

"If I can find a quiet place. No matter where I go, one of the Counselor's staff is always nearby, keeping an eye on me."

"You can use my place if they're done with negotiations for the day. I can do my daily paperwork in the office downstairs. I'll ask whoever is on guard duty to stay outside on the stairs. Will that work?"

"It feels as much like home as anyplace I've been," he said, "so yes."

Her heart crumbled. He deserved so much better. But she couldn't stick around forever to make sure he got it.

With Eugene safely set up in her apartment and the guard at the bottom of the steps, Lori headed for Counselor Carlson's RV. What Eugene had said about

Elex could be verified easily with the right connections, and she'd be willing to bet Carlson had those connections. The information held a kernel of truth, but she was convinced there was more to the story.

For her own amusement, she plotted a new way to sneak into his RV while sitting outside waiting for him to get off the phone. She wondered how the walls of the pop-out were fastened and if there'd be a way to remove one side. It probably couldn't be done without using power tools, so she abandoned the idea. The roof might be a better way in.

"Your turn," the guard said as she studied the ladder attached to the rear of the RV. It was the same man she'd snuck by, and she hoped she hadn't gotten him into too much trouble.

"Thanks," she said as she scooped up a stack of paperwork, the supposed reason for her visit. "Is anyone scheduled after me or am I the last one for the night?"

"The last one. Try to keep it short. He's been burning the candle on both ends."

"Got it."

Carlson was in the kitchen area opening a bottle of water when she came in. "You caught me," he said as he raised the bottle to his lips. Half of its contents were gone by the time he lowered it.

"It's good to stay hydrated."

"What do you need, Miss Grenville? I hope it's easy because there's a situation developing on the West Coast and I have a conference call in ten minutes."

"I'll keep it simple then—how do you find out if someone is a stockbroker?"

Carlson pulled out his cellphone. "There's a database available on line. Who do you want to check out?"

"Elex Destin. According to Eugene, he's with a pack in New York, working as a stockbroker."

"I should have known that," he frowned as he poked at his phone. He jerked his head towards the refrigerator. "Help yourself. The signal out here is weak, so this might take a while."

She followed his example and got herself a bottle of water and waited while he fiddled with his phone.

"He's not registered," Carlson said as she finished off the bottle. "But perhaps he's working for a firm and isn't actually a stockbroker. There are a dozen or so wolves on Wall Street, and many of them have only loose alliances with their packs, preferring to work alone."

It sounded like a time-intensive job to contact each of those wolves to see if they knew Elex. "You have any friends at the IRS to check if he's filed any tax returns?"

"I do, but I won't get an answer tonight. Where did you get this information?"

"Eugene. He opened up to me today." As Lori recited the rest of the story, Carlson started pacing.

"He really doesn't know his parents?"

"It seems that way. I'm hoping his *other* remembers and tells him."

"Talking Hyrum into teaching Eugene how to do that was brilliant."

"I was about to reveal myself when Hyrum showed up. It ticked me off to no end that Eugene had never been taught the trick. I'm not sure how I'd handle things without talking to mine."

"The more I learn about the Destins, the more I'm tempted to call for an open challenge for pack leadership. It is clear his people are not happy, but feel powerless to do anything about it. Who knows what lies he is feeding them about the outside world."

"What's holding you back?"

"It would be risky. With Elex missing, no one is strong enough to replace him."

"Eugene's not ready."

"He's making progress but he's not there yet. I'd be sending him to his death."

"I haven't been able to pick up any useful intel during my nighttime runs."

"You've been in the village?"

Oops. She hadn't meant to reveal that. "Only twice. Very early in the morning. Their sentries are good, but not good enough. They aren't as good as your guards."

"And yet, you managed to get by mine."

Lori tried unsuccessfully to hide her smirk. "Yeah, I did."

Carlson started pacing again. "Elex is the key here. If he can be located, the entire dynamic of this situation will change. I'd love to find out what his thoughts on his grandfather are and if he has potential to be the alpha."

"It would be fun, wouldn't it? To escort the legendary Elex into the bar and see how his grandfather reacted?"

"Only after I made certain he wouldn't continue his grandfather's style of leadership. That could spell doom for the Destin pack."

No, she thought, you want someone who will back your policies. But was that truly any better?

From the darkness at the end of the building, Lori studied the setup. She hadn't been gone that long but the guard at the bottom of her stairs was a different man. She didn't recognize him as one of Carlson's men. In fact, he looked like one of the Jaeger pack who had been to the bar a few times.

The lights were on in her apartment. Not unexpected if Eugene was there. But the figure moving past the window wasn't Eugene. It was difficult to say from the shadow on the curtain, but Lori's gut told her it was a female.

Which didn't make the intruder any less of a threat. But why announce her presence with the stationing of the guard? It didn't add up. Lori decided to treat it as a casual visit, at least until she found out differently.

She backtracked and circled the building. The other side was well lit and if the guard was doing his job, he'd see her coming. If he bothered to look up from his phone. The light from the screen shone on his face and she recognized him.

"Hey, Rory," she called. "What are you doing here?"

"It's my day to play guard dog," he said. "She's upstairs and wants to talk to you."

"Princess? What has she done to upset her father now?"

He shrugged. "No idea. As far as I could tell, everything's been smooth sailing. 'Course, she's been avoiding him because he's been in a bad mood."

"Is he still upset because I claimed sanctuary?"

"He's more uptight because he's wasting his time in these meetings. He'd rather be planning how to destroy the Destins than how to get along with them."

"Which is the reason Counselor Carlson stepped in. I know you wolves say its tradition, but what happens when someone gets killed? Is it worth it to claim the dubious honor of taking over land from another pack? Land that doesn't even legally belong to either one?" Lori's research showed that much of the land claimed by the two packs was actually BLM property.

"When you say it like that, it does sound a bit crazy."

"Next time—if there is next time—I might not be here to patch up everyone. It's too dangerous for me to be involved in an all-out pack war."

"Where would you go?"

Lori shrugged. "Wherever the wind sends me."

"I don't understand how humans do that. Just pick up and leave. Having no sense of belonging."

"We find ways to make our own little packs. We join groups, churches, make friends at work, or find people who fight for the same causes we believe in."

"It sounds like a lot of work. I like the idea of a pack better."

"You're lucky you have a good pack. Not everyone does." It seemed better to hide her personal opinion of the Jaeger pack's leader. Or her own memories. "So, I better go see what your pack leader's daughter wants."

"Good luck," Rory said with a smirk. "I'll be down here waiting if you need help."

That wasn't likely to happen, Lori thought as she climbed the stairs. She rattled the doorknob to alert Princes that someone was coming in although it was possible that Rory already let her know.

Princess waited while Lori closed and locked the door before she spoke. "I need your help," she blurted out.

"I assumed that's why you're here. What do you want?" Although Princess was pale, Lori didn't think she'd been crying.

"Can you get me on Counselor Carlson's staff? Please? Like you did for Steve?"

Lori sat on one of the chairs at the table and waited for Princess to follow her example. "Two things. I didn't 'get' Steve on Carlson's staff. He did that all by himself. I don't have that kind of influence. And haven't you noticed the staff is all male? I'm pretty sure that's deliberate."

A puddle of moisture formed in Princess' eyes. She blinked it away. "I never thought about it. In that case, I need my money. Please."

"Where are you going to run away to? And how?"

"You can't tell anyone. Promise?"

"Of course."

"I've heard rumors. Something about a group called the 'Free Wolves.' Silly name, 'cause we're all free, right? I'm going to find them."

"What good will that do?"

Princess frowned. "I don't know exactly. I guess they get people to safety or something."

"That's an awfully big gamble. You don't know who these people are or what they do or where to find them." Lori wanted to make sure that Princess wasn't doing this on a whim and would change her mind in a day or two.

"But I have to take the chance!" Princess got up and started pacing, "I can't stay here."

"Why not?"

"My father. I'm sorry, 'Elder Jaeger' as he demands I call him by his title now, has decided the best way to get Counselor Carlson off his back is to offer me up as a sacrificial lamb. Killing two birds with one stone, he said, because he no longer has to worry about me. He wants me to be Elex Destin's mate."

FIFTEEN

"He wants you to marry Elex, a guy he's never met? And aren't you cousins? How's that going to work?" Lori asked.

Princess got paler. "That's the thing. No marriage involved. Strictly mating to produce children." Tears boiled in her eyes. "I'd be no better than an incubator. He found something in the pack archives that made him think it was a good idea. Talked about keeping bloodlines pure."

"An actual marriage would be illegal."

"Yeah. So, Elder Jaeger told me I can expect Elex to marry someone else. And whoever he married would be the alpha female, not me."

It sounded like a story from the Middle Ages. "Carlson will never go for it."

"They won't tell him."

"Has Elder Destin agreed to this crazy idea?"

"Not yet. Elder Jaeger sent him a message after the meetings today. But I was ordered to pack a suitcase and be ready to go."

"I'm surprised they allowed you to come here."

"No one besides Rory knows I'm here. Madame

Rose thinks I came to retrieve a necklace I left behind in the bar." Princess reached into her pocket and pulled out a necklace with a wolf pendant. "I really did leave it here. It was my mother's. I wore it to work one day and didn't want to take a chance of it getting broke so I took it off and stuck it in the file cabinet in the office."

"She's in on this too? Doesn't she believe Eugene is Elex? Or is she playing both sides and has her own agenda?"

"I don't know what she's up to. She didn't tell me and I was afraid to ask."

Lori was calculating the best escape route. She had three layers of security to get through. Rory would be the target of Jaeger's wrath. She had no plan, no burner phone to call for help, and the nearest station was hours away.

"What did you bring with you?" she asked. "Clothes, purse. ID?"

"I've got my purse in Rory's truck."

"Are you willing to leave everything else—and I mean everything—behind?"

"You're serious."

"Yes. How good of an actress are you?"

Princess' eyes widened. "Madame Rose says I wear my heart on my sleeve, so not very good."

"We'll do this the hard way then." Lori dug around in her cupboard until she found the box she'd stashed there shortly after moving in.

"You'll hate me for the next hour and a half," she said. "But if everything goes right, you'll thank me for the rest of your life."

"What are you talking about?"

"Your way out of here. Take two pills and in fifteen

minutes you'll start cramping like a bad monthly cycle. Then it will get worse. That will give me the reason I need to drive you to the hospital in Gillette."

"Then what?"

"The less you know the better. Are you sure you want to do this? Once we leave, you can never come back."

"My father will never find me?"

"I can't guarantee anything. You have to decide whether it's worth the risk to try or stay here and be miserable."

Princess sat, head down and her hands folded together as if in prayer. "It's my last chance, isn't it?"

Lori nodded. She couldn't wait too long for Princess to make up her mind. Every second they wasted made it more likely Rory would come pounding up the stairs and the opportunity would vanish.

"Do I take a red pill or a blue one?" Princess tried to grin, but her mouth didn't cooperate.

"Neither. You get gray. Give me your hand." Lori dropped two pills in Princess' outstretched hand. "Do you need a glass of water?"

Princess popped the pills into her mouth, tilted her head and swallowed. She coughed and swallowed again. "That was rough. Fifteen minutes, you said?"

Not as rough as it was going to get. "Yep. That gives us a few minutes to get ready." She crawled under the table and came back out with an envelope in her hand. "Your money. Tuck it in your pocket."

Next, she grabbed several plastic bags. "Barf bags," she explained. "I hope you won't need them, but better to be prepared."

"How much longer?" Princess asked.

"Believe me, when they start working you'll feel it.

We've got a long ride ahead of us so I suggest making a pit stop."

With Princess behind a closed door, Lori gathered up a few more things from their scattered hiding places and loaded them into her backpack. There was a good chance she wouldn't be coming back.

"Ouch! God-damnit!"

The pills must have kicked in. It was time to put the rest of her plan in motion. Lori ran down the steps. "Rory," she called. "Get me Princess' purse from your truck. Hurry!"

He appeared to have been sitting on the bottom step, leaning against the railing, half asleep. Good. She could use that to her advantage.

"Huh?"

"Her purse. We need it."

"Why?"

"I'm taking her to the hospital. I'll meet you at my car in a minute. Go!"

She ran back up the stairs and met Princess at the door. "I hate you," Princess hissed.

"I know. Now lean on me."

The height difference made it difficult, but in between cramps, Princess and Lori made it down the stairs. Rory stood at the bottom, holding a pink purse. He looked anxiously at the two of them.

"Shouldn't the Counselor's medics take a look at her?"

So, he'd finally woken up. "They don't understand female issues," Lori argued. "And I'm sure Elder Jaeger doesn't want two unmated males to examine her. Our best bet is to get her to the hospital."

"I'm coming too."

"You can ride in the back. I'll drive and she'll be up front with me."

Princess bent over, in the grasp of another cramp and groaned.

"You're holding things up." Lori grabbed the purse. "You need to go tell Madame Rose what's going on. We'll meet you at the hospital." As she talked, she guided Princess towards the car. She opened the passenger door and pushed to help get Princess in.

"What do I tell Madame Rose?" Rory asked, clearly torn between stopping them and getting Princess help. Princess picked that moment to vomit. Lori jumped backwards and avoided getting any on her shoes.

"That it may be a ruptured cyst, or something more serious. Hopefully not appendicitis. I can't tell. The doctors will have to make the call." She slammed the door shut and ran around to the other side. "Now go!"

It took two tries to start the car. As Lori put it in gear, she watched the fuel meter swing to 'full.' Things were going her way for a change.

Carlson's guards waved to her as she pulled away and she waved back. They were only there to stop people from getting in, not from getting out. The Jaeger sentries opened the gates for her before she even rolled down her window. Rory must have *sent* them a message.

Now that they were on their way, she could tell Princess a few more details. "There's a side effect to those pills. Besides the pain. It blocks your telepathic ability. You can't talk to anyone, but they also can't talk to you. It'll last only as long as the cramps do."

"You make it sound like a good thing," Princess said between gritted teeth.

"It is. That way your father or anyone else can't intrude into your mind to force you to return. You're temporarily immune to alpha power."

"What will that do? They're going to come to the hospital."

"I'm counting on it. Here's what will happen. We'll get you checked into the ER, you'll be wheeled to the back behind locked doors before your father or Madame Rose get there. They'll be forced to stay in the waiting room, where I'll be. A nurse will come out and fill us in on your condition every so often, but they won't be allowed to disturb the doctors at work. You're over eighteen, so even though they'll demand to see you, you have a right to say no. By the time morning comes, you'll be gone. The doctor will release you, you'll slip out the back door and disappear."

"Where will I go?"

That was the part that still worried Lori. She didn't know if the Free Wolves' contact at the hospital was on duty or not, or even if she still worked there. As she drove through the darkness, broken only occasionally by the flare of headlights coming from the other direction, all she could do was hope.

"Where is she?"

Lori looked up from the cup of coffee she held grasped in both hands to see Madame Rose. She hoped she was the picture of misery. Reddened eyes, traces of tears still on her cheeks, her hair askew.

"The doctor is checking her out. I'm not a relative, so they won't tell me anything. Where's Elder Jaeger?" Madame Rose's driver was at the front desk, arguing with the receptionist. "I don't think he'll have any luck either," Lori added, jerking her chin towards the desk.

"She *will* tell me."

Good luck with that, Lori thought. She'd been watching the receptionist dealing with other patients, family, and visitors. No one got by her.

What Lori knew and Madame Rose didn't was that the receptionist was a Free Wolf sympathizer. A quick exchange of passwords had assured Lori of her authenticity. While not a shifter herself, she was aware of the cause and had assisted with a passenger's escape once before. Although she didn't show it, she was looking forward to thwarting Jaeger's efforts to get to his daughter.

The receptionist and Madame Rose had a long conversation. Madame Rose eventually gave up and took a chair across from Lori.

"Any news?" Lori asked.

"She says we have to wait for Edgar. He should be here soon."

Lori emptied the cup of coffee down her throat and got up to refill it. It was going to be a long night.

"What do you mean, she's gone?"

Lori had fallen asleep leaning against the wall sometime after Jaeger had shown up. A glance at the clock revealed it was seven in the morning. She made a show of yawning and stretching. "Who's gone?" she asked Madame Rose.

"How could she have left two hours ago?" Elder

Jaeger stood at the desk in front of a different receptionist. Lori had slept through shift change.

The receptionist pounded on her keyboard. "The records show she was released two hours ago. Maybe she didn't know you were here?"

"Or she's out in one of the cars sleeping." Lori yawned again. "I know the last time I was in the ER I didn't get much sleep. They kept waking me up to draw blood."

The two drivers dashed out the door without waiting for orders from Jaeger.

"Check your records again," demanded Jaeger.

"She's the only patient we had named Princess. Or Jaeger. There's no way I'm confusing her with another patient. I'll have one of the nurses check the room she was in and make sure it's empty. Please have a seat, it'll only take a minute."

The receptionist hustled through the doors, using her badge to unlock them. Jaeger tried to follow her, but a security guard stopped him. "Please take a seat, sir." the guard repeated.

Jaeger went to stand by Madame Rose. His eyes fastened on Lori. "This is your fault," he spat.

"Look, I don't know what's going on, but ask Rory, she was in bad shape when I brought her in. Even with her ability to heal quickly, I can't imagine she could walk out of here on her own. I thought she was dying last night, she was in so much pain."

Madame Rose huffed out a breath. "Rory told me the same thing."

Jaeger's face went blank. "She is not in the cars."

"Have them check the car we came in. I left it unlocked."

A moment of silence. "She's not there."

A man in a long white coat came into the waiting room. "Mr. Jaeger?" he said, consulting a clipboard. "I'm Dr. Sanchez. Princess is your daughter?"

"Yes," Jaeger grunted.

"I'm sorry, there must be some misunderstanding. She left a couple of hours ago. I remember her saying something about going home."

"What was wrong with her?" Madame Rose asked.

"You are her...?"

"Grandmother," Madame Rose said.

"Princess is over eighteen, and she signed paperwork that we are not allowed to share her medical records with anyone. Not even her parents. I'm sorry, but that's the law."

Lori was concerned that Jaeger was going to grab the doctor and shake him. The security guard had been observing the conversation, and he came and stood by the doctor's side. Jaeger could have taken them both on in wolf form, but he didn't dare shift and reveal himself.

"I'll tell you this much. It wasn't anything serious. She's probably embarrassed by the results and will tell you when she's ready."

Lori wondered how much experience the doctor had with soothing disgruntled parents. From the sound of it, quite a bit. That made her life so much easier.

The receptionist returned to her desk. "She wasn't in the room."

The security guard pulled out his radio, "Code purple," he said. "Code purple," He turned to Jaeger and Madame Rose. "Don't worry, folks, if she's still in the hospital, we'll find her."

Madame Rose let out a small scream. Jaeger looked

as if he was ready to tear the guard apart. Lori tried to figure out how she could stop him.

"If you'll take a seat, we'll update you in a few minutes," the guard said, oblivious to the immediate danger.

Lori stepped between them. "You need to organize a search of the city," she said. "Call up your contacts. You must have allies here." She knew they wouldn't find anything.

"Yes," Jaeger said. "Yes." The guard was gone so he turned to the receptionist. "Call me if you hear anything. Anything."

"I'll drive back the way we came," Lori said. "Stop at every little place along the way and see if anyone remembers her."

Fat chance of that happening, she thought. With a two hour or more head start, Princess was well on her way to a safe house. Within twenty-four hours, she'd be buried so deep in the Free Wolves' system of hideouts that no one would ever see her until she chose to make an appearance. Lori patted herself on the back for another successful rescue and added a gold star to her imaginary scoreboard.

SIXTEEN

"I want to know how you pulled that off," Carlson said, handing her a bottle of water. She'd snuck in using the under-the-bed way again, making the meeting undocumented. He made it easier this time by sending one of his guards off on an errand.

"I haven't the foggiest idea what you're talking about."

With Princess still unaccounted for, the negotiations remained at a standstill but Carlson's work continued. The mounds of paperwork on the kitchen counter made that clear. Jaeger had declined to attend any more sessions while searching for his 'beloved daughter.' Lori suspected he was too embarrassed to show up and try to explain to Elder Destin what happened.

His attempts to find Princess were amateurish at best. Although he'd spread the word to other packs in Wyoming, an experienced private investigator wasn't hired until three days after her disappearance. And until the investigator suggested it, he hadn't tried to get her cell phone records. Which proved fruitless because Lori confiscated Princess' cell phone outside the hospital when they arrived. The phone was buried in one dumpster, the SIM card in another, and the battery ended up in Lori's pocket to be added to her collection.

"Sure you do." Carlson grinned. "How did you make Princess vanish?"

"Who, me? I stayed in the waiting room in public view the whole time. I'm devastated she's gone and spend hours and hours trying to find her." She put the back of her hand to her forehead. "I can't even sleep worrying about her. How was I supposed to guess her plans? I can't read minds. She took advantage of me and I'll never forgive her. I could have lost my job because of her! Or my life! How dare she?" Lori added dramatically.

The life part was truer than Carlson guessed. Lori honestly thought Jaeger might kill her when Princess wasn't located in the first twelve hours. It took the efforts of several of his men to talk him down and convince him Lori was working as hard as anyone in the search effort. One had reminded Jaeger that she was still part of Eugene's sanctuary, and to kill her could unleash the wrath of not just the Destin's but packs from all over the country.

Carlson laughed, then sobered up. "You took a major risk for her."

"In case you hadn't figured it out, that's what I do. It's my way of paying back the original women who helped me escape."

"What pack did you run from?"

That information would follow Lori to her grave. "Privileged information. And you're not that privileged."

"We're on the same side, but in different ways. I'm

trying to bring the packs into the modern world so women like you and Princess don't need to run."

"While I appreciate your efforts, they're too slow. And there are always leaders like Jaeger and Destin who don't want to change."

"I'm half-tempted to let them destroy each other."

"You won't do that because they'll be the last ones to get hurt. And they are both equally bad as far as I can see. Any luck locating Elex yet?"

Carlson shook his head. "My contact is on vacation. I've started making inquiries to pack leaders in the area and so far no one has heard of him."

"Sounds like someone joined the Free Wolves." she joked. The moment the words left her mouth, Lori realized what they implicated. "Holy shit," she whispered.

He handed her his cell phone. "Call," he urged.

"Nope, not from here and not from your phone."

"Then how?"

"I need an untraceable phone I can destroy after making the call. I might get one in Sheridan, but Casper would be better."

"Consider it done. I'll get it for you tomorrow."

"If one of your staff buys it, it's not untraceable."

"Then we need to get you to Casper."

The cover story was she needed to pick up a unique wine for a dinner Carlson wanted to host for Jaeger, and the closest store carrying it was in Casper. She took off early in the morning in a rental car borrowed from Billy. She needed as much time as possible because along the route she'd be stopping to make changes in her appearance.

The clothes were easy. A t-shirt at one convenience store, a pair of sweatpants at a truck stop. She picked up the makeup she needed at a drugstore along the interstate. The one thing she couldn't get was a realistic looking wig and she didn't have time to dye her hair, so she made do with a series of hats.

By the time she entered the department store in Casper, she didn't look anything like the woman who left Charity earlier in the day. She looked at least fifteen years older with a vaguely Hispanic heritage.

She picked out the most basic phone the bored clerk pointed out, telling him it was for her mother. A twenty slipped across the counter convinced him to activate it for her from the store line. It only came with thirty minutes pre-loaded but they were more than enough for her purposes.

"Wind here."

"Shadow here. Did you get my package?"

"It was a nice surprise."

"Thanks. I need another favor."

"You have a second passenger?"

"No. I want to find out if someone was a previous passenger."

"Name?"

"Elex Destin."

"I don't recognize that name. I'll do some digging. Where can I contact you?'

"Don't. Get the message to Counselor Carlson. Or Fairwood to pass along. Whichever is more secure."

"Priority?"

"High. Believe it or not, we're collaborating to avoid a pack war."

Wind chuckled. "Breaking the rules again, eh, Shadow? Don't worry, I'll handle this one personally."

"Thanks. Shadow out."

By the time she hit the wine store, Lori no longer appeared Hispanic. When she pulled into Charity, she'd shed the extra fifteen years and all the new clothes.

Patience is a virtue, Lori reminded herself. She'd waited all morning for a chance to talk to Carlson, but since he'd ordered Jaeger and Destin to meet with him, he didn't have the time to spare for her. She prayed the meeting would result in a breakthrough, but doubted it.

Eugene seemed to sense her mood on their daily run. He stayed in human form so they could talk. "What's bothering you?" he asked.

She had a handy excuse. "I'm still worried about Princess. I suppose if she was in trouble we'd know by now, but I'd like to hear she's okay."

"They say no news is good news."

"My grandmother used to say that. I stopped believing it when I was a teenager and my mother left on a trip and never came back."

"What happened to her?"

Lori thought she was over that old wound, but the tears in her eyes reminded her it would never heal. "I never found out. I've searched through tons of websites, trying to find her name somewhere, even on a death certificate, but nothing." Even the Free Wolves, with their far-reaching network, had been unable to locate her.

"It may seem meaningless, but I'm sorry."

"At least I knew my mother. You don't even have that."

"I figured it was only my failing human memory, but even my wolf doesn't remember her."

Either his wolf suffered from PSTD as well or he'd been ripped from his mother shortly after birth. "Are you talking to your wolf much?"

"We're getting to know each other. There aren't many people here I can talk to. I mean, there's plenty of people but I'm an inconvenience to most of them. They all have things to do and I'm in their way most of the time."

"I haven't done much the last few days either. It's not like I can reopen the bar, and there's only so much cleaning to do." With the repairs and improvements the contractors completed, she didn't even have a wish-list of things to fix. "I'm catching up on my reading."

"The Counselor gave me a few books to read but I'm not making much progress. They're about war and politics."

"His favorite topics." Lori wondered if that was Carlson's way of helping Eugene prepare for a role as an alpha. "You're welcome to borrow any of my books." She couldn't imagine him reading her drugstore romances, but she had a few science fiction books that might interest him.

They reached the high spot they'd adopted as the end point of their daily excursions. She settled into an area beside a rock that sheltered her from the worst of the wind without blocking the sun. Eugene, being larger, didn't enjoy the same benefits.

The only thing wrong with it, in her opinion, was

that Hyrum knew where it was, and made a point of checking on them every day. He'd lope by in wolf form, nod his shaggy head, and keep going. It was annoying. Lori was tempted to find a new 'favorite' spot for no other reason than to irritate Hyrum. But with Princess' disappearing act still a sore subject, it wasn't a good plan.

"How soon do you think he'll show up?" she asked.

"Hyrum? Anytime now." Eugene must have read her thoughts. "We don't have to wait for him if you don't want to."

"I'd prefer that neither of us gets in trouble," She shrugged. "Sounds like we're a couple of teenagers worried about curfew, doesn't it?"

"Pack protocol can make you feel that way." Eugene frowned. "Especially when you're an omega. But I've heard betas say the same thing."

"I don't believe you're an omega."

"You keep telling me that. But I've been treated like one my entire life so it's hard not to accept that I am."

"You can't let how other people treat you define how you think of yourself. What does your wolf say?"

"He says I need to 'find myself' whatever that means."

It meant his wolf didn't want to force him into believing something he wasn't ready for. Wise wolf.

"My wolf also says that you are more than what you seem to be and to trust you."

This was dangerous territory. Did his wolf know of her dual nature?

Eugene stood and stretched. "He won't say anything else about it."

Very wise wolf, Lori thought. She considered telling Eugene her secret, but instinct told her it wasn't the right time. Once he no longer needed sanctuary and she was free to leave, maybe she'd let him in on it.

"Speaking of Hyrum..." Eugene said.

There he was, and Eugene had spotted him first. That was new. Hyrum shifted into man form and ran up the hill. "You need to return to the bar immediately."

"Don't we even get a hello, how's it going? All we get is 'return to the bar?' Whose orders?" Lori stayed right where she was.

"Elder Jaeger."

"He sent you to do his dirty work, eh? Then the answer is a big fat no. He doesn't have authority over either one of us."

"He is an alpha," Eugene pointed out, as if she'd forgotten.

"Not my alpha. Not yours either, Eugene. So, what does Elder Jaeger want?" she asked Hyrum.

"He didn't tell me"

"He ordered and you jumped."

"That's my job."

"But not ours. Tell him we'll come when we're ready."

Hyrum stared down at her. "That's not a good idea. I should pick you up and carry you back, little human."

"But you won't. This is my choice. Give Elder Jaeger our regards and tell him we'll be back shortly."

"I hope you don't regret your choice." Hyrum shifted back to wolf form, snarled, and ran off.

"Was that smart?" Eugene asked when Hyrum was out of hearing distance.

"Tell me why Elder Jaeger would order both of us to return."

Eugene wrinkled his forehead as he thought. "I don't know. Maybe he has news about Princess?"

"Do you really think he'd share it with either one of us?"

"No."

"Exactly. I smell an ambush. I'll lay odds his men are waiting along the trail, hiding behind a rock or down in a gully." And Hyrum was involved in the plot. Or was it another way for Jaeger to test Hyrum's loyalty?

He shook his head. "That doesn't make sense. We're not a threat."

"You underestimate yourself. And me. I might not be able to tackle him in a physical battle, but there are other ways of undermining an enemy. And you—he's getting older—and if you had more experience in battle you might be able to take him one on one."

"Only an alpha can beat another alpha."

Her point exactly. "If there is an ambush, he won't be anywhere in sight. He'll be sitting in the bar drinking Counselor Carlson's whiskey, and his betas will do all the work. Think about all the empty land between here and there. Do you think anyone would ever find our bodies?"

"Elder Jaeger wouldn't order our deaths."

"I hope not, but I prefer to take precautions I don't need than to be unprepared."

"So, what's your plan?"

This was the perfect opportunity to see if Eugene could think like an alpha. "What would you suggest?"

"We can't run away."

That was the omega talking.

"We head back, but we don't take our normal route."

He was still thinking, so she waited.

"If we were both wolves, I'd propose that we would split up, but I won't leave you alone."

"I appreciate it."

"They'll be looking for either a wolf and a human or two humans. We can't change that."

They could, but it would be her ace in the hole that she hoped she wouldn't have to use.

"We take a different route home and circle around and get to the bar from a different direction."

"Can your wolf guide us?"

He took a moment. "He says he can."

"I'll carry your clothes. Even we humans are good for something." Another time she'd tell him about the sentry teams at other packs where one ran as human and one as wolf. The human carried the clothes and the weapons, while the wolf used its better senses to scent out an intruder. That lesson could wait.

Seventeen

"They don't look friendly," Lori whispered.

Wolf-Eugene nodded his head in agreement.

From a small rise, they'd spotted a mix of men and wolves in a gully near the trail Lori and Eugene normally traveled. The men carried weapons, including various makes of rifles. Although they had a wolf stationed near the road, no one guarded their rear flank. Mistake number one.

Mistake number two was the fact the men were talking among themselves. Not mind-to-mind, but with loud voices. Even the wolves were yelping and snarling.

Lori counted six of them. Four men, two wolves. She would have adjusted the ratio evenly, but that was personal preference. All were Jaeger pack members but none she counted as friends. That eased her mind.

In the distance, Lori spotted the sun glinting off the metal roof of the bar. Mistake number three. That close, they were in mental range of a strong wolf.

She explained it to Eugene in the barest of whispers. "Have you ever talked to Counselor Carlson mind to mind?"

He nodded vigorously.

"I want you to try to reach him. Tell him what's happening. Think you can do that?"

His eyes took on a sad look and he rocked his head back and forth.

"It's not that far. You don't need to see him to talk to him. You remember what his mental signature felt like?'

He cocked his head, closed his eyes, and shivered. His whole body stiffened and he whined.

"When you find him, send him a picture of what's going on and try to explain to him where we are." She didn't know how skilled Eugene-wolf was at 'talking.' Some wolves were limited to pictures and feelings. She didn't get a response and hoped he'd reached Carlson.

After a long couple of minutes, he shook himself and panted. She pulled a half-empty bottle of water from her backpack and poured a little into her hand. He lapped it up, his rough tongue tickling her palm, then he looked for more. She repeated the motions until she emptied the bottle. Mental speech could be as exhausting as a long run.

"Did you find him?"

A nod, and then his mouth curved into a wolfish smile.

"Is he on his way?"

Another nod.

"We'll wait here."

He placed his head on his paws and wiggled his belly. Getting comfortable, she assumed. It sounded like a good plan.

Eugene-wolf heard them first. No surprise, because his wolf hearing was better than her human sense.

She'd hoped Carlson would be with them, but he didn't lead the group. The four men surrounded Eugene and her, observing the situation. When they held a mental conversation, the desire to drop her shields and listen in tempted Lori. The need for caution won out.

One stripped, switched to wolf form and slithered his way towards the gully. He lay behind a rock and Lori wondered what he was up to. "He's trying to catch their conversation," the man beside her said quietly. "We need to verify their intentions. Maybe they're just out for a picnic."

She covered her mouth to stifle a chuckle. The tactic made sense. They didn't want to be accused of starting a fight for no reason.

When they moved, they did so with a speed that astonished her. One moment men, the next their clothes lay scattered on the ground and in another they were wolves. They hurled themselves into the gully and Eugene, still wolf, went with them.

The Jaeger pack men didn't have time to pull their guns from their backs. One wolf jumped on each, dragging them to the ground. In the next instant, each wolf had a human throat in his mouth. Death was imminent.

The fifth wolf faced off the two Jaeger wolves. It seemed like unfair odds, but he was bigger and stronger than both of them. Yet, the two of them working together might be able to take him down. Lori held her breath and waited.

One of the Jaeger's wolves snarled and attacked. The onslaught was met with an open mouth full of jagged teeth snapping at its hindquarters, and a paw swiping at its tail.

When the second of Jaeger's pack joined the battle, Lori had a hard time telling who was who amid the dust cloud they created. But since the rest of Carlson's bodyguards didn't appear worried, she decided it must be going in their favor. It didn't take long for one of the smaller wolves to limp away, nursing a mangled front leg. The second of the smaller wolves soon followed, one ear ripped to shreds.

The winner shifted back to human form, and Lori could see that he hadn't escaped without a few small wounds of his own. They didn't seem to bother him when he walked over and collected the guns. "We're heading back to the bar," he hollered as the wolves backed away and let the Jaeger men up. "You want to bring our clothes down here and come along?'

Lori stood, brushed the dirt off her clothes and carefully made her way through the rocks to where the group waited. Ignoring the dirty looks from the Jaegers, she waited while Carlson's men got dressed. She trailed along as the bodyguards herded the Jaegers toward the bar.

The man who had talked to her dropped back to walk alongside her. Although he and the others were all built the same, tall and muscular, the turtle tattoo on his neck marked him as unique. She sensed he was the leader of the expedition. "Are you okay?" he asked.

"Fine. You're in worse shape than me,"

He chuckled. "I'm a fast healer." He jerked his head towards Eugene. "The boy did good."

Lori had stopped thinking of Eugene as a boy, but surrounded by these hulks of men, it was clear he hadn't obtained full growth. "He needs more training. Can you and your friends help him out?"

"Sorry. Anything that distracts us from protecting the Counselor is out."

"Who's guarding him now?"

"The other shift. We're technically off duty, but this sounded like fun."

"I've been trying to figure out how many of you there are. The way you rotate shifts and personnel it's almost impossible to sort out who is who."

"Thanks. That's what we aim for."

"Is it also part of the strategy that you don't introduce yourselves?"

"You're one smart lady, Miss Grenville. A little too smart. That's why we don't trust you. What's your game?"

So, Carlson hadn't shared her secret. "I can't say. But everything changed when I claimed sanctuary for Eugene. If it helps, I consider the Counselor an ally and will do everything I can to protect him as well."

"You'll understand if we don't take your word for it."

"I don't expect you to. But can you tell me what will happen when we get back to the bar? What's the protocol for a pack leader that breaks sanctuary?" She'd never heard of a situation like she found herself in at the moment.

"We'll find out soon enough."

So, he didn't know either. Lori refrained from smirking. She didn't want to get on his bad side.

What was Elder Destin doing there? Lori had anticipated this would be a meeting solely between Jaeger and Carlson. Throwing Destin into the mix created a whole new opportunity for chaos.

Turtle—since he didn't have a name, that's what Lori called him in her thoughts—looked unhappy as well. "As much as I don't trust you, I don't trust him more," Turtle whispered. "We can't get any information about his pack and we've tried."

"What do you need to know? Eugene might be able to help."

"We asked him. He's not talking. We have aerial photos of their village, but we'd like to get a feel for it from the ground."

"I can get you in." Lori kept her voice as casual as if they were discussing the weather.

Turtle grabbed her arm and pulled her out the back door. Not wanting to draw attention to herself, she went along willingly. "Do you mean that? How?"

She nodded. "I'll have to get Carlson's permission first. He asked me not to make any more trips there. I've been trying to locate their archives. What are you looking for?"

"Randy Jaeger."

"He's dead. At least, that's the rumor."

"Who told you that?" Turtle's whole body tensed.

"A little birdie. I can't confirm it. I'm trying to get information on his son, Elex."

"As is the Counselor."

"Is he? Maybe we should pool our intel." If Carlson hadn't revealed their alliance, neither would she.

"When?" Turtle asked.

The sudden shift confused her. "When what?"

"The Destins. When can we go?"

"Tonight. If what goes on in there," she jerked her head towards the bar, "doesn't interfere."

Stuck in the hallway, Lori couldn't see over the shoulders of all the men who squeezed into the main room of the bar. Where had they all come from? Turtle looked down at her with a broad grin. "Want me to get you a chair to stand on?"

At least he hadn't offered to pick her up like some little kid. "I'm going to head upstairs and relax. Someone can fill me in later."

"No can do. You're a witness."

She didn't want to be subjected to scrutiny by the unfriendly crowd. "Then I really shouldn't be here until I'm needed."

"It's not a human trial. We don't follow the same rules."

Lori had witnessed one 'trial' as a child. It started as a discussion that rapidly become nothing more than a free-for-all with the strongest side winning. Would Carlson allow that to happen? Even as strong as his bodyguards were, would they be enough of a force to protect him against two packs? She'd have a huge target on her back, no one to watch out for her and no shotgun.

"Counselor Carlson wants you up front."

This seemed like as good of a time as any to remind Carlson that she didn't take orders from him.

"Oh." Turtle grinned. "He said to say please."

Lori had to hand it to Carlson. He was slick, real slick. She couldn't refuse him without making both of them look bad. She had one last out. "I can't push my way through this crowd."

"Stick with me. I'll get you there."

It amazed her how the crowd split once Turtle made his presence known. He coughed loudly, and as the men turned to look, glared. The ones closest to him stepped back, pushing against the next row, and a path appeared. Turtle strolled through the opening, exuding confidence and danger. Lori followed in his wake, considerably less comfortable.

At least she didn't have to stand next to Carlson. His bodyguards filled those spots. It would take more than silver buckshot to take them down. They stood at parade rest, but Lori sensed their readiness to spring into action.

Two more bodyguards took position behind Carlson, and two others a few steps on either side of him, forming a semicircle with him at the apex. Eugene claimed one end of the semicircle while someone had placed a chair on the other end for her. Jaeger faced Carlson, alone. Although pack members contributed to the small crowd inside, and others peered in through the windows, none were allowed to stand beside him.

"Your pack stands accused of breaking the rules of sanctuary. Twice that can be proved, and once that can only be suspected." Carlson addressed Jaeger. He got right to the point and ignored any social niceties that might be expected. "Explain to me why I shouldn't remove you from pack leadership as it is clear you are either implicit in the action or ineffective in leadership."

Jaeger wasn't having any of it. He waved a hand in the air. "Rumors. Lies. I'm surprised that a man of your wisdom can't see that." A trickle of alpha power followed the words. Did Jaeger really believe he could influence Counselor Carlson?

Carlson appeared not to notice and stood as solid as a rock. "You forget I witnessed the first attack. Do you deny those men are Jaeger pack members?"

"They acted without my approval," Jaeger protested.

The onlookers appeared split on the truth of the statement. A mixture of mutters and grumbles rumbled underneath a layer of nervous laughter. Carlson waited patiently for the noise to die down. "It is possible," he noted. "A symptom of poor pack leadership, but possible. But what of the men today? Did they also operate without your knowledge? After all, you sent for Eugene and Miss Grenville."

Lori caught her breath. Jaeger had to realize he was digging himself into a hole.

"What do you know of the lone wolf that attacked Miss Grenville?" Carlson asked.

"No one knows who that is. He isn't one of my pack. For all I know he's a Destin," Jaeger answered with a self-satisfied smirk. "You can check the pack roster. No male is missing."

"Elder Destin has also denied knowing the identity of the deceased attacker."

Whose body lay decomposing somewhere in the middle of the desert, Lori thought. A fitting end. His death hadn't been made public but Jaeger didn't react. Was there a leak among Carlson's staff? Carlson's stoic expression remained unchanged.

"I'm also aware that your daughter hasn't been located. How many other females has the pack lost?"

Ouch. Talk about moving in for the kill. Accusing a pack leader of not protecting his females was the supreme insult. Lori had never seen that side of Carlson.

Jaeger looked as if he'd been punched in the gut. "Three."

"Well, perhaps they are with the missing Destin heir. Where is Elex, Elder Destin?"

She hadn't seen the Destin pack leader enter the bar. With a little 'guidance' from yet another of Carlson's bodyguards, Destin stood beside Jaeger. The men glared at each other, but neither stepped away. To do so would be a sign of weakness.

Carlson stood perfectly still. Lori wasn't even sure he was breathing. What was he waiting for?

The bodyguard standing behind Destin coughed and Lori realized Destin hadn't answered Carlson's question. If Destin thought he could avoid revealing Elex's location, he was severely testing the limits of Carlson's patience. And power. There was no question about who would win. The only question in her mind was if Carlson already knew the answer.

The silence stretched out long enough that she wondered if Destin would answer. She wasn't sure how Council rules worked in this situation. Did Carlson have the right to force him to speak?

Then she felt it. The little undercurrent that tickled at the back of her brain, so subtle she almost missed it. It easily could be attributed to stress or the weariness of a long day. A mere thread of alpha power, not aimed at her, but she was more sensitive than most to subtle shifts in the atmosphere around her. The unique awareness to the use of alpha power saved her life once.

Destin reached up and swatted at his ear as if it itched, Jaeger rubbed his left shoulder with his right hand. So, Carlson was pressuring both of them. Everywhere she looked, men were reacting as if the bar had been invaded by swarms of gnats. Even Carlson's bodyguards were twitching. But why didn't it affect her?

Carlson looked around the room with the barest of smiles. He caught her eye and raised an eyebrow as if her lack of response surprised him. She nodded to signal she knew what he was doing.

Like a light switch being flipped, the irritating prickles stopped. Everyone stopped scratching. The bodyguard behind Destin coughed again.

Destin spread his arms open, almost hitting Jaeger in the process. Lori thought it was accidental, but wasn't sure. "Everyone knows where Elex is," he said, molasses dripping from his words. "He's in New York working with a Wall Street stockbroker."

"Are you sure you want to stick to that story?" Carlson asked. "The first rule for successful lying is to make it believable."

Destin appeared unfazed. "Ask anyone in my pack."

"Who of course believe the story you told them. But they don't have friends who own Wall Street firms, do they?"

"You insult my pack." Lori gave Destin credit for not backing down. She wasn't sure if Carlson aimed to trip him into revealing more information, or was trying to get Destin to confirm some tidbit of knowledge.

"But what will your pack say when they find out Elex is a janitor at the firm and not a stockbroker? Or, at least, the last time he checked in. How long ago was that, Elder Destin?"

Lori caught her breath. Not that there was anything wrong with the hard work a janitor did, but it wasn't a normal job for an alpha. She wasn't the only one in the room who reacted. Members of the Jaeger pack appeared amused while Destin pack members either frowned or wiped all expression off their faces. She wondered if any of them, especially Destin's betas, were aware of the situation.

She turned back to catch Carlson's response. It might have been her imagination or a trick of the changing light coming through the window, but he appeared larger and bulkier than before. An angry wolf on steroids. "Elder Destin, you insult the Council of Wolves with your lie," Carlson said, and a growl played under his words. "Elder Jaeger, you have violated the traditional right to sanctuary. Both of you insult the Council with your obvious efforts to waste my time here. It is my duty and my right to defend the honor of the Council and to challenge both of you. One on one or two against one, it makes no difference to me."

EIGHTEEN

Outside, a wolf howled and Lori shivered. Was Carlson serious?

"I will give each of you the opportunity to change my mind. If you want to, of course." Carlson smiled, allowing his canines to show. "Perhaps you'd rather fight, and that's fine too."

Where they all came from, Lori didn't see, but suddenly every one of Carlson's bodyguards filled the bar, forming a semicircle around Destin and Jaeger. They formed a wall of muscle and determination so the two leaders had no chance of escape. She'd been maneuvered to the outside of the wall, leaving her vulnerable.

She couldn't get out either, with no way to force her way through the men that filled the bar. Not that it was any safer outside. Even her apartment wouldn't be a haven if the assembly turned into a free-for-all.

If she wormed her way to the office, at least she could lock the door and push the desk against it. She took a step backward and ran into a brick. At least, a man's chest masquerading as stone. "Sorry," she mumbled.

"It's okay, little human, I should have told you I was here."

Hyrum? Why wasn't he guarding Elder Jaeger instead of sneaking up on her? She couldn't ask because Carlson started speaking. The rest of the room quieted.

"Your silence is all the answer I need. I'll expect resignations from both of you within forty-eight hours. Neither of you is suitable for continuing pack leadership. I will accept recommendations for your replacements as there is no clear heir for either pack. However, the Council will not be bound by your choice."

Did Carlson have the authority to make that decision? The room erupted into growls and snarls as well as an underswell of cautious cheers. How many of the men envisioned themselves as the next alpha? In contrast, Hyrum was noticeably quiet. Not that Lori didn't understand. No matter who became alpha for the Jaeger pack, Hyrum was likely out of a job and a home.

She reached backward to find his hand, planning on squeezing it to show her sympathy. Instead, she found a clenched fist. She stroked it lightly, just once, trying to convey her message. Then he disappeared, his sudden absence unexpected. Had she done something wrong?

When she turned to see where he had gone, she realized the bar was being emptied. Jaegers filing out the front door, Destins out the back. How had she missed the message? And what was she supposed to do?

The human wall in front of her thinned out, and she saw four of Carlson's bodyguards directing the mass exit. Another four made sure the two pack leaders didn't leave. The rest remained in positions to protect Carlson.

Except one. Turtle.

"Counselor Carlson would like me to escort you to your apartment," he said. "Several of us will be outside to make sure you aren't disturbed. He said to convey this as a request, not an order."

Lori shut her mouth. She'd opened it to protest, but there wasn't anything she could complain about. Not complying with Carlson's wishes would make her appear ungrateful. She recognized the manipulation but decided it wasn't the time or place to put up a fight. He had enough issues to juggle already.

Held under protection was a lot like being held prisoner, Lori thought, peeking out through a crack in her curtains. She had an emergency exit plan that would get her past Carlson's bodyguards if she decided to leave, but wasn't sure the situation warranted her disappearance. Yet. She wanted to see how the packs responded to Carlson's orders.

The escape plan would be made easier by the fact the Jaeger pack had pulled its sentries from the area around the bar. Even a trip to the Destin village might be easier as Destin and his betas debated their next steps, leaving less experienced pack members to guard their borders. On the other hand, it would be the perfect night for a raid if either pack leader decided to strike one last time to determine who was king of the hill. Or in this case, the desert.

A raid would also be the perfect cover to attack her. Eugene would be safe, she thought, protected by Carlson's staff. No one in their right minds would take on Carlson directly. She turned away from the window to begin choosing what to take with her.

The loud and steady march of footsteps on her stairs told her it wasn't an enemy approaching, but she hid as much evidence of her task as possible in the few seconds she had. A moment of lowering her shields revealed it was Turtle approaching her door and brought a smile to her lips. Had he been designated as her liaison or was it a futile effort on Carlson's part at matchmaking?

At the knock on the door, she slid her emergency backpack under the bed and made an appropriate amount of noise on her way to the entrance. "Who's there?" she asked. If she got lucky, he'd slip and tell her his name.

It didn't work. "I've got a message from Counselor Carlson," Turtle said through the door, "May I come in?"

She unlocked, opened, and held the door for him. He took a step inside and looked around. "Place barely looks lived in," he said.

"No sense in getting it all cluttered when I don't know how long I'll stay." A handy excuse. She tried to sound sad. That usually kept anyone from asking more questions.

It worked this time. At least, Turtle didn't pursue the topic. "The Counselor would like to talk to you," he said. "He emphasized that I should say 'please.'

He also said to tell you to come in the back door, whatever that means."

Lori knew exactly what it meant and hid her smile.

"He also asked if I can tag along." Furrows creased Turtle's forehead. "Something about if you can figure it out so can an unfriendly."

Lori looked him up and down. "Sorry, no can do. I understand what Carlson wants, but the truth is, you're too darn big."

"I'm not *that* big."

"Look at me and say that with a straight face."

His response was a crooked smile.

"Tell you what. I'll take you along part of the way. If you promise to do exactly what I say. Deal?" Lori held out her hand.

Turtle shook it. "Deal."

To Lori's surprise, Turtle kept up with her. In fact, the trip to the RV seemed too easy. There wasn't the normal amount of Carlson's staff scurrying around, doing whatever they did when they were off-duty.

She didn't have to lower her shields to catch him muttering to himself each time they slipped by a guard. Or when she timed things to roll under the RV without being caught. It took him a bit longer to join her.

She scooted on her belly to where the outside storage compartment door was, hoping it would be unlocked. Turtle was right behind her. "It's the end of the trail for you," she whispered into his ear. "See you inside."

"Where are you going?"

She waited until the legs of the sentry made their

turn and moved away. "I don't want to ruin the surprise. We had an agreement, right?"

He nodded.

"I kept my end of the deal, now it's time for you to keep yours." She put her finger on his lips while the guard made another pass. At the proper moment, she removed her finger and gave him a shove. "Go!"

From inside the storage compartment, Lori listened to footsteps crossing the RV and the voices greeting Turtle when he entered. The noise made the perfect cover for her next move, slipping through the hatch and ending under Carlson's bed. He'd left the light on but had closed the door so she didn't worry as she lifted the board that let her into his room.

Feeling more than a little smug, she sat on the edge of the mattress and lowered her shields to *send* Carlson a message. *"I'm here."*

"That didn't take you long," he replied. *"Sit tight. I'll come and get you in a minute."*

At least he had a new book on his nightstand, the biography of a recently deceased president. Still not her first choice, but better than the previous reading material. She lay stomach down across the bed and opened the book.

By the time Carlson *sent* her a gentle mental shove, his way of alerting her that it was time for the show to begin, she was on the second chapter. She closed the book and plastered a smile on her face. At least one of her secrets was about to be revealed.

Carlson opened the door enough that she could listen in to the conversation. "How do you think you're going to get into Destin pack territory let alone the village? The few of you that have been there went in the main gate."

"That girl said she could get us in," said a voice Lori didn't recognize. "I doubt it's possible, but she claimed you know about it."

Someone else chipped in. "Right. I don't believe it for an instant. Sure, she's pretty badass for a human but what does she know about stealth intrusions?"

"I wouldn't underestimate her," yet another man said. "I'm convinced she had something to do with the Jaeger girl disappearing."

Lori wished she could see their faces so she would know who was on her side.

"I've asked Miss Grenville to join us," Counselor Carlson said. He pushed the door open the rest of the way. She took it an indication she should join the party. "What do you say? Care to lead a group of my guards to the Destin village tonight?" he asked as she made her appearance.

Lori ignored the soft gasps from throughout the RV. Far to the back of the group, she spotted Turtle shaking his head and grinning. "What's the rush?" she asked. "Tomorrow night would be better. That gives me time to select a team and work out the logistics."

"How long have you been here?" asked one of the guards.

"Long enough to appreciate the new book Counselor Carlson is reading." She turned to him. "Nice choice, by the way. You still get your politics and strategy but a story goes with it."

Carlson's eyes twinkled. "I thought you might like it. As to your question, the men are convinced that delaying the trip would give Elder Destin the time he needs to destroy what they are looking for."

"And that is?"

There was a private exchange Lori couldn't *hear*.

"Look, if you want my help, you need to be upfront with me."

"They still aren't convinced you can assist them," Carlson said.

Lori drew in a deep breath. Wasn't it Carlson's job to convince them of it? What was he waiting for?

Turtle broke his silence. "After that little demonstration? I left her on the ground under the RV. I haven't figured out how she appeared in the bedroom. If she can get inside with none of us seeing her or catching her in the act, she can get us into the Destin village. So, I'm going to tell her." He glared at the group for a long moment, challenging someone to object. No one did, so he turned to Lori.

"We're worried about their weapons."

"They have guns? In Wyoming?" She lifted the back of her hand to her forehead. "What a shocker! Anyway, I bet that each of you has at least two guns right now." Concealed, but she'd spotted a giveaway bulge or two.

"It's not that they own guns. It's the kinds they have. Sven overheard a discussion about a new shipment of RPGs."

"They were discussing blowing up coyotes as target practice," said a man with a shaved head and a large mole above his left eye. Lori finally had a name to attach to a face. "I had the impression they weren't practicing for fun."

She knew nothing about RPGs other than what she picked up from news reports, but that explained the area she'd found where the ground was riddled with holes. "What would they need them for?"

"Can you imagine what would happen if they used them during a raid on the Jaegers?"

It didn't take much for pictures of destroyed houses and children with burns all over their bodies to flood her mind. "I'll take four men. We go tonight. You guys decide who goes with me."

Turtle came up to her while the rest of the guards debated who would get the glory of going. "Do you know where the armory is in the village?"

"I've only surveyed the location from a distance, at night, so no. But I spotted several buildings that aren't houses and it shouldn't be hard to narrow down the choices."

Carlson pulled out his phone. "I wonder if the village shows up on satellite images."

"While's he checking, I'd like to hear how you got into the RV," Turtle said.

"If I reveal my secret, I'll never be able to use it again," Lori protested.

"That's the point. If you can do it, so can someone else, and they might not be on our side."

"I asked you to sneak in to prove a point," Carlson said, still staring at his phone. "You should never need to do it again."

Fair enough, Lori thought. "One of the outside compartments open up into a space under the bed. It's a tight fit, but I can make it."

"That's why you said I couldn't go with you," Turtle said. "I'm too large for the space."

"Exactly." There were a few advantages to being small. "You can fix things by locking the cover, although it would be easy to pick. I'd fill the storage space and nail down the plywood hatch."

Carlson nodded. "Make it so, Number One."

"You didn't just say that," Lori giggled.

Turtle grinned. "It's not the first time. We usually ignore him."

"I've got it!" Carlson said, ignoring the jibe and handing Lori his phone. "It's not clear, but might help."

Looking at the roofs of the buildings didn't give Lori any hints as to their role. She passed the phone to Turtle.

"These aren't houses, but what they are used for, I can't tell you," he said pointing to three different places on the screen. "One of them has to be the armory, but I won't bet which one."

"We'll figure it out when we get there." Lori raised her eyebrows. "Who's going with me?"

NINETEEN

"Whose car are we taking?" Turtle asked as he adjusted the straps on his backpack. The other three men copied his moves. "Or do we need to take two?"

The remains of sunset in the otherwise-darkening sky gave Lori enough light to examine the group. The shadows cast by the three RVs that formed a horseshoe around them provided some privacy. Although the men didn't have nighttime camo like hers, they'd each come up with dark clothing that would work well for the mission.

"No cars. We go on foot or paw the whole way. Why do you think I wanted the packs light enough for your wolves to carry?"

"How are you going to keep up with us?"

She still had a surprise up her sleeve. "You'll find out when it's time. First, we need to sneak out of here like teenage kids going to a kegger. We'll meet up at the draw west of here on the border of Jaeger territory. You all know the spot, right? See you there in twenty minutes."

Each man would get to the rendezvous point on their own. Except for Turtle. He was tagging along with her. He claimed it was to make sure she didn't run into any issues, but she was convinced it was because he didn't trust her. She didn't blame him. If she was in his shoes, she wouldn't trust herself either.

Although she'd taken the hardest route out of the area, it didn't present much of a challenge with no guards from the Jaeger camp to dodge. Turtle stuck with her and they reached the designated meeting place with time to spare. Lori used the extra time to scout the surrounding countryside to make sure there weren't any unexpected tagalongs.

With the team reassembled, Lori revealed the next step. "It's about seven or eight miles cross country to the boundary of Destin pack territory. More like ten miles if you include all the detours we'll make."

"Not a problem for our wolves." Turtle apparently was the designated spokesman for the group of men. "But what are you going to do?"

"Lead the way. There's something else you haven't been told although Counselor Carlson knows." She paused, building up the suspense. "I'm a Free Wolf. So if any of you can't work with me and want to abandon the mission, now's your chance."

The announcement went as well as expected. Not well at all, which didn't surprise Lori. After all, people saw the Free Wolves as enemies of the Council, despite Carlson's support of certain members of the movement.

When the fangs dropped and claws sprouted, she

forced herself to stay calm and made a show of adjusting her backpack. These men were the elite, and they only needed a moment to regain control of their emotions. When they were ready to talk, she would be as well.

"So, what kind of shifter are you?" Turtle asked.

"Wolf."

"No, really."

"Wolf." Lori shrugged. "Even in wolf form, I'm small, but that's the way it is."

"Then why can't we smell or *hear* you?'

She moved away the mental blocks that kept her secure. "*Try now.*"

Four voices flooded her brain and she held up her hands. "*One at a time, guys!*"

"*How do you do that?*" asked Turtle.

"*Training. And it's not perfect. A strong alpha can break through. Carlson can. But there's no time for twenty questions. We need to get going.*"

"*Will you be able to keep up with us?*"

Lori grinned. "*You forget, I'm leading the way. You have to keep up with me.*"

It had been so long since Lori had shifted in the presence of others that an unexpected wave of shyness hit as she removed the camo top. But the men were too busy removing their own clothes to pay any attention to her so she quickly stripped off her pants and tucked the outfit into her backpack. One final check of the straps and then she reached out to her *other*.

The shift brought the familiar rush of joy. She loved being wolf but there were too many times she had to deny herself the freedom *it* brought. A sacrifice she made willingly to assist others but a loss just the same.

"*Why are you helping us?*" Turtle asked as she picked up the pack with her mouth.

"*I have my own mission. If I can find the pack's records, I might figure out Eugene's ancestry. I'm convinced there's more to his story than even he knows. It would be a bonus to find out where Elex is. Despite the Counselor's allegations this afternoon, I don't think he knows.*"

Turtle bobbed his shaggy head. "*You think we can do both?*"

"*No. But your mission is more important in the overall scheme of things. I can live with that.*" She surveyed the small line of wolves, each with a pack in their mouth, and resisted the urge to raise her nose and let loose a howl. With a flick of her tail, she set off at an easy lope, a pace that would burn up the miles and leave them the energy for the final push.

It was too quiet, Lori thought as she surveyed the village from the top of the little rise. She hadn't spotted a single sentry in the few minutes since they'd arrived. Everyone was back in human form, but talking mind-to-mind was more secure.

"*I can't believe the Destins are this careless,*" Turtle sent.

"*They aren't. This feels like a trap.*"

"*How did they find out we were coming?*"

"*Not us. The Jaegers.*"

"*That could be, but we should be able to see something that gives away their positions.*"

"Unless there are booby traps set up," suggested one of the other men.

"We didn't bring equipment to check for those." Turtle frowned.

"Wouldn't the lights in the village be off if was a trap?" Lori asked. *"Everything seems normal."*

"So why else would they withdraw their sentries?"

"Because they don't need them?" Even as the words left her mouth, Lori realized they made no sense. Every pack she'd ever been around always had at least a minimal security presence no matter what.

She listened as the men debated their next move. They were the experts in the situation, not her. She'd gotten them this far and if she wanted to, was free to walk away. But she wouldn't do that. There was too much at stake and whatever she could do to help, she would.

"Have you ever been in the village?" Turtle asked, breaking into her ruminations.

"The outer edges, but I know how to get farther in without being spotted."

"Thanks. You can head back now. We're going in, but it's better if you don't. We'll make our own way back when we're done here."

Lori wasn't sure if they were trying to protect her or if they still didn't trust her. *"There are a few tricky places between here and the village. You still need me."* Besides, she wanted to find the pack records.

"I figured you might say that. I'll go first to watch out for traps, and you follow behind me to give me directions. The rest of the guys will trail you. Will that work?"

She didn't see why not. *"There's an antelope trail a few yards east. It'll get us about halfway there."* And hopefully, any traps on the way would have been triggered by wild animals.

The closer they got to the Destin village, the more nervous Lori became. It was like Christmas Eve, as quiet as a mouse. The village should have been in turmoil as its residents debated who their new leader should be. Or, deciding to stand up to the Council and keep the current leader.

With one paw, she nudged Turtle's shoulder. "*I'm going out on a limb here, but do you have anyone watching the Jaeger village? And a way to reach them?*"

"*Why?*"

"*What are the chances the two packs are collaborating to attack Counselor Carlson?*" That would certainly explain the lack of guards, although it didn't explain the lack of activity. Unless they were all getting a good night's rest before making a bold daytime assault.

"*Shit.*" Creases formed in Turtle's forehead. "*It's possible, but I can't reach the guys keeping an eye on the Jaegers. We're too far away.*"

"*It's a crazy idea anyway. Neither of those two alphas is a match for you guys.*"

"*With the strength of the two packs combined they are capable of overwhelming us. Not easily, but it's possible based on their numbers.*"

"*That makes it all the more important that we find the weapons.*"

They were different now. It was evident in the way

they moved, each movement taut and tightly controlled. It was as if they'd been out for an easy evening run that turned into a fight for their lives. Which, Lori thought, it had.

At the edge of the little cluster of houses, the men split up. It would be faster to locate the building used as an armory by spreading out. Lori stuck with Turtle. The others could stick up for themselves in a fight but she had no weapon other than her quick thinking.

There was one advantage to it being a wolf shifter village over a human one, Lori thought as she and Turtle slunk from one shadow to the next. No barking dogs, no pets at all, unless there was a bird or fish or two inside one of the houses. Nothing to raise an alarm as they threaded their way through the narrow streets.

The houses reminded her of a historical photo. Small, wooden buildings that hadn't seen a new coat of paint for too many years. Other than that, they seemed to be well maintained. No cracked windows, no broken-down steps, even a few flowers planted in front. It looked like a movie set.

Without warning, Turtle rammed her to the ground and threw himself on top of her. She panicked, flashing back to the moment when the dead wolf lay on top of her, and struggled to push Turtle off.

"Hold still. We have company."

Lori hoped her movements hadn't been heard by the boy wandering down the street. To calm herself, she counted to ten slowly and then counted backwards to one. At least Turtle wasn't covering her nose and mouth and she could breathe. When he finally rolled away from her, she stopped herself from hitting him.

"*How about a warning next time?*" she sent, knowing her anger would carry over into her mental voice.

"*Sorry. It was instinct.*"

She brushed herself off. It wasn't much of an apology, but the only one she'd get. "*At least we know someone is alive.*"

"*I was thinking the same thing. But there's a building just ahead, looks like a public building, not a house. Doesn't look like an armory though.*"

The wooden bench out front with pictures of books carved into the sides was a dead giveaway. "*More like a library. I wonder if that's where they keep the pack records.*" She edged around Turtle, plotting a path to the doorway.

"*Save it,*" he sent, swatting her hind quarter. "*They found the weapons.*"

Even in the village of her birth, Lori had never been in the armory. As an under-sized female, pack leadership assumed she'd have no interest in fighting. She wasn't even good for breeding and her only future would be taking care of other women's children.

So, she had no basis for comparison as she looked around the large room with concrete walls. How many rifles did one pack need? Or handguns and grenades? Along with the other unidentifiable weapons. But Turtle and the others knew exactly what to do as they began the job of removing guns from their cases.

Now she understood why each man brought along a tool kit. Besides using one to pick the lock on the front door, they were removing small metal parts from each weapon before returning the item to its case.

Then the part they'd removed would be twisted out of shape and discarded on the floor.

"What can I do to help?"

"Patrol the perimeter and warn us if anyone approaches. I can't believe they left the place unguarded with only a simple padlock to secure it. Take a gun if it makes you feel any better. There's plenty to choose from," Turtle sent.

She switched back to human form. After eying a shotgun, she chose two small revolvers. She wanted something she could carry easily and hide if needed, although the form-fitting camo suit didn't give her many options. One gun ended up in her waistband while the other was clutched tightly in her hand.

The name 'Shadow' hadn't been plucked from the air for her, she'd earned it, and she proved it, slipping from one dark spot to another as she prowled the outside of the cement block building. A mere whisper in the night, she kept all her senses tuned for the slightest hint of change.

The second time around, she found the trouble she'd anticipated. The same boy that she and Turtle avoided earlier. Was he the pack's only sentry? If so, she felt sorry for him. But he had to be stopped before he opened the front door of the armory. As she *sent* a message to warn Turtle and the others, she devised a plan.

TWENTY

Lori bent over and, with her left hand, grabbed a handful of pebbles from the gravel forming a path between the armory and the house next to it. With a flick of her wrist, she hurled them to a spot behind the boy before she dropped to the ground. They struck the pavement. He swiveled as he tried to figure out what created the noise.

The temporary diversion, one of the oldest in the book, should have given the men the time needed to lock the door but assumptions were killers. She pulled out the large rock that was sticking into her ribs and hefted it to judge its weight. From the ground, it would be difficult to give it a good toss.

She rose to a crouch, still not an ideal posture, but better. She aimed for a spot across the street and released the rock with a sidearm pitch. The rock clattered against the porch of a nearby house and the boy switched directions again. Lori resumed her watchful position on the ground.

"All secure in there?" she sent to Turtle.

"Yeah, thanks for the warning."

"He's headed back your way. Hopefully, his duties

only include rattling the door and making sure it's locked. I don't see that he has any keys."

"*Roger that. I'll be standing by, just in case.*"

Lori tracked the boy as he gave up on identifying the source of the sounds and returned to his patrol. His path led him to the armory and he wiggled the handle. When nothing happened, he continued up the street.

She released a small puff of air as she got to her feet and wondered how often his route would bring him back her way. While he was on duty, she could relax a bit. A more experienced sentry would present a bigger problem.

At least his presence kept her awake. Like clockwork, he came by every twenty minutes. By his sixth rotation, she started to worry the men inside were taking too long. They needed to get out of the village before the first rays of the sun reached the horizon.

"*Almost done?*" she sent, watching the boy check the door again.

"*Give us five more minutes,*" Turtle responded.

That would work for Carlson's purposes, but it wouldn't help her personal mission. "*I'm headed over to the building I think is the library and pack archives. I'll meet you at the same spot we entered the village.*"

"*Be careful.*"

"*I will.*" She only had one chance at this and needed to get it right.

The unlocked wooden door creaked as Lori pushed it inwards. She left it half-open to cut down on the noise and allow light to sneak in. Even so, she used her wolf's eyes to examine the room.

After sticking the second revolver in her waistband, she picked up a random book laying on a nearby table and frowned. The front cover was torn and dust drifted to the floor when she turned it over. Other books were in the same shape, apparently no longer wanted. A layer of brown dirt coated the floor. Did no one in the pack read?

She didn't have time to be outraged at the thought. The unused library was the most likely spot to store the pack's archives unless someone had taken them into their home to preserve them. Most packs guarded their records with a fierceness akin to a fervent religious experience. If the archives were located in this abandoned building, it reflected poorly on the alpha.

Two smaller rooms branched off the main one. The first room Lori peered into appeared to have been used by the children of the pack, based on the undersized chairs that lay overturned on the floor. The second room, no bigger than a closet, had been an office. A desk and filing cabinets filled the small space.

With only a few minutes to spare, if the archives didn't jump out at her, she might never find them. Would they be in a file drawer or tucked away in the desk? The desk seemed like the easiest place to start.

The first two drawers she yanked open held nothing but dust. The middle one was locked, and no matter how hard she tugged, remained closed. A stack of empty manila file folders lay crumbling in the next drawer. She rifled through them anyway, not wanting to miss anything.

The last drawer didn't open when she pulled on the handle the first time. She was about out of luck and out of time. She jerked the handle, putting more strength into it, and the drawer popped open. More file folders filled the drawer. Why would anyone need that many? Or were they only the top layer, hiding something underneath?

She put a stack of them on the desk and uncovered more. She put a second bunch with the first. Underneath she uncovered an old leather-covered binder with a rusty lock. Was it the pack records? Or someone's old diary? The darkness hid its secrets, so she grabbed it, tossed the rest of the files back in the drawer, pushed it shut, and hustled out of the building. She couldn't be late for the rendezvous.

Her hands full, she used her heel to close the door. Its hinges squealed in protest and she cringed, praying no one would hear.

"Did you find what you were looking for?" Turtle asked as the group left town, Lori in the lead.

She was preoccupied with stuffing the binder into her pack, worried that her wolf would tire before they got home. *"I don't know yet. Haven't had a chance to take a good look. How about you? Did you disable all the weapons?"*

He chuckled. *"I want to see their faces when they realize their big bad toys that go boom won't do anything but click. Unless they have an arms expert, it'll take them forever to figure it out. To replace the missing parts will take even longer. We left enough working guns for hunting and basic self-defense, but they won't be able to mount a raid soon."*

"Will you do the same to the Jaeger's weapons? I can get you to their armory."

"That'll be up to Counselor Carlson to decide."

It would only be fair. Lori didn't like the idea of the Jaeger's having an advantage over the Destin's. Or leaving them with guns that could be used to attack Carlson and his staff.

A short distance from the village, they stopped to make the shift to wolf form for the long run home. Lori fit her clothes in with the binder, but had nowhere to put the two revolvers. Too bad, because they were the perfect size, and the engraved roses on the handles gave them a feminine touch.

With a large jagged rock, she dug a shallow hole under a clump of sagebrush. She'd bury the guns, mark the spot, and come back later and retrieve them. Either that or an archeologist would uncover them a hundred years from now and concoct a story about how they got there.

"What are you doing?" Turtle asked.

"They're too heavy for me to carry."

"You could ask for help."

"I hate to impose." Besides, she was so used to doing things for herself, the thought hadn't crossed her mind.

He switched back to man form and picked up the revolvers, adding one to his pack and the other to one of the other packs. *"No imposition, it's as simple as that."*

Lori's energy fizzled out by the time the group stopped at the initial meeting spot. The sun was breaking the horizon but she wasn't worried about anyone seeing them. Still, protocol decreed they make the final leg of the trip one by one. As leaders of the expedition, she and Turtle should be the last to leave.

In human form again, each member of the team dressed in silence. Lori had observed the effect before, a mix of pride at a successful mission and sadness it was over as the adrenaline faded. Turtle's face bore the familiar blank expression as he reported in.

"Counselor Carlson requests you return to your apartment and get some sleep," he sent. *"A guard has been assigned to make sure you aren't disturbed."*

Or that she didn't leave without someone knowing about it. Lori didn't have the energy to fight. All she wanted to do was to examine the binder. Hopefully, it contained more than old receipts and unpaid bills.

She might have agreed to follow Carlson's instructions to go home, but that didn't mean she wanted to make things easy for him. Crouched behind a car, she eyed the large man sitting at the bottom of her stairs, one of the bodyguards. It wouldn't be easy to get past him unseen, but it was possible. After the long night though, she wasn't sure she had the energy or the desire.

Besides, her secret was out. How long until the news of her dual nature reached the ears of people who shouldn't know? She stood, brushed herself off, and strolled the short distance to the building. She nodded to the man and headed up the stairs.

As she climbed them, his eyes burned a hole in her back. Yes, it was time to disappear. Hopefully, Eugene would forgive her for not sticking around. As she opened her door, she was cataloging what to pack. First, she needed a nap.

The scream of bullets whizzing by her head woke Lori. She rolled off the bed and crawled underneath it. She struggled to pull the thin mattress off the frame and position it against the wall. The protection it offered was mostly a placebo, but better than nothing.

A too-near boom rattled the window, followed by the hiss of rain striking the glass pane. Lori laughed uneasily. They'd been blessed by a rare Wyoming thunderstorm. In her half-asleep, half-awake moments, she'd dreamt the thunder was enemy fire.

The storm changed her plans. She wouldn't take a chance on being out in the open and being struck by lightning. Her time wouldn't be wasted, however. She'd use it to look through the 'borrowed' binder.

While waiting for a pot of water to heat to make a cup of tea, Lori wiped the accumulated grime from the leather cover. Even stored away in the closed drawer, Wyoming dirt found a way to coat the surface. It made Lori doubt the book was the pack's records because surely babies had been born in the past several years.

With a cup of mint tea at her elbow, she examined the small lock. She shouldn't need her full tool kit to open it. A bit of luck, some vegetable oil and the screwdriver from an eyeglass repair kit should do the job.

It took a lot of jiggling, a lot of patience, and a few curse words, but she finally heard the soft 'click' she'd been waiting for. Lori held her breath as she opened the book.

The spidery, faded writing on the first page revealed she chose well. 'Destin Pack History 1906.' She released the air in her lungs, picked up the cup of tea, and flipped the page. Some archivists treated pack records like the 'begats' in the Bible, others recorded in story form. Which would she find?

She ended up with a combination of both. As the handwriting changed as archivists came and went, so did the style of record keeping. She'd heard of pack historians staying in the position for eighty years or more, but not with the Destins. The longest time Lori identified one person maintaining the records was ten years. She wondered if she should mention it to Carlson but decided it would be a waste of time. In the overall scheme of things, it didn't matter.

Without an exact date of birth for either Eugene or Elex, she didn't know where to start. She guessed Eugene to be eighteen or so, but Elex must be older than that based on Elder Destin's claims of his career. As she flipped through the yellowed pages, she struggled to read the words. The last archivist's handwriting was sloppy and the numbers ill-formed as if they'd been written in a hurry.

She scanned for familiar names. Although she'd not gotten close to any of the Destin pack who'd worked as servers, she knew their names at least. One or two of them must be close to Eugene's age. Their records should help her locate his.

Her eyes hurt and her head throbbed when she closed the book and pushed it away. How could the alpha-to-be's birth not have been recorded? How many other names were missing besides Eugene's? Had their births been recorded with the state?

She closed her eyes, crossed her arms on the tabletop, and rested her head on them. The only other thing she could think of was to interview the oldest mothers of the village. At least one should remember the births and would be willing to share the secret. Finding *that* one in the short amount of time left was an impossible task.

It was a blow to her ego to be so close and fail. What had she overlooked? With one more peek, maybe she'd find the information she wanted. She shook her head, re-opened the binder to a random page, squinted her eyes and started reading.

This time, she spotted Hyrum's record of birth. But he was more her age, not Eugene's. She tore a strip from a napkin to mark the spot, thinking that perhaps he'd like to see it, then turned a random number of pages forward.

TWENTY~ONE

"That's when I noticed the missing page," Lori told Carlson. "Cut cleanly, almost all the way down to the binding. Probably with a razor blade. No way it was an accident."

He ran his finger down the small remnant of the missing page. "I agree. This is deliberate."

"What we can't tell is if this was Elex's birth record or Eugene's. I couldn't find either one listed."

"I can't locate Elex. None of my sources found any information on him. I can't even swear that he's still alive."

Lori flashed back to the wolf she'd killed. "You don't think...?" she asked.

"No," Carlson answered, reading her mind. "If that was Elex, someone from the Destin pack would have known. My theory is he was a renegade, hired by one of the packs to do the job. Which pack, I can't tell you."

That didn't help. "So, where's Elex?"

"He may have changed his name or moved overseas. Clearly, he doesn't want to be found. If I understood why not, it would help me figure out where he went."

"If Eugene's memory losses are due to abuse, who's to say Elex wasn't abused too?"

"The favored heir abused? They usually are spoiled rotten."

The sound of the rain hitting the roof of the RV soothed the tension. Although the initial storm had passed, the rain remained. Since Lori wouldn't be going anywhere for a while, a visit to Carlson helped to pass the time.

"The first thing that comes to mind is he didn't want to be alpha," she said. "As crazy as it sounds."

Carlson frowned. "Being an alpha is not something you can turn on and off, Miss Grenville. Certainly, a beta can have hidden alpha tendencies that arise when called for, but once you are alpha you can never be beta again."

So said the supreme alpha of the wolves in North America. Lori didn't allow the grin to reach her face. "I get that. What if he wasn't alpha material and got tired of pretending?"

One of Carlson's eyebrows raised. "That's an interesting theory. Especially as Eugene was raised to be omega when he is clearly alpha."

"If this was a book, the last chapter would reveal they'd been switched at birth." Lori laughed.

The piercing stare that Carlson fixed on her made Lori want to slink away.

"Say that again," he demanded.

"What? The switched at birth thing? It was a joke!"

He tapped the book beside him. "A missing man, an abused alpha, and a page removed from the pack records. Add those things together and what do you get?"

"It's too far-fetched to be believable. They aren't

even the same age. And a mother would realize if her cub got switched with another." Lori had never had a baby, and never expected to, but was convinced she'd know her own child no matter what. Just like she'd recognize each and every passenger even after they changed their appearance.

"I'm not an expert on the subject." He grinned. "One of the few things I have no personal experience in."

For a moment, Lori felt sorry for him. No mate, no children. The price of being able to stay neutral in negotiations. But no one forced him into his role, he'd chosen his life as surely as she'd picked hers.

"What we need is to find the pack's midwife and see if she can clue us into what happened," Carlson mused. "But I haven't met a female from the Destin pack yet. It's as if they are kept locked up in a cloister. I'm surprised you haven't gone in to free them."

She smiled broadly. "Give me time."

"I don't want to hear it." Carlson covered his ears and winked. "If you don't tell me about it, I can act surprised when it happens."

She hoped she wouldn't have to do anything, that the change in pack leadership would be all that was needed. As much as she wanted to, she couldn't go charging into the village and lead the women out like Peter Piper.

"Can't you tell Elder Destin that you want to talk to the pack's midwife? Or maybe the alpha female? One of them might tell you the story behind Elex and Eugene."

"If I'd asked a few days ago..." Carlson shrugged. "After yesterday? Not a chance."

Which reminded her of another burning question.

"Are your men going to raid the Jaeger armory tonight?"

He subjected her to another of his intense stares. Not wanting to back down, she held his eyes in a steady glare as long as possible. The subtle pressure began, gnawing at the back of her brain. "Submit!" it screamed. As the pressure increased, she couldn't help herself. She blinked and looked away.

"What was the point of that?" she asked.

Carlson leaned back in his chair and crossed his arms. "A reminder that no matter how good you are, there's a reason I can't tell you everything. If I can 'influence' you, it's possible for others to do so."

He was right. "So, when I see them slinking around the bar tonight, headed towards the village, I'll ignore them. Got it."

"You won't see them."

Did that mean there wouldn't be a raid or that he was confident in his men's abilities? Either way, he wouldn't tell her, so she didn't bother asking. Instead, she picked up the Destin pack book and stood. "This will give me something to do while I'm not watching for your men," she said, hoping Carlson caught the teasing note in her voice.

Carlson stood too. "I don't want you to think I didn't appreciate your help last night, Miss Grenville."

"But?"

"Some things are better left to experts."

Lori frowned. "Are you calling me an amateur?"

"My diplomacy has failed me again. No, I don't believe you are unskilled. There are things you could teach my men. A weapons expert you are not. Stay home tonight, keep your door locked and your curtains closed. Please."

"I'll keep your advice under consideration, Counselor." She wouldn't promise him anything.

As Lori heated leftover spaghetti, she mulled over the strange turn in the conversation. It was if a switch flipped and Carlson changed from friend to a mere acquaintance who was annoyed with her. Her simple question about the possibility of a raid shouldn't have been enough to cause such an abrupt change. Not unless he worried the raid would go badly.

In that case, she refused to stay in her apartment, cowering behind the wooden table tipped over on its side. If there was going to be a battle, she'd be part of it. She didn't have her shotgun anymore, but she had the revolvers she'd acquired from the Destin armory. And the full brick of ammo Turtle gave her. Silver, of course.

She wandered downstairs to throw a bag of garbage in the dumpster and to verify a guard still patrolled at the bottom of the stairs. She didn't recognize the man pacing there, but sent him a chin lift to acknowledge his presence. Had Carlson brought in reinforcements? From the burning feeling at the base of her neck, she knew his eyes never left her until she closed the apartment door.

The decoy boxes in the closet, stuffed with rocks and paper, were the first to go. Stacked along the exterior wall of the bedroom, they'd serve as a weak layer of protection against stray bullets.

She moved the clothes hanging in the closet to the bed. The few that were part of her escape supplies got put in the largest backpack she owned. She'd abandon the rest.

It took a few minutes to pry out the nails from the floor. She'd left them poking up, not pounded all the way in, and they pulled out easily. When finished, she sat back on her heels and rested.

She discovered the trapdoor and hidden staircase while cleaning in the downstairs office and guessed it was used to spirit females up to the apartment by the building's original builder. At some point, it got turned into storage space, but now all it held were cobwebs and dust. No one knew about it but her. It would be her escape route if she needed an unseen way out.

Sleep would be impossible, so Lori occupied herself with combing through the Destin pack records again. The number of infants and young children that died in the beginning made her eyes tear. A mix of accidents and disease took more than their share of young lives. Inexperienced shifters in wolf form had been hunted as trophies.

The stories during the Depression were worse. The pack's attempts at cattle ranching failed followed by an even worse failure at farming when they found out the land didn't have any water rights. Pack members left to find work and the pack almost dissolved.

When she stopped reading long enough to get a drink of water, she glanced out the window over the kitchen sink and realized that the only light came from the bar's outside fixtures. Not a sliver of brightness came from any of the RVs. Except for the dark blotches they created against the horizon, Lori wouldn't have known they remained parked in their usual spots. She turned off her lights to make it seem as if she was asleep. With a silent plea that nothing would happen, she sat on the floor with her back against an interior wall, her pack at her side, and began the wait.

On the battlefield, it would be a suicidal move. But Lori wasn't in battle, she told herself, so it should be safe. She opened her mind to *listen* for the normal babble of a million conversations.

And *heard* nothing. It seemed as if she were the last person left alive. Or that hell on earth was about to be unleashed. She suspected the latter.

Halfway down the hidden staircase, she caught the first 'POP' of gunfire. The anticipated barrage of answering shots didn't happen and Lori tried to convince herself the sound had been a figment of her imagination. The echo of a second shot reverberated as she forced open the sliding panel leading into the downstairs office. She almost missed the sound, masked by the groan of the panel grinding into its slot. Silence followed.

So, it was just a sentry taking potshots at a prairie dog to relieve the boredom of a midnight shift. And the silence in her mind was because everyone else slept. She could hope.

But the years of fighting and fleeing had scarred her, and hope didn't belong in her vocabulary. Only plans and action. Both of which were in short supply at the moment.

She crept down the short hallway and peeked out the back door. The light was dimmer there and would be her choice for escape. That was, if her guard joined the rest of his team. If not, she'd be stuck sneaking out the front door.

The long shadow cast by the man sitting at the bottom of her stairs brought some comfort. The moment Counselor Carlson was threatened, he'd be gone. His relaxed presence meant everything was going according to plan.

The front windows of the bar provided a more direct view in the direction of the village, so Lori threaded her way through the barren room. No one had touched it since the disastrous meeting and tables were piled to the sides with chairs stacked on top of them. She pushed aside her sadness, knowing she'd never re-open the bar to customers. She'd come to like the place.

The rain had ended and a few wispy clouds rolled by the crescent moon, playing peek-a-boo with the stars. The perfect night for lovers to stroll through the desert. She wondered if Elder Destin allowed pack members to choose their own partners.

Lulled into a moment of complacency, she almost fell asleep. She needed several cups of hot coffee, but without turning on a light to find the supplies, couldn't make a pot. Instead, she resorted to doing jumping jacks, stretches, and occasional marches across the room and back.

She caught it from the corner of her eye. The flare that streaked upwards and lit the night sky. Who fired it and who it signaled to was only a guess she didn't have time to make.

Because the world exploded.

TWENTY~TWO

The first grenade detonated near the bar, shattering one of the windows, covering Lori in shards of glass. Protected by her clothing, the only injuries were minor scratches to her face and hands. She darted outside, not trying to hide her exit. The next missile might hit the building and obliterate it within seconds.

The screams of a hundred voices assaulted her at the same time and she staggered under the blow before she erected her shields. For a moment, she stopped thinking clearly. Who needed her help first? Carlson? Eugene? She settled on her guard. He needed to be told he didn't need to risk his life looking for her in a burning building.

His look of shock as she rounded the corner was her reward. "How?" he stuttered, then shook his head. "Never mind. They warned me about you. What's our next step?"

"*Our* next step?" she asked.

"Yep. My orders are to stick with you no matter what."

"What do you know about what's going on?"

"It was supposed to be easy in, easy out. There's no news about what went wrong."

"Is Carlson safe?"

An engine gunned and a car tore out of the parking lot. "He will be in a few minutes."

There was another explosion nearby and Lori and the man simultaneously threw themselves to the ground. "That was bigger than any grenade I've ever seen," he said.

Great. "The Jaegers must have their own stockpile of RPGs."

He growled. "We need to find shelter."

"Sorry, there's nothing around here but gullies big enough to be foxholes."

"That won't do us any good." He stuck out his hand as they got to their knees. "I'm Jace."

"Lori." They shook and climbed to their feet. "Got any other ideas, Jace?"

"I can't reach any of the other guys."

"Eugene?"

"The kid? No. But my range is pretty short. He might have left with Counselor Carlson."

She hoped so. It made her life easier. "Well, I won't wait for the fight to come to us. Let's go see what damage we can do."

He grinned. "I like the sound of that."

She took the lead as it was his first day on the assignment. Plus, she knew the way to the Jaeger's armory. It was her best guess as to where the rest of Carlson's bodyguards might be. At least if they were trapped there, they wouldn't run out of ammo.

Every few minutes, they'd stop, open their minds

and *listen*. But neither of them had any luck with making contact with the other bodyguards. Lori limited herself to reaching out for only one mind, Turtle's. Another onslaught of too many voices could take her to the ground.

Halfway to the village, they stumbled across the first victim of the fight, hit by a multitude of bullets. Lori knelt by the wolf to assess its wounds, but it was dead, its eyes staring blankly at nothing. She gently lowered its eyelids and closed its mouth. She hoped someone would do the same service for her body.

"You recognize him?" Jace asked, kneeling beside her.

"Not in this form."

"He's not one of ours." Jace rubbed the left ear. "We notch our ear so we can be identified."

That provided only minor comfort.

The second victim managed to drag himself a few feet towards the village before succumbing to his wounds. Lori made a cursory check for breathing and a notch in the ear before they moved past. "What happened to raiding for the glory only, not to kill?" she asked no one in particular.

"Someone didn't get the memo."

A burst of gunfire forced them to roll into a nearby ditch. Lori listened for the splatter of bullets striking the ground, but heard only faint thuds. They weren't the target.

She used the opportunity to *reach* for Turtle again. And found him.

"*Where are you?*"

"*In the Jaeger armory. Safest place to be right now.*"

"*Who's fighting who?*"

"The Jaegers are attacking us. And the Destins are attacking them."

"Someone is attacking the bar too. Carlson is out and safe."

"Where are you?"

She ignored the question. *"What can we do to help?"*

"We?"

"Me and Jace."

"Unless there's a company of Rangers handy, the best thing for you do is head to Charity and hole up there."

"At least you have enough weapons to last."

The sudden silence bothered her. There was a temporary halt in gunfire so he wasn't under attack.

Then he returned. *"Someone cleaned out the armory before we got here. Our only weapons are what we brought."*

They wouldn't last long. *"We'll figure something out."*

"Give Counselor Carlson my regards the next time you see him. Tell him it was a privilege working for him." He disappeared from her mind and Lori swore under her breath.

"What?" Jace asked.

Lori relayed the conversation. "No way in hell I'm leaving them there."

"I agree in spirit, but what can the two of us do? I only have one gun and not enough ammo to last."

"I brought two." Lori slid the straps of her pack off her shoulders and retrieved the revolvers.

"Still not good enough."

"There's a back way to the armory. We can get there without getting caught."

"And do what? Outfight two packs at once? You're crazy."

That was exactly what she intended to do. "Do you have a better plan?"

At the sound of nearby footsteps, they froze. "Grenville," a voice called. "Where are you?"

Eugene? Where had he come from? She popped her head up from the ditch. "Here. Quick."

There wasn't enough room for them to lay side-by-side, so Eugene laid the opposite direction. With their heads together, they didn't need to yell to have a discussion. "Why aren't you with Carlson?" Lori asked.

"I refused to go. This fight is about me. I need to be here."

Lori couldn't scold him for being foolish when she was using much of the same reasoning. "How did you find us?"

"Your scent. It's different today and so I could track you."

Lori realized she hadn't showered since the previous night's mission. After running in wolf form, the effectiveness of the special soap ended. That meant he knew her secret. "I'm sorry I couldn't tell you before. About what I am."

"Are you still my friend?"

"That hasn't changed. We can talk about the rest another time. After we figure out a way to rescue Carlson's men."

"I'll help if you let me. What's the plan?"

She filled him in on the situation.

"I saw a rifle a little ways back," Eugene said. "I'll go get it." He popped out of the ditch before Lori could stop him. It seemed longer to her, but he was back in three or four minutes, a rifle in his hand.

"Hugo must have dropped it," he said, crawling back into the ditch.

"Hugo?" Lori asked.

"One of the dead guys I spotted. I bet he shifted hoping his wolf was strong enough to heal him. Didn't work."

"You don't sound upset," Jace said.

"Nope. He was a Class A bully. One of Destin's betas, thought he was better than everyone else."

Lori didn't like how casual Eugene seemed about the death of one of his pack members, but without knowing the whole story, she wouldn't pass judgment. "Did you know the other one?"

"I spotted two more. Didn't recognize either one. They must have been Jaegers."

"So, neither side is playing by the rules. That means we don't need to either."

"What do you have in mind?" Jace asked.

She needed a plan, and fast. "Give me a few minutes to think about it."

Lori gave thanks to whatever gods listened that they didn't come across any dead or injured women or children as they made their way to the village. She gave up checking each body they came across because it slowed down their journey and she didn't have first aid supplies anyway. Jace and Eugene took time to collect weapons and ammo but she preferred to travel light.

Avoiding the main road meant the trip took longer, but it reduced the chances of running into an enemy. The fight had consolidated at the center of the village and the trio only had to dive for cover when a one-on-one battle bled into the surrounding countryside. The combatants they watched were fighting for the win and not the kill so Lori didn't feel the urge to step in and stop them.

Lori reached out for Turtle each time they came to a halt, wanting to tell him help was on its way. Each time, she found nothing. Each time, she had to remind herself that he was fighting for his life.

Her destination was an alleyway between two houses at the edge of the village. She'd spotted it on one of her trips to visit with Madame Rose. Cluttered with abandoned trash cans and tumbleweeds, it seemed the perfect way in.

They huddled in the shadow of a rickety wooden fence as two wolves tore by, one nipping at the heels of the other. Something about the bigger one in the rear tugged at Lori as if she should recognize him. "Do you know them?" she whispered to Eugene.

"The one in front is Roy, a Destin omega. He's no match for the wolf following him. He was right to run."

"I hope he'll be all right."

"The big wolf won't waste his time on an omega. We need to move before he comes back," Jace said.

"It's not much farther." Lori tilted her head and listened to make sure they were alone. "We can stay in the shadow of the fence until we get there."

Dry weeds underfoot made moving silently impossible. Each stealthy footstep resulted in a 'crunch.' A good sentry would hear them—if there were any left.

The alley, when they reached it, was in worse shape. "We can either make a little noise for a long time or lots of noise for a short time. What'll it be?" she asked.

"We go fast," Jace answered. "If anyone was around, they would have confronted us."

Lori didn't need convincing. There were too many obstacles for a flat-out run, so she took off at a quick trot with the two men close behind. She slowed near the end when she spotted a dark shadow where no shadow belonged. The air shimmered and the shadow morphed into a man.

"Come out, little human. Your friends too."

Hyrum? Why did it have to be Hyrum? She didn't want him to get hurt, but if he stood in the way of the rescue, there'd be no way to avoid it.

She signaled to Jace and Eugene to stay where they were before stepping forward herself. "I need you to do me a favor and move aside, Hyrum. Don't ask any questions, just do it. Please."

"Not gonna happen. Tell me what you're doing here."

In the dim light cast by a distant street lamp, she studied his face. "Those are my friends in the armory. I'm going to break them out."

He snorted in derision. "You and what army? No matter how good your two friends think they are, they can't take on a whole pack."

"How much of the pack is left, Hyrum?"

He crumbled. His shoulders dropped, his knees buckled, and he closed his eyes. "The women and children left before the fighting started, but I don't know how many of the men are still alive."

"Where is your alpha? Shouldn't you be by his side?"

His lips formed a tight line. "He left with the women. Claimed his job was to protect them."

"He's a coward. He started this fight and then ran." Jace spit out the words with contempt as he came to stand beside Lori. "The betas could guard the women. His job is to protect the pack. He should be here."

"He has abandoned his pack. The pack is no more," Lori said solemnly, pronouncing the traditional words. They should have been said by a member of the pack, but as a Free Wolf she considered herself a member of every pack as well as a member of no pack.

"He has abandoned the pack. The pack is no more," Jace repeated.

Tradition required three people to bear witness to the action. Lori held her breath and waited. Would Hyrum join them?

He shook his head. "It was bad enough when you claimed sanctuary for the boy, human. Now you try to use another tradition against us?"

Lori held out her wrist. "There are things you don't know about me. Smell me."

"What?"

She dropped her mental block. "*Smell me, Hyrum.*" she sent. "*I am not only human, I am wolf. I am both.*"

He stepped backward. "You can't be a shifter. What kind of trick is this?"

Lori took two steps forward and shoved her arm under his nose. "*Smell me.*"

TWENTY~THREE

Even naked, Hyrum could kill her before Jace or Eugene could stop him. Standing there defenseless, with her arm raised, Lori waited for his reaction. Because of his height advantage, her neck was bared to him as she stared into his eyes.

With a groan, he grabbed her arm and pressed it against his nose. "Wolf. How is that possible?" Abruptly, he flung her arm away. His fangs descended and he snarled. "What are you?"

She fell, but Jace caught her before she hit the ground. "I'm a woman on a mission," she said, allowing her own fangs to drop. "And you're in my way."

"You don't really believe the three of you can rescue the invaders in the armory?"

"Just like I didn't manage to get Princess out of here and hidden so deep her father can't find her."

"Rumor has it the Free Wolves did that."

"Bingo."

Hyrum blinked several times. His eyebrows knotted as he considered her statement. "I almost believe you can rescue your friends."

"Would you like to help?"

His solemn expression cracked. "For the chance to see you in action, yes."

Hyrum shifted back to wolf form to act as the long-range eyes and ears for the group. The heart of the battle that still raged was on the way to the front door of the armory so he led them down back paths towards a side door.

Even with his help, the path wasn't clear. He refused to fight Jaeger pack members so Jace and Eugene handled most of the dirty work. They stuck to the old standard of fighting to prove who the better fighter was, so Lori declined to use her revolvers. One group of three they came across included a young man, ragged and worn out, but not ready to give up. While Jace and Eugene fought his companions, Lori engaged him. She wasn't a fighter, but knew a few basic self-defense moves. Still, his size and strength were too much for her and despite her best effort he backed her up against a wooden fence. He moved in to strike a disabling blow when she recognized him. He'd been one of her patients the night of the original Destin raid.

"*How's that scratch on your right leg doing?*" she sent as he raised his fist.

The question was enough to make him miss and hit the fence. She ducked under his arm. "*You're still favoring your left, I see. You might want to get it checked out. It should have healed by now.*"

He swung again but his heart wasn't in it and his blow went wild, striking nothing but air. He fell to the ground and looked up at her. "*What are you doing here? Why aren't you with the other women?*"

"*If you want to find out, come with me and my friends.*" Lori extended her hand to help him up.

"*I can't betray the pack.*"

"*Your alpha has fled. The pack is no more. I can help you find a new one.*"

He grabbed her hand and she pulled with all her strength. Someday he'd make a good beta.

"*What are you doing here?*"

"*Rescuing friends. Want to help?*"

Jace and Eugene tied up the men they'd fought, using strips from their shirts. The cloth wouldn't last but it put them out of action long enough for her purposes.

"I*t looks like you are on the winning side here,*" the boy sent. "*I'll stay with you.*"

The door Hyrum led them to was locked and he didn't have the key. Yet another indication that Jaeger didn't trust him. A swift examination convinced Lori that even with the right tools, she didn't have the knowledge to pick it. And Turtle still wasn't in communication.

"What if we shoot it out?" she asked.

Jace shook his head. "Won't work like in the movies. We can try but all we'll do is draw attention to ourselves."

"Can we break it down?'

"It's hardened steel," Hyrum said. "You'll hurt yourself."

There had to be a way in. They were too close to give up now.

"Maybe if we knock they'll hear us."

"This door opens into a small office that's kept

locked. The interior walls will muffle the sound and they can't get into it anyway."

Hyrum wasn't being much help. "Got any other ideas?"

A flurry of nearby gunshots forced them to hug the exterior wall. A group of twenty men blocked the front of the building, occasionally firing toward the door, keeping Turtle and the others inside. If they were still firing, that meant Carlson's men were still alive. She needed to get in. With all the doors out of the question, that left entry through a window. The only windows were two stories up with bars over them. Even if she stood on Hyrum's shoulders, Lori wouldn't be able to reach them. "I need a trampoline."

"Even you aren't small enough to slip between the bars," Jace pointed out.

She turned to Tony, the young man. "Kids always figure out how to get into pack buildings. What trick do you know?"

He shook his head. "We used to use the bathroom window, but got caught and they blocked it. That was a couple of years ago. I wouldn't fit anymore. But you might."

"Is there only one shared bathroom, or are there both men's and women's?"

Tony's face lit up. "They're separate. I've never been in the girls' room, but I don't think they touched it."

Hyrum grunted. "We only put bars on the boys' room. Elder Jaeger didn't want to put out the extra money for both."

"Can we get there without attracting attention?"

"There are four men guarding that side of the building."

They needed a distraction. Lori realized she was the only one in the group able to pull it off.

In wolf form, Lori rolled around in a puddle left by the afternoon's rainstorm, thoroughly coating her fur. With her light brown fur matted with mud, she appeared almost as small as a child at first shift.

"You don't have to do this," Jace *sent.*

"I'm the only one who can. Now I need you to cut my paw. Just enough to make it bleed." She held up her left front paw and Jace pulled out his knife.

"Is that necessary?" Hyrum pushed his way between Lori and Jace.

"The blood is what makes my act believable." The wound would heal soon enough.

"Then cut me. I'll bleed for you."

She didn't know what to say or how to react. In one way it was sweet of Hyrum to make the offer. Was he trying to protect her or did he think her incapable of handling the slight pain?

Jace didn't give Hyrum time to reconsider the offer. He grabbed Hyrum's paw and raked his blade across the top. Lori dropped to the ground next to Hyrum so he could rub his paw on her front shoulder.

"I'm not sure that's enough," Hyrum looked at his paw. *"But it's stopped bleeding."*

"As long as I smell like blood, I'll make it work." Lori didn't want anyone else to be hurt for the sake of her upcoming act.

"You sure you want to do this?" Eugene hadn't

liked the plan from the start. *"We can figure out a different way."*

Lori was tired of arguing. She batted him playfully on the hip, hiding how touched she was by his concern.

"He's right. We can find another way. You're putting yourself in danger." Jace's deep voice was meant only for her.

"I'm aware of the risks. Sometimes you have to sacrifice a pawn to win the game."

He looked her in the eye and nodded once. *"Good luck."*

She needed all the luck she could get.

Her left front paw raised slightly, Lori limped down the gravel walk on three legs. Every three or four steps, she'd put the 'injured' paw on the ground and whine. The four men were more intent on tracking the battle happening on the main street then guarding the pathway, so it took her awhile to get their attention.

From a few yards away, she whimpered loudly. One of the men turned around and reached for his gun. Lori laid down, put her head on her paws and sniveled.

The second man turned and swatted the first man on the shoulder. "It's just a scared kid. Put your gun away."

"What's a kid doing here? Didn't they all leave?" the first man asked.

Lori hoped the men were unfamiliar with the children of the pack. Her gambit depended upon it.

"I'm not surprised they missed one in that mess." The second man held out his hand like one would do to a stray dog. "What's your name?"

"*Rosie.*" She whined and licked her paw. Many female cubs were named after the female alpha so it was a safe choice.

"Shit! A little girl and she's hurt! What are we going to do with her?"

"Take her to the school. That's where the wounded are," the first man answered.

"Have you seen the shape some of the guys are in? That's all she needs, to be mixed up with that."

"She can't stay here. A couple of women didn't leave, maybe she's one of their kids."

The second man knelt beside her. "Rosie, can you tell me who your mother is?"

Lori *sent* an image of one of the female customers of the bar.

"That's Hannah," the first man said. "She's gone. She helped Madame Rose get everything into the car. Madame Rose probably yelled at her so much that she forgot her own kid."

So far the men hadn't moved away from the post. How could she get them to leave?

At another burst of gunfire, she whimpered and put one paw over her eyes.

"That does it," said the first man. "The school is the safest place for her. You go with her and make sure she gets there. The rest of us will stay here."

Not the perfect scenario, but it would be easier for her tiny group to disable three guards than four.

"Come on, Rosie," said the second man. "Let's go."

Lori rose with feigned caution, took a step, yelped and fell.

Without a word, the second man scooped her up. "I'll carry her," he said. "Don't worry, Rosie, we'll take care of you."

She wasn't worried about herself. Once they got to the school, she'd find a way to sneak out. All she had to worry about now was Jace and the others slipping in through the bathroom window at the armory.

The stench of spilled blood filled Lori's nose as she eased her way past another victim. How many had died needlessly in the battle? She longed for hands to wipe away her tears but she was still in wolf form. Her backpack and hopefully her friends waited for her. A few more streets, a few more corners and she'd reach the designated gathering point before the sun rose. There'd be time to slip out of Jaeger territory unseen.

The pack's medic didn't have the time to deal with the little wolf with a scratched paw. He stuck her in an office with a blanket and a bowl of water and told her he'd be back to check on her later. That suited Lori just fine. She didn't plan on sticking around anyway. But she'd seen the damage done to both Jaeger and Destin pack members and wasn't able to help.

She reached out for Turtle. And found silence. If he was safe, surely he'd answer.

The last two blocks to the meeting spot took far too long to travel. There were pairs of Jaeger men patrolling everywhere and Lori needed to duck and hide every few steps. Had she been betrayed?

Once past the last house, she moved faster. The patrols weren't running outside the village. Yet, even straining her wolf's hearing, there was no hint of Carlson's bodyguards.

She belly-crawled the last stretch, sensing one person at the chosen location. His scent was familiar. Eugene. What had gone wrong?

"*Eugene. I'm coming in.*"

He jumped up and looked for her. "*You're safe!*"

She shifted and walked the last few feet. "*What happened?*"

"*I'm not sure. Everything was going well when there was a burst of gunfire and Jace told me to run. I was the last one outside.*"

"*Did you get the weapons and ammo in?*"

"*Yeah.*"

A few supplies were better than none.

She pulled her clothes out of her backpack and got dressed. The desert was no place for a human to walk around barefoot. "I'm going back," she said as she tucked the revolvers into her waistband. "Are you with me?"

"Are you crazy?"

"Am I crazy to care about people I barely know? To put my life on the line for those people? I guess most folks would consider me crazy, but that's just the way I am. Have a nice life, Eugene."

"You can't go in alone."

"I can and I will."

"I'm going with you."

Lori ignored the small surge of alpha power that accompanied his words. "Let's get something straight right now. I don't care how alpha you are, I'm in charge. Got it?"

Lori didn't like being in charge. She preferred to work in dark corners, hidden from the light. The only plan she could come up with was a full-on frontal assault. Go in with guns blazing and mow down anyone who tried to get in her way. But she didn't know how many enemies she and Eugene would be facing or if they had enough bullets to go around.

She mentally clicked off how many men belonged to the Jaeger pack and how many were injured or dead. They *might* have enough rounds for one per man. But what if they also had to battle Destin pack members? In her heart, she knew the rescue attempt was a fool's errand. But she was determined to try.

As they threaded their way to the armory, she realized they had a secret weapon. Eugene. He was alpha. And if she convinced at least a few of the men they came across to swear loyalty to him, they stood at least half a chance of being successful.

TWENTY~FOUR

"Your alpha has fled. The pack is no more. Swear allegiance to your new alpha." Lori had lost track of how many times she'd repeated those words, but ten men, mostly omegas, swore allegiance to Eugene for the moment. Eight more lay tied up alongside the street after refusing to break their loyalty to Jaeger. Three more were injured with wounds that even a shift couldn't heal. She'd rather shoot them in the kneecap then kill them when they attacked after being challenged.

Eugene was worn out. She hadn't realized how much physical energy it took to 'influence' people using his power, and he wasn't an expert in its use. If it came down to a physical fight, he'd be in bad shape.

Jaeger's betas were the ones holding Turtle and the others hostage. In his state, Eugene wouldn't be able to convince them to drop their weapons let alone submit to him. Their biggest battle was yet to come.

She no longer tried to sneak around unnoticed. At an even twelve, they were too large of a group. If she could get this man to join them, it would make a baker's dozen.

"Come on, Clark, you know Jaeger didn't care about us," one of the men said. "And do you want to take a chance on one of the betas being put in charge? We'll still be at the bottom of the totem pole. At least with the kid, we can start over."

Clark hesitated before dropping his head. "The alpha has abandoned the pack. The pack is no more. Hail to the Alpha."

Eugene nodded. "Welcome to the new pack, Clark. Will you follow me in battle?"

"I will." Clark shook his rifle in the air then asked sheepishly, "What are we fighting for?"

"We're going to rescue Carlson's bodyguards," Eugene explained. Despite her earlier statement, Lori did her best to let him be in charge. She was beginning to believe that not only did they have a chance of completing the rescue, Eugene might be able to hold the group together afterward.

One more block to take control of, and it looked suspiciously empty. Where were the patrols? A movement halfway down the block caught her eye. Two men emerged from the shadows. They carried guns but held them away from their bodies.

Lori stopped, confused by their actions.

"Hey, Eugene," one called. "We heard rumors you were coming this way. We cleared the path for you."

"Seth! Ira! What are you doing here?"

They must be Destin pack members. She waited for their answer.

"They told us the packs worked out a truce," said the taller one. "We came to help get things ready for a celebration."

"But they attacked as soon as we drove in," said the other. "We didn't even have guns."

"Or a chance. Then another group appeared from nowhere and defended us."

"They were the biggest guys I've ever seen. And man, could they scrap. But as good as they were, there were too many of the Jaegers for a fair fight."

"So, they holed up in that building."

"We picked up these guns and we've been doing what we can to cause trouble but now that the sun is coming up we're leaving."

Who had betrayed them, Jaeger or Destin? Or had the two collaborated to make Carlson look bad?

"You're welcome to join us," Eugene said.

"Us? You realize most of those guys behind you are our enemies, right?" the second man asked.

Lori didn't expect the roar that arose. "The alpha has fled. The pack is no more," the band chanted in unison. "Hail to the Alpha."

The taller one shook his head. "I always knew there was more to you than they let on. I'd like to join you but we're still bound to Elder Destin. As far as I know, he isn't dead."

"You aren't slaves," Lori said. "You can leave the pack anytime you want. If you have a family to support, you can bring them with you."

"Families? Right. Because we're omegas and aren't allowed to have mates."

"That won't be true in my pack," Eugene said.

The two men exchanged glances. "How do we sign up?" the taller man asked.

They were fifteen as they moved into the street in front of the armory. A ragtag bunch of omegas against the elite of the Jaeger betas. But, if Carlson's guards joined the fight, they stood a chance of winning. Lori still couldn't sense Turtle or any of the others. Were they dead?

"Look who's come to play," called one of the Jaeger men who lined the street. The lone streetlight revealed the bad news. Twenty men, including Josef, formed a gauntlet between Lori and the armory. She should have guessed he'd be involved.

"Your alpha has fled," she called, her voice as steady as a rock. "The pack is no more. Stand down."

"He'll be back, don't worry. And then the big bad wolf can eat you for breakfast, Goldilocks."

She didn't answer, too busy watching his gun hand to worry about his lame threat. It wasn't the rifle slung across his back that worried her, but the prominent bulge under his left arm. In an old-fashioned showdown, who would win?

Eugene cleared his throat. When he spoke, his voice dropped an octave lower than normal.

"Your alpha has fled. The pack is no more. Drop your weapons and join me or face judgment."

In her peripheral vision, Lori caught some of the Jaeger men shuffling their feet. Although betas, they weren't strong enough to face the challenges necessary to take over the alpha spot. Still, she doubted any of them would abandon their positions. At least, not until they identified a winner in the upcoming fight.

Josef sneered. "Run home to your mommy, boy. Oh, that's right, you don't have one."

"Where are your manners?" Lori asked. "It's not a good idea to insult an alpha."

"Let the 'alpha' speak for himself." Josef raised his hands and made air quotes. "Your presence insults me, human. This is wolf business."

To shift would leave Lori vulnerable long enough to be killed. She ignored the temptation to reveal her *other*. "I stand by Eugene."

"Let your blood be on his hands then." Josef reached for his shoulder harness.

She was faster after all. Before he drew his gun, hers nestled in her hand. As he raised his, she squeezed the trigger. She fired a second time without waiting to see where—or if—the first shot hit. She ignored the sudden sting in her left shoulder, threw herself to the pavement, and shot a third time.

With a course yelp, Joseph crumpled.

Lori searched for another target. What she found was mass confusion as a mix of wolves and men attacked each other. She didn't dare fire again for fear of hitting a friend. In this battle, she was useless.

Eugene's fledgling pack didn't stand a chance, although he held his own against his opponent. The rest weren't fairing as well. One wolf—she thought it was either Seth or Ira—lay on his back, his throat in his opponent's mouth. And still no sign of Turtle and the others.

It was her fault. All of it. She should never have tried to rescue Turtle. Or claimed sanctuary for Eugene. Or come to Wyoming. Guilt and despair brought an onrush of tears. She gagged holding back a sob. If any of Eugene's followers died, or Eugene himself, it would be her fault.

She reached out for Turtle one more time. Carlson's bodyguards would help even the odds. All she found was silence.

She should have known better. The men were loyal to no one but Carlson. They'd only pretended to be her friend to use her skills and knowledge. Now they didn't need her anymore.

A new sound reached her ears. The chuf-chuf of helicopter blades breaking the air. She rolled over to see two copters hanging above the street. One slowly descended. There wasn't room for it to land, but its rotors whipped up a tornado of dirt and debris.

She stared in fascination as the side panels slid back. Before they were fully open, a shower of small objects were hurled to the ground and exploded in a flurry of loud bangs and bright lights. Lori raised her arm and covered her eyes to protect them.

Simultaneously, the doors to the armory flung open. Turtle led the charge to the street. Through narrowed eyes, Lori saw each of Carlson's bodyguards wore a pair of sunglasses. A trickle of hope picked at her wall of despair.

A second round of flash-bangs covered the street. Then ropes dropped to the ground and men dressed in military gear rappelled down them. She crawled her way to her knees, fighting the weakness in her left side, clutching a pistol in her right hand. She prayed the newcomers were on her side but would be prepared if they weren't.

The fights halted as man and wolf alike recovered from their momentary blindness. Unchallenged, the soldiers took positions along the street. The first helicopter rose and moved away. In seconds, the second helicopter took its place. Only two men descended from it. They stood in the middle of the street, arms crossed; as if waiting for something or someone. The wind whipped up by the helicopter blades nearly blew her away, but they seemed oblivious to it.

She didn't expect the wave of alpha power that blanketed the area and sent her back to the ground. Eugene wasn't that strong. She didn't think anyone was that strong. It seemed as if it came from half a dozen directions all at once. Up and down the street, men and wolves fell to the ground and rolled over onto their backs.

One more rope dropped from the helicopter. A man followed, dressed in a black shirt and black pants. He had a black hood partially pulled over his face and didn't appear to be carrying any weapons. Either he was the bravest man she'd ever run into or a fool. Until she saw what he planned to do next, she wouldn't decide which.

The helicopter reversed direction and rose. Its downdraft sent dust and debris into the air and Lori closed her eyes to protect them. When she reopened them, the Jaeger men were either surrendering or running away. That should have made her happy. But with long, determined strides, the man in black headed her way. And that scared her.

Out of energy with nowhere to run, no place to hide, she sat on the ground and waited, her gun by her side. She had a few bullets.

He stopped and placed a hand on Turtle's shoulder. Turtle was busy wrapping cloth around Josef's leg but stopped immediately. They exchanged no words, but after a minute, Turtle nodded. The man continued his walk.

The closer he got the surer Lori was she knew him, his confident stride the giveaway. She struggled to rise to her feet to show him the respect he was owed but felt too drained to make the gesture.

She almost missed it when Josef pushed Turtle

away and shifted. Josef launched himself into the air with a mighty leap, heading her direction. She reached for her gun, but it was no longer by her side. In her effort to stand, she must have pushed it away.

The man in black turned seconds before Josef would have reached him. The air 'popped' and a large black wolf replaced the man. Shredded cloth fluttered in the air. She'd never seen such a fast transformation.

Josef's rear leg collapsed on his landing. He tried but failed to skid to a stop before running into the larger wolf. The black wolf growled and raked Josef's chest with his claws.

It didn't dissuade Josef. He backed off long enough to shake off the pain and sprang again. His jaws snapped as he tried to find something to bite. The black wolf moved at just the right moment and Josef ended up biting air.

Then the black wolf went on the offensive. He whirled, and his teeth found a hold on Josef's tail. He bit down hard. Josef yelped and tried to run. The black wolf didn't loosen his grip and Josef fell flat on his face.

The bigger wolf released Josef's tail and walked backward two steps, waiting to see what Josef would do. If Josef was smart, he'd roll on his back, bare his throat and give up. He wasn't that smart.

Instead, he twirled on his good rear leg and head-butted the black wolf. The crash of skull meeting skull made Lori wince. When both wolves staggered, she held her breath. Why was no one rushing in to help? But that would go against every unwritten rule of wolf-to-wolf combat.

The black wolf recovered first. He raised his head towards the rising sun and howled. All around, other wolves joined in the song. Before the echoes died away, he charged.

Josef couldn't retreat fast enough. The black wolf was everywhere, it seemed, snapping and snarling and biting. All the vulnerable spots became his targets—the ears, the neck, the muzzle. Every time Josef tried to protect himself, the bigger wolf found a new spot to attack. It only took a few minutes until Josef whimpered and tried to run away.

This time, it seemed as if the bigger wolf would allow Josef to leave. He was several yards away before the black wolf sprang into action. He rammed Josef in the side, knocking him to the ground and bowling him over. In no time at all, he clenched Josef's soft neck in his mouth. All the black wolf needed was to apply a little more pressure and Josef's throat would rip open.

Josef lay panting and helpless. His eyes rolled into their sockets. Drool dripped from the side of his mouth. The bigger wolf shook his head once, then once again. He yawned and walked away.

Before Josef could react or shift back to human form, Turtle and two other men were on him. They tied his legs together and wrapped his mouth to form an impromptu muzzle, making sure that he had no means of attacking anyone again.

The black wolf licked his paws, cleaning off Josef's blood before shifting back to man form. With no covering over his face, Lori's suspicion was confirmed. She tried without success to get to her feet, but he walked over and sat down beside her.

"So nice of you to drop by, Counselor," she said.

Twenty~Five

"You didn't think you'd get to have all the fun, did you, Miss Grenville?" Counselor Carlson asked. He pulled on a pair of sweatpants one of his men brought him.

"How did you convince your bodyguards to let you come? You could have been hurt." Lori swatted away a mosquito and groaned at the sudden rush of pain.

"You're the one who's hurt. Let me take a look."

It was strange having the leader of all the wolf packs in the country hovering over her like a nurse. He clucked when he examined her arm.

"I'm sure it's nothing. I probably pulled a muscle," she said.

"You're bleeding. This looks like a gunshot wound. How did you manage to get in the way of a bullet?" He gestured to one of his bodyguards to come over.

Great. Another man in her way, "I might have had a fast-draw contest with Josef."

"I wondered who shot him. You won, by the way. He may have shot you once but you hit him twice. Made my job too easy."

Only a few scratches marred his skin to show he'd

been in a fight. "Right. Remind me to never run into you in a dark alley."

"You'll need to stay out of alleys for a while, I'm afraid." He patted her on the knee. "I have to go take care of business. Promise me you won't leave on your own."

"I'll make sure she doesn't." Hyrum, clad in a pair of jeans, walked out of the shadows and hunched down beside her. She admired his well-defined abs, then gave herself a mental slap. She had more important things to worry about. She shivered in the early morning chill and wondered why neither man was affected by the cold.

Hyrum knelt behind her and wrapped his arms around her midriff, avoiding her left arm. "I'll keep you warm, little human." He chuckled. "I can't call you that anymore, can I?"

Lori didn't have the energy to protest. She didn't want to, anyway. His warmth seeping into her back comforted her. It was a move a friend would make and didn't mean more. In a few days, she'd be gone.

All of Lori's meager possessions were packed and ready to go. With the inside of the bar destroyed by looters, there wasn't a reason to hang around. Except Carlson extracted a promise from her that she would stay for a week. That, and Hyrum clung to her like ivy to a brick wall, playing at being her personal guard.

Besides, she was curious about how it would all work out. With both of the old pack leaders out of the picture, and Eugene having only a small group who swore allegiance to him, the tension was thick enough to cut with a chainsaw.

In the shade of a large canvas pavilion, chairs formed a semi-circle, a table at their head. She grabbed a seat as far away from the table as possible before the crowd arrived. It offered minimal protection for her left arm, still in a sling.

Now, every chair was filled and more people sat on the ground around the pavilion waiting for the action to begin. Of course, Hyrum claimed the chair next to her. She hadn't been able to slip away from him.

The number of women in the crowd outnumbered the men five to one. They gathered in small groups of three and four, talking among themselves while waiting for the meeting to begin. Lori recognized only a few of them, and couldn't determine if the others were Destins or Jaegers. A few children ran around on the outskirts of the gathering, playing tag and throwing beach balls back and forth. The atmosphere reminded her of waiting for a famous rock band to take the stage.

Carlson had been gone for several days, leaving a large contingent of his bodyguards behind to keep order. If anyone knew where he'd gone for sure, they weren't saying, so rumors were rampant. Everything from him being on his deathbed to him being spirited off on a special mission for the government.

The second idea held more truth than most people realized. The morning after the battle, Lori overheard a conversation about the men in the helicopters being a special ops group, a squad of alphas without packs working together. Together, they'd been responsible for the surge of power she felt the night of the fight, a coordinated attack. It wasn't out of the realm of possibility that Carlson needed to repay the favor he'd received when he 'borrowed' the team.

Eugene and his small pack gathered off to one side of the pavilion. A few more men joined after the battle, mostly omegas from the Destin pack, but she was tickled to spot Rory among them. So far, all the members were male, which didn't bode well for its future. Lori caught more than one woman checking Eugene out, so there was still a chance to make the pack work once he found a place to settle.

An abrupt change in the alertness of Turtle and the other bodyguards was the first clue something big was about to happen. They switched from being relaxed and chatting with each other to silent and focused in a heartbeat.

When the two black stretch limos pulled into sight, the crowd fell quiet. Murmurs started as the bodyguards formed a ceremonial line between the cars and the pavilion. People craned their necks and the rustling in the audience got louder as one of the car doors opened. Sighs of disappointment filled the air when two ladies got out and guards escorted them to their seats.

Madame Rose climbed out first. Lori gasped when she saw how much the matriarch aged in the short amount of time since Lori last talked to her. Her salt-and-pepper hair had gone white. The cane she used to walk with was no longer for show. Her clothes, always perfectly pressed before, appeared to have been slept in.

Lori didn't recognize the second woman, although her face seemed vaguely familiar. She stared at the ground as she followed her escort, so Lori didn't get a really good look at her.

When the two took their seats, she expected the limo to pull away so the second one could pull up but that didn't happen. Instead, Turtle walked over and opened the passenger side door of the second car.

The murmurs died down again. Lori, like everyone else, expected Carlson to emerge. Instead, a man in his twenties dressed in jeans and a t-shirt exited from the car. Lori sensed he was a shifter, but looked too thin to be a wolf. She decided to withhold judgment because she didn't look like a wolf either. There was something familiar about him, as if she'd seen him before, but she couldn't figure out when or where.

The man walked up to the first limo and opened the front passenger door. The oldest woman Lori had ever seen emerged. Her face was as wrinkled as a raisin, her hair silver done up in a bun, her back bent, and when she shuffled away from the car, her feet barely left the ground. She took the man's crooked arm for support and they ever-so-slowly made their way to the spots reserved for them. The crowd got noisier as the pair got closer. "Savta!" someone called loudly. The old woman looked up and waved before sitting.

"Do you know who that is?" Lori asked Hyrum in a whisper.

"She is Savta, the Destin pack historian," he answered, his voice reverent. "I remember her from when I was very young. She was ancient then, I can't imagine how old she is now. I heard she was dead."

"And the man with her?"

"If he's a Destin, he's too young for me to have known him."

That should have satisfied Lori, except that she kept hearing 'Elex' from various parts of the crowd.

Had Carlson pulled off a miracle and found him? That explained why he looked familiar. But he looked as little like an alpha as Eugene did when she first saw him. The day had just gotten twice as interesting.

But the person the crowd waited to see hadn't made his appearance and Turtle still stood, rigid, by the limo. He leaned forward and extended his hand. Carlson didn't need any help. It must be part of the show.

She almost missed it when Carlson exited the limo because everyone else was on their feet and stretching their necks to catch a glimpse of him. When he raised one arm high in the air, the crowd roared its approval. If not for the security line formed by his bodyguards, he might have been crushed as people reached to shake his hand or just touch his sleeve.

He put on a good show. He'd discarded the slacks and polo shirts he'd worn for his stay and dressed in a custom fitted gray pinstriped suit. She thought he looked as good as any male star walking the red carpet at a Hollywood awards event. Maybe it was his way to make the packs feel important, that they mattered to him and the Council.

He took his time getting to the table stacked with paperwork waiting for him, shaking hands and kissing a baby along the way. Once seated, he looked around, smiling, until the talking died down. "Thank you all for coming today," he said.

Lori wondered how he made himself heard without a microphone. When he spoke again she realized he used a combination of verbal and mental speech. "You will be the determining factor in the decisions being made today," he continued.

He waited for the cheers to die down again. "As you

know, Edgar Jaeger left pack territory the night of the most recent raid."

"He has abandoned the pack," half of the audience roared. "The pack is no more."

Carlson raised his hand, a plea for quiet. "The Jaeger pack can still be saved if a suitable alpha is found. But before we address that issue, we must also acknowledge the status of the Destin pack. Elder Meshach Destin has officially resigned his position as pack leader."

"He has abandoned the pack. The pack is no more," roared the other half of those gathered.

It took a bit longer to regain control, but Carlson waited patiently. "It is normal to request pack members who wish to be considered for the honor of becoming the new alpha to present themselves for challenge at this time." He stopped speaking when the chant of 'Elex! Elex!' started somewhere near the back.

He stood and started pacing in front of the table. The crowd noise turned into soft murmurs. "Before that happens, I want to tell you a story." Carlson put his hands behind his back and took a spot behind the three women who came with him. "Many of you know the first part.

"Years ago, one of the first Counselors was faced with the rivalry between the Destins and the Jaegers. He proposed the radical idea of swapping boys from the two packs as a symbol of friendship. As Madame Rose can attest, the exchange of young men did not go as planned. The wrong Jaeger son went to the Destins."

The crowd hissed. Even if they didn't know that part of the story, they recognized it was a deliberate move.

"It didn't turn out as expected. The Destin pack benefited from the strength of Randy Jaeger while the Jaeger pack had lesser leadership from Edgar Jaeger.

"I am aware of the rumors Randy Jaeger was murdered. Those rumors are not true. Sereh, his mate, is here and can bear witness to the sad truth. He had a massive heart attack that killed him before he was able to shift in hopes his wolf could heal him. My personal physician autopsied his body and assures me there are no indicators of anything else." Carlson laid his hand on the shoulder of the woman Lori hadn't recognized and passed her a handkerchief. She dabbed her eyes and kept it, clenching it in her hand.

A chant rose. "Elex, Elex, Elex."

Carlson paused until others in the crowd shushed the ones chanting. Lori found herself sitting on the edge of her chair waiting for the story to continue. She was puzzled by Elex's—if it was Elex—lack of reaction. Shouldn't the heir apparent be acknowledging his supporters? Waving to the crowd and smiling? Instead, he sat quietly beside Savta, his head down.

There'd been no mention of Hyrum's part of the story either. Sure, he wasn't an alpha, but he was loyal to the core and she'd grown to like him. She felt bad that he was being ignored. She reached over and put her hand on his knee. A friendly gesture of support, that was all. He put his hand over hers and squeezed slightly as Carlson started talking again.

"Of course, as Randy and Sereh were close growing up they fell in love and chose each other as mates. That's the way you've heard the story, right?"

A stray beach ball headed Carlson's direction followed by a little girl. He scooped up both the ball and the girl, sent the ball flying towards the crowd but held on to the girl. "But that isn't what really happened. Randy and Sereh, while friends, had no romantic interest in each other. The mating was ordered by Meshach Destin to ensure his line would remain strong.

"As dutiful pack members, Randy and Sereh accepted the pairing and made the best of it. When Sereh got pregnant, the pack rejoiced. When it was discovered that she was pregnant with twins, the pack worried."

As they should have, Lori thought. Twins in shifters, although rare, frequently resulted in the loss of one if not both of the babies.

Carlson put the little girl on the ground and watched as she ran back to her mother. "Unfortunately, one of the twins died at birth. The other survived, was named Elex and proclaimed the heir to the position of alpha. That's the story the pack was told."

"It's not true."

TWENTY~SIX

It took a long time for quiet to return. Carlson knelt in front of Savta until the many voices stilled. "This part of the story is not mine to tell. You need to hear it from a witness. Someone who was there. Savta, as both midwife and pack archivist at the time, can tell you what really happened."

The old woman put one hand on Carlson's shoulder and struggled to rise. "You can sit and talk," he told her.

"Naw, I always tell stories standing. Too old to change now." Her voice was soft but strong, without the quaver Lori associated with old people.

Laughter rippled through the front of the assembly. "We can't hear in the back!" someone yelled.

Carlson came prepared for everything. He only had to raise his hand and a guard came running with a portable mike. Speakers were already set up.

"Never used one of these things before," Savta mumbled as Carlson attached the mike to her collar. "Getting old ain't all it's made out to be."

The laughter was more widespread the second time. "Am I loud enough now?" Savta asked.

"Loud and clear," someone called.

"Good. Everyone settled in? Let me tell you a story. The story of the birth of Elex and his brother. The story of joy and loss and deceit."

It seemed as if Savta threw a spell over everyone as she started her tale. Lori felt the flow of power surround her as the woman spoke. Not alpha power, but it commanded attention in a different way.

"I expected the birth to be hard," Savta continued. "Sereh had problems throughout the pregnancy and the fact that she bore twins made it that much harder. Several times I thought she might die before the babies were born.

"What I feared more, however, were the intentions of Meshach, then Elder Destin. I overheard him talking to his betas about the potential for rivalry between the children should they both be boys. He wanted to make sure the weaker child didn't get in the way of the stronger one. He mentioned the old ways when the second child would be killed so the first could be nurtured and thrive. Of course, it wouldn't matter if one was male and one female—or both were female.

"I never thought he'd carry through with those threats."

She took a sip from the bottle of water Counselor Carlson handed her.

"But I made plans anyway," she continued. "In case he lost his mind. Sometimes what is good for one outweighs the potential needs of the many.

"When Sereh went into labor early my plans went awry. I'd arranged for the second baby to be fostered with the Casper pack if needed, but my friend was out of town. And with the labor going poorly, I didn't dare leave Sereh's side to make a phone call. Especially not with Meshach hanging around, acting all concerned."

Savta spit on the ground. "I knew he didn't care about his daughter that much, except as a breeder. He'd thrown his wife out of the pack when she didn't produce a male heir and Sereh's baby was the only way for him to pass on his legacy, what there was of it. And Randy Jaeger was gone, sent away by Meshach to negotiate with an alpha in Oregon about buying timber or some such garbage. A bogus excuse, a way to separate Randy and Sereh.

"When the first baby arrived, we rejoiced for it was a boy. Sereh, despite the pain of more contractions, named him Elex, for he was to be a warrior. The first born, the alpha to be.

"That was all Meshach cared about. When he left to announce the news, Sereh had yet to deliver her second child. She was weak at that point, with no strength left to push. I worried that if she didn't have a Caesarian section, both she and the child would die. I didn't have the skill to do the procedure and the hospital was too far away.

"But somehow, she found the strength for a final push and a second son made his appearance. Sereh named him Elon, because he would need great strength to survive."

She took another sip of water and glanced around the crowd as if searching for someone. Her eyes settled on Eugene for a moment.

"Sereh passed out after that so it made the next part of my job easy. While she slept, I took the second baby from the bed and carried him to another woman of the pack whose own child was getting ready to wean. She never knew whose baby she fostered because I returned before Meshach came back to check on his daughter. I told him that the second child died in birth. And may the gods forgive me, I told Sereh the same thing. I hope she'll forgive me."

The crowd gasped and all eyes shifted to Sereh, who buried her face in Carlson's handkerchief. Her body shook but she stayed silent.

"Randy never found out either," Savta continued. "And I gave Elon a different name so no one would tie the two together. When the foster mother died in an accident, Elon got passed to yet another woman of the pack.

"Elex grew and thrived, but to his grandfather's disappointment, never showed interest in taking over control of the pack. At least, not when I lived here. But that's all of my story. The rest is Elex's. Now I'm tired. Is there someplace I can take a nap?"

Carlson knelt in front of her again as she sat. "Soon, Savta. Do you have any proof of your tale?"

"Of course I do." She chuckled and reached for the over-sized purse by her side. "I took the page from the archives when I left. Didn't want anyone else to discover the secret." She pulled out an envelope and handed it to Carlson. "Here ya go."

He scanned it and held it up so the crowd could see the single yellowed sheet of paper. "I'm in possession of the book this page came from. It is the true record of the birth of Elex and Elon.

"One more question, then you can take your nap, Savta. Who is Elon?"

"Ha! I thought a smart man like you would have figured that out by now."

Lori was sure she'd figured it out. All she needed

was confirmation from Savta. She leaned forward even further and waited.

"I did a good job hiding him," Savta said. "Even changed his birth date and birth year and people believed me."

She glanced around the crowd with a smile, enjoying her moment in the limelight. "He's here, ya know. Older and bigger, but I recognize him. Elon is Eugene. And as I suspected from the moment the boys were born, Elon is the alpha. Meshach chose wrong."

The perfect opportunity for Lori to slip out and leave would have been during the ensuing commotion. But with Hyrum still holding her hand, she was as stuck as a stamp on an envelope. Besides, the fun wasn't over.

Carlson himself escorted Savta to one of the RVs for her nap. Eugene—or should she call him Elon?—was surrounded by new admirers. Mostly female, but all he seemed interested in was getting to where his mother and Elex sat.

Madame Rose tried to talk to Sereh and Elex, but they ignored her. Well, not so much ignoring, as not paying attention. Their attention focused on Eugene. She felt bad for Madame Rose. She was Elex's and Eugene's grandmother and no one had acknowledged her.

Lori stood and pulled Hyrum up with her. At least, she tugged on him so he'd know he was welcome to come along. "I'm going to go say hi to Madame Rose. She looks like she needs a friend."

"Not now," he said. "The Counselor is on his way back."

She was a little jealous that he could see over the crowd. One of the advantages of being tall. The only time she ever had that experience was with a group of kids. Little ones, at that.

Carlson sat on the edge of the table and casually crossed his legs. The wolf in sheep's clothing. Or was he the wolf in wolf's clothing? Lori giggled silently. He waited for everyone to get settled and quiet down.

He looked around, making sure everyone's attention was on him. "When a pack leader resigns, he either has an heir in place or the alpha position is thrown open to be contested for by the males of the pack. In rare cases, the position is opened nationwide. That's why we are here today. Two packs need alphas.

"However, another factor is in play. I could disband both packs. Normally when I do so, it's because there aren't enough females to keep the pack going. That's not true in this case. The packs have enough women, but after the battle the other night, the supply of men is low. We can fix that by bringing in young men from other packs.

"I would prefer finding leadership locally, so if there are worthy candidates from either the Destins or the Jaegers, let them present themselves now."

"Elex! Elex!"

Carlson glanced at the young man and quirked an eyebrow. Elex shook his head. "I believe Elex declines the honor," Carlson said.

"We want to hear it from him!"

Lori twisted, trying to identify the speaker. Elex stood and cleared his throat. His lips moved but no sound came out. Turtle rushed over and handed him the portable mike.

Elex coughed again, clearing his throat. The

speakers squealed and he put his hand over the mike for a minute, then tried again. "My name is Elex Destin," he said, his voice getting stronger as he talked. "Those of you who knew me growing up probably remember me as a loud-mouthed bully. I didn't realize it until I was away from here that it was my way of trying to live up to Elder Destin's constant demand I act like an alpha. Still, it was wrong and I'm sorry.

"In fact, that's the reason he sent me away. He thought if he dumped me off on another pack I'd discover my inner-alpha. Instead, it convinced me I wasn't an alpha. And those stories about me being a big-shot stockbroker in New York City? Lies. All lies. You want to know what I really do? I'm a marine biologist, studying the effects of how the interbreeding of farm-raised salmon and wild salmon are affecting the long-term survival of the species. I spend most of my time on fishing boats miles offshore on the Pacific Ocean.

"Sorry, but I don't want to be your alpha. In fact, I don't want to live here. I like the ocean, not the plains. You need to find someone else to be your leader." He handed the microphone to Carlson and they shook hands.

"Are there any other contenders?" Carlson asked as Elex sat beside Sereh.

Would anyone suggest Eugene? Why wasn't he saying something? Someone should have briefed him on the protocol for becoming a challenger for one of the positions. Then Hyrum tightened his hold on her hand and Lori wondered if he was thinking of making a play for the Jaeger spot. Before he could stand, two women walked towards the front of the pavilion.

"Why do we need an alpha? We're strong women and don't need a man to tell us how to run our lives."

A few women cheered. Certainly not a majority of those present.

"*You?*" Carlson asked, suddenly present in her mind.

"*Nope. I have nothing to do with this. I like these ladies.*"

"There is merit in the proposition. But how you will support and protect the pack?"

"We have a few ideas. Sell hand-crafted items on the internet. Heck, someone got rich selling tumbleweed. There're plenty of weeds here." She indicated the prairie with a broad sweep of her hand.

An excited buzz rose from the other women. Lori wondered if they realized how hard running a business was. Still, she felt sure the Free Wolves would help them get it off the ground.

Eugene conferred with his group. "We'll offer protection." He strode forward and addressed the women. "My people will operate as a traditional pack, but as your allies, we'll keep you safe from others. That way we can stay in our ancestral home without the curse of either the Jaeger or Destin name."

For the briefest of moments, Lori saw the shock on Carlson's face, but he recovered in an instant.

"We could sell home-baked goods," another woman added. "The diner in Charity is always looking to buy my pies. Maybe other places would carry them too."

"Organic eggs. Chickens don't care that we are shifters," suggested another.

"We can call ourselves the Mid-Wyoming Cooperative."

"Are Jaeger women welcome?"

So, these were all Destin women with the ideas? No wonder Elder Destin hadn't allowed them to come to the negotiations. He'd known they weren't happy and was afraid they would say so to the wrong person.

The first woman who had spoken up walked up to the table and grabbed the mike, casting a sideways glance at Carlson as she did so. Her old jeans and t-shirt didn't come close to matching his suit, but her self-assurance was evident in her upright spine.

"Absolutely," the woman said. "In fact, we can put it in the rules that both Destin and Jaeger women are supervisors or managers or whatever term we use for our representatives." She grinned. "Heck, we can make one up. Supreme Goddesses of the Plains."

"When you decide on a name," Eugene said. "We'll name our pack something similar to show our support. The Mid-Wyoming Pack has a nice ring to it. Those of you who want to stick around but be part of a traditional pack structure, talk to either me or one of my lieutenants after the meeting." He waved his hand towards his small group of followers.

Interesting choice of words. Lieutenant instead of beta or second. What else did Eugene have in mind as far as changes?

"Let's take a vote," said the woman with the mike. "Oh, and for those of you who I haven't met yet, I'm Abigail. That should be our first agenda item, getting to know each other. All in favor of setting up our own organization, raise your hands!"

"You've lost control," Lori sent to Carlson as she watched the wave of hands rise in the air along with corresponding cheers.

"This has the Free Wolves written all over it," he replied.

"*I had nothing to do with it, but I'm sure we can find experts to come in and help them get things going. It'll take more than home-made pies to succeed.*"

"*The Council will help Eugene to get his pack organized.*"

"*A joint venture? This is a step beyond what happened with Lapahie Enterprises. Will the Council approve?*"

"*I doubt it. I'll make it happen anyway.*"

"*They'll need funds to get started. I suspect there's little left in either pack account.*"

"*Seed money. Good idea.*"

Twenty-Seven

All Counselor Carlson had to do was uncross his legs and stand and everyone's eyes were on him. "I will seek approval for Council monies to lend to the new organization to get it started," he said. "You'll need a satellite internet connection and infrastructure changes to make this work, along with legal advice to draw up the needed paperwork. The Council has more than its share of lawyers, and I'm sure one or two will enjoy a trip here. In addition, with Eugene's approval, we'll supply experts to assist in the training he and his pack need."

That will allow the Council to keep control of the situation, Lori thought with admiration, as well as develop new loyalties. All while looking like a benevolent friend. Nicely done. Too bad she wouldn't be able to tell him so in person. It was time for her exit.

With all the people she'd revealed her secret to, she needed to take a long break before accepting a new mission. There was a cabin deep in the woods of northern Florida—or was it in Georgia?—where she could hide as long as needed. Time enough to change her hair, get a new set of contacts in a different color, and for people to forget her name and her face.

Hyrum dropped his hold on her hand, distracted by the building excitement. She took her hand off his knee and rested it on hers for a moment to see if he'd notice. When a group of women entered the pavilion to get closer to the discussion, she joined them. But only for a few steps. She split off and blended in with another group, then another, until with one backward look to make sure she was invisible to Hyrum, she slipped out the opposite side.

Her backpack and a few other items she didn't want to leave behind were stowed in the pack's old car. She'd take it as far as possible, at least to the Wyoming border, then abandon it and get a message to Carlson to pass it along to whoever was in charge. They could retrieve it and put it to good use. She hoped to spend a day or two with the ranger at Devil's Tower. It would be a shame to leave the state without seeing the monolith. She regretted never making it to Yellowstone but a trip to the park would take her the wrong direction.

No one took notice of her as she made her way to the parking lot. The pathway wasn't empty, but the women were busy with small children and the few men were huddled in a group passing around a cigarette. With luck, they wouldn't even remember her going by.

"You," she heard as she reached for the car door. Lori sighed and turned around, plastering a smile on her face.

"Madame Rose! How nice to see you."

"You!" Madame Rose hissed again. "It's all your fault!"

"What's my fault? Are you okay?" Lori was concerned because the old woman wobbled as she approached.

"It's your fault that my son lost his pack. It's your fault I'm no longer the alpha female. It's your fault I'm going to lose everything."

Had someone told Madame Rose her secret? When she looked closer, Lori saw tears streaming down Madame Rose's face. She was tempted to offer the old lady a hug, but instinct stopped her. "I gave you two grandsons. That should count for something. And no one said you have to leave. I'm sure you're welcome to stay and either join Eugene's pack or the new group."

Madame Rose drew herself up to her full height. "What? You expect me to spend my time working for someone else? This is your fault, and you will pay."

"How is this my fault?"

"Everything was fine until you showed up. Don't think I didn't hear the others talking. They tried to hide it from me but they failed. If you weren't beholden to a man, why should they be? That it was unfair that my Edgar never allowed them to choose their own mates. He was doing what was best for the pack and they should have known that."

"It's a different world. You can't stop people from wanting their freedom. Packs have to change too."

"No. You took it all from me. And the fools I sent to kill you failed so now I'll do it myself. I will take it all from you. People still do my bidding and they will take your body out to the desert and dump it. Let the coyotes and vultures tear it to bits. No one will ever know."

Did Madame Rose just claim responsibility for the attacks? Stunned, Lori wasn't prepared for the shift—

the shimmer in the air, the crackling of bones. Taken by surprise, she missed the chance to shift herself so now she was at a disadvantage.

At least the wolf showed her age, not only in the gray fur, but also in the slowness of her movements. *"You don't have a shovel to protect yourself this time."* The wolf that was Madame Rose bared her teeth and stalked towards Lori.

But Lori had time to read the wolf's intentions and slid across the hood of the car when it pounced. Its nails scraped against the metal as its claws slid down the side, like fingernails on a chalkboard.

"You can't win this," Lori said. "You're past your prime. The spirit may be willing but your wolf doesn't have the strength. I don't want to hurt you. If you don't want to stay, I'm sure Counselor Carlson can find another pack for you to retire with."

"Oh, yes, you're Carlson's pet human, aren't you? You don't think he plans on keeping you when he leaves, do you?" She sidled along the front of the car and Lori moved around to the tail end.

"No one 'keeps' me. I go where I want when I want."

"You sound like one of those 'Free Wolves' people talk about. More like 'Free Fools'. We wolves can't exist without a pack."

They moved again, one on either side of the car. "Don't insult the Free Wolves," Lori said. "You don't know anything about them."

"And you do?"

Lori had had enough. She wished she hadn't worn her best jeans to Carlson's meeting but she could replace them down the road. As Madame Rose stalked around the back of the car, Lori reached out for her *other* and became wolf.

The howl that rose in the air didn't come from her throat but from someone wandering through the parking lot. Lori didn't care, let them watch. When Madame Rose stuck her nose around the end of the car, Lori clawed it.

Madame Rose sat back on her rear haunches and yelped. "*Stay out of this. This is between me and the human.*"

"*There is no human. I am other, I am wolf, and I am free.*" Lori broadcast her words. She didn't care who discovered her secret.

Still, the cheers that rang out surprised her. She snuck a glance around to see a small crowd. That gave Madame Rose the break she needed and she sprang.

But Lori was not only quick, her wolf was smaller and lithe. She jumped sideways and avoided the attack. When Madame Rose skidded to a stop, Lori bit her tail.

In battle-speak, it was an insult and Lori knew it. Her plan was to get Madame Rose flustered. She didn't want to fatally hurt the older wolf, but to break her spirit so she would submit.

Lori bristled when a larger wolf came trotting up to her. She bared her teeth and snarled. "*This is my fight. Stay out of it.*"

"*It's me, Hyrum.*"

As if she wouldn't recognize him. "*I've got this covered. Stay out of my way.*"

The temporary distraction gave Madame Rose a chance to dart in and nip at one of Lori's ears. She yelped, twirled and kicked out with a rear claw, raking it across Madame Rose's side. The injury didn't slow the older wolf, and she twisted and came back towards Lori, teeth snapping.

At the last moment, Lori leaped upwards on all four paws, a trick she'd learned from a fox-shifter. She landed on Madame Rose's back and bit her neck, then, before Madame Rose could shake her off, she jumped off on her own. Another move meant to demoralize instead of injure.

It confused the old wolf long enough for Lori to take the offensive. She rushed in and body slammed Madame Rose hard enough to knock her over.

"That's enough!" A roar filled her head.

Carlson. Who dragged him in? *"When she submits,"* Lori growled back. *"She took responsibility for trying to have me killed and threatened to murder me and dump my body in the desert."*

"She is old and weak."

"And that's why she's not dead already." Lori sidestepped as Madame Rose rushed again. Almost as an afterthought, she stuck out one paw and tripped the older wolf. Madame Rose faltered and fell nose first.

Lori ignored the laughter from the onlookers, her attention focused on Madame Rose. Would she give up? There was no way she would win this fight. Lori hadn't even tried for her throat yet.

Carlson, in human form, stepped between them. *"It's over. Madame Rose, the Council will determine your punishment."*

"I don't answer to the Council." Madame Rose's muscles tensed. *"They betrayed me when they took my son."* She snarled and leaped. Carlson jumped out of her way.

Lori was prepared. She hunched down as close to the ground as possible. When Madame Rose charged at her, Lori was in the perfect position to attack the exposed throat of her rival.

She could have gone for the kill. It would have been easy as the skin around Madame Rose's throat was thinned by age. But Lori didn't have it in her.

Instead, she nipped hard enough to draw blood but not to tear the skin. Then, because she felt like it, bit down again, this time harder. When Madame Rose yowled with pain, Lori scrambled away.

She didn't go far because in two steps she ran into a solid mass of fur and muscle. *"The Counselor said the fight was done. If you attack again, I'll sit on you,"* Hyrum sent.

The absurdity of the statement drained the last bit of anger out of Lori's soul. She pictured the gigantic gray wolf hovering over her, pretending to sit but afraid to, knowing he'd hurt her. Besides, two wolves had corralled Madame Rose, so she was no longer a threat. Lori raised her head and yipped, a sound as close to laughter as she could get in wolf form.

With one hand on the door handle of the car, Lori took a minute to watch the sun set. It seemed fitting, the hero in white riding off alone into the night. Except she was dressed in black jeans and a t-shirt.

There was no need for her to sneak off. After Madame Rose was dealt with by Carlson and his guards, she took the time to say a proper goodbye to everyone she cared about. The list had been short, but that was normal. She'd missed only one person—Hyrum.

He disappeared after the fight. It made sense if the

only reason he'd hung around was his need to protect her. She didn't need protection anymore, so why would he stay?

The engine started with its usual whine. She threw the car into reverse and twisted her head to check that no one was behind her. With Carlson's staff getting everything packed up and preparing to leave, there was an unusual amount of traffic and she didn't want to hit anyone. So, she didn't pay much attention to the almost-new pickup that parked alongside her. The layer of yellow dirt and the Wyoming standard cracked windshield gave away that it didn't belong to one of Carlson's men.

Until the large man swung open his door and climbed out. She hadn't even known Hyrum owned a truck. When he knocked on her passenger side window, she put the car back into park and leaned over to roll it down.

"Nice rig," she said.

He grunted. "Thanks. I bought it a few years ago but hardly ever drive it."

"I wondered where you went," she said, "I wanted to tell you goodbye."

He leaned over and rested his arms on the window frame. "How far do you think this piece of junk will get you?"

"Devil's Tower, with any luck. If not, as far as it will go. Beats walking."

"I can think of a better way for you to get there."

"Wyoming isn't a safe state for me to run across."

"No running, no walking, no hitchhiking." Hyrum jerked his head towards the truck. "We go together."

Lori turned off the car. "Aren't you staying? I heard a rumor that Eugene wanted you to help him organize security for the new pack and the women's organization. You'd be perfect for the job."

"He asked. I declined."

She didn't understand. How could he pass up the shot to make a place for himself with a new pack? She climbed out of the vehicle and walked around to the front. He followed suit and they met in the middle.

"Why?" she asked.

He scratched his cheek. "I want to explore Yellowstone."

There must be more to it than that. "Devil's Tower is in the wrong direction."

"I know. But since I answer to no one but myself, it doesn't matter."

Lori felt a flutter of joy. It was like watching a baby bird taking its first flight.

"You made me realize something very important," he continued. "All my life I've been tied to a pack, even when that pack didn't acknowledge me. The past couple of days, no one's been giving me orders and I haven't ordered anyone around. And I liked it.

"I've got a bit of money saved and I grabbed a tent and sleeping bag from pack supplies. We can go back and get another one. I thought about taking two but I didn't want to assume anything."

Lori didn't want to make any assumptions either. "What are you saying, Hyrum?"

"I want you to teach me how to be free. How not to say yes every time someone asks me for a favor. How to go where I want when I want. We can start out as friends and if somewhere along the road we become more than that, it would be okay with me."

Was he hinting at the two of them becoming romantically involved? "I can't promise I'll be a good traveling companion. I've never done anything like this before." Still, she found the idea illogically appealing.

Hyrum smiled. "Me neither."

Lori realized how long it had been since she had done anything on a whim. Her whole life was plotted out so she could help others. "Yellowstone, huh?" she asked. "Can we go see Old Faithful?" Then she rose on her tiptoes and pulled his head down to hers.

It was time she taught herself how to be free.

EPILOGUE

Lori stiffened under the heavy weight crushing her into the ground. She sucked in a deep breath, preparing to scream. But a loud snore brought her to full wakefulness, and she released the extra air and smiled. Overhead, a few stars fought to shine in the brightening sky. Sunrise was only a glimmer on the eastern horizon, but too soon it would wake the world to another day.

She pushed against Hyrum's limp body, hoping he'd roll over so she could get up without waking him. She wanted to hit the showers before the rest of the tourists began their morning routines. If they were going to spend a long day on the road, she preferred starting out feeling fresh. It might be cool in the mountains of Yellowstone, but by the time they reached the Wyoming prairies, temperatures were predicted to be in the eighties.

It had been Hyrum's idea to spend their last night in the park sleeping under the stars instead of in the tent. Unlike normal humans, they didn't need to worry about bugs biting in the middle of the night. Their scent worked as a natural insect repellant. Still, they'd pitched the tent in case of rain.

And Lori didn't need to worry about getting cold, either. They'd zipped their sleeping bags together, and Hyrum's warmth kept her as cozy as a heater. Another day, she would allow herself to drift back to sleep, cocooned in his embrace.

Instead, she reached for the zipper on her side of the bedroll. Before she made her escape, a strong arm wrapped around her chest and tugged.

"Where are you going, little wolf?" Hyrum whispered in her ear. He yawned and Lori's hair fluttered as he blew out a breath.

"Trying to get an early start," she whispered back. She flipped around so they were face to face. "We have a long day in front of us."

"I know just how to get it going."

She planted a peck on his cheek. "And get us busted for putting on a lewd display in public?"

"I didn't think this sleeping under the stars thing through, did I?" he grumbled.

"You'll survive."

"If we stop at the Cooperative on the way to Devil's Tower we can sleep in a bed tonight."

"No can do. I can't go back to anyplace where I'd be recognized."

Hyrum sat up and chilly air rushed into the sleeping bag. "You say that so casually, but it sounds like a life sentence."

Lori hadn't looked at it that way. She'd always considered it as an unfortunate side effect of her work. "It's not that bad. I know where I'm welcome and where I'm not. One day I'll be able to return to the Cooperative, but it's too soon for them to have weeded out the supporters of the old ways. There's bound to be at least one person who resents the changes, and I prefer not to become a target for their unhappiness. I should have warned you about the dangers of being involved with me, but it's been a long time since I allowed myself to have a relationship."

She pulled herself to a sitting position, expecting Hyrum to put his arm around her waist. When he didn't, she realized what she needed to do. Even if it hurt.

"This is your easy out." Lori pulled her knees to her chest and rested her chin on them. She blinked away a stray tear. "I understand this life isn't for everyone. But if you'll give me a lift to Devil's Tower, I'd appreciate it. After that, I'll be safe and you'll be free."

"Why do you do this, Grenville?"

The switch to calling her by her last name stung like a hundred paper cuts. "I have a whole spiel about rescuing other women from a life of misery. Or I can try to convince you I'm out to change the world, one person at a time. But the truth is, I'm still trying to find my mother. Intellectually, I know she's dead." Lori shrugged. "Enough years have gone by that even if she wasn't mistreated by whatever pack she ended up with, she might have died of old age by now. But there's a part of me that won't let go. So I keep looking."

"Do you plan to ever try and find your mate?"

Lori watched as the sun peeked over the horizon. "When I was a kid, I bought the idea that everyone had a predestined mate. Then I realized that most matings were forced, not fated. I stopped dreaming."

"What do you call this?" Hyrum placed one hand on the small of her back and moved it in small circles.

"You and me? I haven't put a label on it but I'm enjoying it for as long as it lasts. I didn't think forever existed. At least, not until I saw Dot and Gavin together."

"Who?"

"Dot Lapahie and Gavin Fairwood. He's a pack leader back East and she runs a school for the Free Wolves. They almost make me believe in fated pairs."

"They're famous. How do you know them?"

"You could say we're friends. I was in the group that helped Gavin rescue Dot when she was kidnapped." She decided not to mention that she did occasional 'research' jobs for Gavin.

The rubbing motion stopped but the hand didn't pull away. Lori *reached* but couldn't sense Hyrum's reaction. Had he blocked her?

"You move in mighty powerful circles," he said after a long moment. "What do you see in a packless guy like me?"

Lori elbowed him in the ribs. "Did you really say that? Did you forget who you're talking to? It's me, the expert on running free. I wouldn't even consider a guy tied to pack duties. That's part of what makes you perfect for me."

In the next second his arms were wrapped around her tightly and his nose was nuzzling the top of her head. "So I'm perfect for you? Tell me more."

She wiggled, but there was no way she'd be able to break free of his embrace. Not that she wanted to. "You want a list of all your good qualities? It'll take a while and we don't have the time. Not if we want to hit the road before the tourists do."

He stopped squeezing but kept his arms around her. "My wolf believes in fated mates. He says you're mine. He told me so the first time I walked into the bar and saw you behind the counter. I told him he was crazy. No human could be my mate. Besides, you smelled wrong."

"Is that why you kept sniffing when you were around me?" Lori chuckled. "I wondered if you had allergies."

"Nope. It was my way of trying to figure you out. You smell different now, and I like it." He stuck his nose into her neck and took a deep breath.

"That will change when I go out on another mission," she told him.

"If you go out on another mission, I'll go with you. You won't need to hide."

That wasn't the way it would work, but Lori decided she'd deal with the issue later. All around them, tourists started preparations for the new day. She and Hyrum needed to hurry if they wanted to beat the potential traffic jams caused by bears or bison along the road.

"We have time to figure it out. It'll be a long trip to Georgia sticking to the back roads. We better get started." She tried again, unsuccessfully, to squirm out of his arms.

He laughed but released her. She felt his eyes watching as she stood and stretched. *"Don't even think about it,"* she sent. *"You are not going to pick me up and carry me into the tent. Not today."*

He grinned sheepishly and stood. *"I'll settle for a kiss."*

"One kiss. Then we pack."

She expected one of his wild, demanding kisses she enjoyed so much. What she got started with a bare touching of lips that turned into a soft but lingering caress that stirred places in her soul she'd forgotten.

When they broke apart, Lori rested her head against Hyrum's chest and listened to his heartbeat while she made up her mind. She reached down and snatched up the sleeping bags. *"What's the good of being Free Wolves if we can't rearrange our schedule?"* She grabbed his hand and led the way into the tent.

THE END

OTHER BOOKS BY P.J. MACLAYNE

Wolves' Pawn
Book 1 of the Free Wolves

Dot McKenzie is a lone wolf-shifter on the run. Can she survive when she becomes a pawn in a pack leader's deadly game?

Wolves' Knight
Book 2 of the Free Wolves

Tasha Roeper knows what it means to protect your own. Torn between tradition and a changing world, will Tasha risk everything to save a friend—including her own life—when old enemies arise?

The Oak Grove Mysteries

The Marquesa's Necklace

Harmony Duprie enjoyed her life in the quiet little town of Oak Grove—until her arrest for drug trafficking. Now she has to figure out who is behind the sinister incidents plaguing her, and why.

Her Ladyship's Ring

Harmony Duprie is back, and so is trouble in Oak Grove.

Her ex-boyfriend Jake is out of prison and a suspect in a murder. Can Harmony clear Jake's name and solve the mystery of her own heart?

The Baron's Cufflinks

What starts as Girl's Night Out ends in murder, and Harmony Duprie is a suspect.

P.J. MacLayne can be reached at:

Facebook
https://facebook.com/pjmaclayne

Twitter
https://twitter.com/pjmaclayne

Google +
https://plus.google.com/u/0/+PJMacLayne/posts

Made in the USA
San Bernardino, CA
27 January 2020